Holding Their Own II: The Independents

By

Joe Nobody

Edited by:
E. T. Ivester
Contributors:
D. Hall
D. Allen

www.HoldingYourGround.com

Published by

PrepperPress

www.PrepperPress.com

Prologue

The pilot looked at the fuel gauge on the cluttered dash of the small Cessna for the tenth time in the last few minutes. The needle seemed to be glued to the capital E, and he knew it wasn't going to move, no matter how many times he checked. He considered the passenger in the front seat and shook his head – *We're not going to make it.* Right on cue, the engine sputtered, spit, and then returned to its steady drone. It was an unwelcome validation that the gauge was neither broken, nor inaccurate.

After a minor adjustment to the rudder, he glanced out the side window at the desolate west Texas landscape below. A seemingly endless expanse of brownish sand accented with bleached, off-white rocks spread out below him. Small, random clusters of dark vegetation littered the ground here and there, but what really drew his attention were the angry, sharp-looking formations of grey and red rocks. His mind visualized their razor-like edges slicing through the thin skin of the aircraft. Despite being above it all, he could tell it was a harsh world down there. Even the hazy outlines of the distant mountains looked gloomy and foreboding.

He pushed down the panic that was growing in his throat and looked at the passenger. "Do you think that was him?"

The passenger was looking out his window, lost in thought. He surveyed the map resting in his lap, and then the pilot. "No way to tell. There was somebody down there for sure, but who knows. Can you get us down?"

One last check out the windows confirmed what they both already knew. The only place to set down was a thin strip of blacktop the charts indicated was Texas State Highway 98. The pilot grimaced and shook his head. "We don't have any choice – here goes." He adjusted the trim and steered the nose so it began to line up with the road below.

From their altitude, the roadway below looked like a piece of dark ribbon stretching to the horizon. As the front of the plane slowly aligned with the makeshift landing strip, the engine protested its lack of fuel by cutting in and out several times and then finally fell silent. The sound of air rushing past at just over 100 miles per hour was a poor substitute for the engine's mechanical hum and reassuring vibrations. The pilot ignored the crushing pressure building in his ears, focusing on the white dashes that now cut the black road in half. Everything he had ever read or heard about landing without power came rushing to the forefront of his mind. He mentally ran through the checklist learned so long ago. He didn't know the wind, and it was useless to radio a mayday – everything else had been done. He

1

squeezed the controls and kept his eyes locked on the improvised runway ahead.

The passenger reached across, put his hand on the pilot's shoulder, and spoke in a calming voice. "You've done well. No matter what, I want you to know that." He then turned and looked at the girls seated behind him. He mouthed the words, *"I love you,"* and then said aloud, "We're going to have a rough landing – better make sure your belts are good and tight."

Despite the overwhelming whistling of the wind outside, everyone in the cabin could hear the whispered prayers coming from the backseat.

The plane was being pulled down by gravity, and the angle was bad. The pilot desperately worked the controls, trying to flare the nose. At the last instant, a pocket of thermal air nudged the powerless craft, causing it to miss its mark by only a few feet.

The small plane hit the pavement hard. On initial impact, the starboard landing wheel snapped off as the plane bounced back into the air. On the second touchdown, the uneven landing gear caused the nose to veer sharply right, and the port wing slammed into the ground. The cabin was heaved upwards as the plane rolled over, still traveling at over 70 miles per hour. The nylon seatbelts felt like they were cutting flesh, and the roar of tearing, screeching metal filled the air. Passengers who managed to keep their eyes open, would have noticed the landscape outside the front windows turn upside down, and then slowly roll back to normal. It took a full five seconds before the momentum bled off, and the plane skidded to a complete stop.

The desert didn't notice the wreck, nor did it care. The small cloud of dust, already settling around the crumpled airframe, was of no consequence. The shallow trenches created by the skidding metal would be refilled by the winds within a season. Even the repeating hiss…hiss…hiss…of a fluid dripping onto the hot engine manifold meant nothing to the desert.

Chapter 1

Bishop stood looking at the rim of the box canyon wishing the plane would magically reappear. When it didn't, he tried tilting his head slightly in a vain attempt to detect engine noise. The sky was empty, and the desert was soundless. The aircraft had clearly made two direct passes right over the ranch, and his mind was working overtime trying to figure out if they could've really seen anything from the air. Bishop meandered into the middle of the ravine, trying to imagine what could be recognized from above.

The camper rested partially underneath an outcropping of solid rock and the canopy of a young pecan tree. A thick film, caused by years of windblown sand, covered the once shiny aluminum skin. Directly behind the camper was the pickup truck. Most of it was obscured by the overhang as well. Besides, the truck was even dirtier than the camper and would probably be difficult to detect from the air. An old camouflage net was strung between the truck and the camper. Bishop had put it there for shade more than concealment. Under the net were two worn, folding lawn chairs with green and white nylon webbing that was beginning to unravel.

Opposite the camper, separated by a flat area of bare sand, was the canyon wall where the Bat Cave was located. A naturally formed rock room created by thousands of years of erosion, its almost constant temperature enabled the couple to carefully store bits of food, tools, and equipment salvaged from their Houston residence. As with its sibling formation, which hid the camper, the sheer cliff face curved inward at the base, creating an area completely hidden from above. A spring dripped constantly from the overhang into a small pool of solid granite. Bishop had dammed the natural drainage creating what they called the hot tub. Both the spring and the entrance to the Bat Cave were difficult to detect from ground level, let alone a fast moving airplane hundreds of feet in the air.

Downslope from the hot tub was their garden. While it was barely sprouting any green at the moment, Bishop wondered if the straight rows of plantings could be spotted from the sky. No doubt the soil was darker, as it was irrigated from the hot tub, but was that enough to cause an aircraft to hone in on their ranch?

A slight rustle from behind signaled Terri had joined him. He recognized the familiar sound of her bare feet on the hard-packed desert floor. A moment later, she exhaled a sigh as she leaned her body against his back. Her fingers interlocked across his chest in a gentle hug, and her head peeked over his shoulder. "What's the matter, Bishop? I mean…besides the obvious."

Bishop's voice relayed frustration. "I'm not sure I need to check on the plane. I don't think the pilot could see anything. I mean, look around…what could he have identified from the air?"

Terri released her hug and moved around to look at her husband's face. While she expected to see concern, his face showed anger. When he finally made eye contact, her expression made it clear she didn't quite follow his thinking.

His tone softened. "I don't want to leave you here alone unless it is absolutely necessary. I've taken enough risks lately, and my luck isn't going to hold out forever. I want to stay here, dry the meat, eat dinner, and then count the stars before going to bed. Remember? We were going to find Orion's Belt tonight. I was looking forward to that."

Terri rose up on her toes and kissed his cheek. "Bishop, if you're sure you won't be worried about someone sneaking up on us, I'm cool with your staying here. I just thought we would both sleep better if you checked things out."

Bishop shifted his weight from one foot to the other, fidgeting with the rifle slung across his chest. His gaze shifted from Terri's eyes to the point in the sky where the plane had disappeared and then back again. The isolation of the ranch was their single greatest peace of mind. Now, without warning or reason, someone had trespassed. At least that's how he felt about it. Terri and he were the only people who knew the ranch was here – at least until now. Stealth was always the best defense, and now their cover was blown.

Their lives had been so tranquil since arriving at their sanctuary. The harrowing trip across Texas to get here had left its scars and shadows, but the routine of surviving was slowly healing them both. Desert living was tough on Bishop and Terri. While they had good water, some supplies, and the old camper for shelter, it still took all of their energy to provide just basic food and security.

The ranch had been their permanent residence for two months now, and some days had been more challenging than others. When Bishop originally inherited the property, he envisioned a remote hunting retreat where he could spend many uninterrupted hours honing his skills. Terri had pictured a rustic hideaway, absent the daily frustrations of city life. For all that the weekend escape had meant to them, the ranch was never intended to be more than a temporary refuge. When terrorist attacks pushed an already crippled United States over the edge, the couple had initially tried to stay in their suburban Houston

4

home. A few weeks after the local government ceased to exist, it become clear they couldn't sustain any longer in suburbia. Food was running short, neighbors were beginning to turn on each other, and martial law had been established in the city limits. The radio broadcasts sought to calm an out-of-control population with the announcement that soldiers would be establishing order and taking control of Houston. But the young couple had no interest in exchanging their family table for work camps and food lines. Deciding the Army's solution didn't sound very palatable to them, Bishop and Terri hurriedly packed as many supplies as they could fit in the truck and set out on their own.

Bishop looked at his wife and nodded. "You're right, as usual. I'll go check it out. I need to get some gear together."

Bishop strode deliberately toward the outcropping, which signaled the entrance to the Bat Cave. He opened the heavy steel door, salvaged from a grain hauler, and waited for his eyes to adjust to the shade. The cool air inside was a refreshing change from the dry heat of the desert. Leaving the door ajar illuminated a path to a far corner where his gear was stored. He needed to start thinking about what to take with him.

The light from outside dimmed slightly as Terri entered the rock room. Bishop looked up and smiled as she came to watch him get ready. She could clearly see from his actions that he was uptight and knew instinctively he was worried about the baby and her. A warm feeling went through her thinking about Bishop being protective of their expanding family. In a way, it was cute and made her feel good inside. On the other hand, she worried it might cloud his judgment. Before everything had gone to hell, the stereotypical father-to-be was humorous. Bringing home a new baseball glove, expecting the newborn to be ready for a game of catch was funny then. Now, Terri wasn't so sure. If Bishop made decisions based on unrealistic concerns about the baby and her, this new world could instantly deliver a dose of harsh reality. *I need to reassure him*, she thought. *He's not even aware he's doing it.*

Terri walked behind him and rested her chin on his shoulder. When he glanced at her, she cleared her throat and declared, "Bishop, I need you to get me some pickles and ice cream before you go."

He stopped working with his equipment and flashed a puzzled look. "What? Are you serious?"

Terri put on her best indignant face when she countered him. "Yes, of course I'm serious! I'm pregnant, and it's my God-given right as a spoiled American woman to crave pickles and ice cream. If you really love me, you'll go find me some."

5

He shook his head and started to laugh. "Very funny Terri, where the hell would I find..." She overrode him with a raised voice. "I don't think it's funny at all! You're not the one who has morning sickness now and stretch marks in her future. I want chocolate ice cream and dill pickles." Her hands came to rest on her hips and her chin jutted out, daring him to challenge her.

Bishop was stunned and started stuttering, "Where...I don't...how..."

Terri turned her back to him, mostly because she was pretending to be mad, partly because she was having trouble keeping a straight face.

Bishop quickly turned and followed, putting his hands on her shoulders. "Baby, please don't be upset. You know if I could go get you anything...anything in the world, I would. There's no way I can find pickles and ice cream, just no way. It's just not reasonable."

Terri sighed loudly and looked up at the ceiling, still keeping her face away from her husband. "Nikki Morrison's husband went several times in the middle of the night to get her peppermint ice cream when she was pregnant. He had to drive clear across town and never complained. I guess he loved her a lot."

Her challenge had the desired effect as Bishop spun her around and looked her square in the eye. His voice was firm. "You can't compare our current situation to Mitch Morrison's little late night jaunts to a nearby Walgreens for ice cream. In case you haven't noticed, things are a little different now. Show me a frigging Walgreens, and by god I'll bring you back enough ice cream to sink a battleship. That's not fair, Terri. I can't spoil you the way I want to. The world has changed, and while I love you more than anything, I can't just simply..."

The corners of Terri's mouth showed just enough of a smirk that Bishop stopped. Her eyebrows raised just a little, and when he saw the twinkle in her eyes, he realized he'd been had. He smiled, shook his head, and looked down at her feet. "You got me."

Her voice softened, and she put her hands on his face. "Baby, the world *has* changed. Our roles have to adapt. It's so sweet that you want to protect me every moment of every day, but you can't. I'm a big girl. We made it this far because we trusted each other's instincts. Don't change that – it works."

Bishop nodded and seemed to be studying his feet. Terri wanted to reinforce her message. She smiled and rubbed her tummy in small circles. "This is a baby, not Kryptonite, so don't let it weaken you," she continued in a steady and reassuring voice. "You *have* to go see who was in that plane.

6

You *have* to trust your judgment." She paused and smoothed his tousled hair with her deft fingertips. "I'll make your favorite soup when you get back, and then we'll find Orion's Belt. I'll wear my pistol and stay close to the cave while you're gone. I need to see how much food we have left in here anyway."

Terri's words seemed to calm him. Bishop reached up and pulled down a laminated set of papers hanging on the wall. He kept an inventory of all of his equipment along with his DOPE, or Data on Previous Engagements, next to the tools. He didn't know how far away the aircraft was, so he intended to pack for an overnight stay in the desert. It had been months since he had done this, and he knew from experience that everything needed to be planned out in detail. The plastic-covered paper had lists of gear and the time it took to do everything from making a meal to cleaning his rifle. He opened a small box on the makeshift workbench, pulled out a clean piece of paper, and began writing out a plan.

Terri padded over to his side for a closer look. A mischievous smile crossed her lips as she asked, "Isn't this like packing for a vacation? Just throw everything in you might possibly need and go? Why do you keep all those lists anyway?"

Bishop laughed and kissed her on the forehead. "Well, just like our vacations, there isn't room for everything. Don't you remember having to repack about ten times whenever we decided to get away for the weekend?"

She playfully swatted him on the arm and feigned a hurt look. "It wasn't *ten times,* Bishop." Terri paused briefly before continuing. "Seriously though, how come you keep all that information?"

Clearly lost in thought, Bishop paused and then inhaled deeply. "Did I ever tell you about Mr. Franklin P. Mossback?"

Terri shook her head and giggled. "No, Bishop. I'm *sure* I would remember a name like that."

He stared into space for a moment before pulling more equipment from the rock wall. He glanced at his watch and turned to Terri. "I bet the plane tried to land on the highway, and I want to get there when the light is at my back. I've got some extra time before I need to leave. So let me tell you about Mr. Franklin P. Mossback, Senior Geologist, HBR."

"Several years ago, before you and I met, I received my first assignment at HBR where I was going to be in charge. HBR had won a contract to explore for natural gas in a remote location known as the *Tri-Border Area*, in South America. Quite the little cesspool of criminal and terrorist activity, it was basically a disputed border region between Argentina, Brazil, and Paraguay."

Terri interrupted him. "Terrorists in South America? Are we talking about Islamic terrorists or rebels?"

Bishop shook his head, "Both . . . and much, much more than that. There were drug cartels, Chinese mafia, homegrown syndicates - you name it. If you were into money laundering, drug shipments, gunrunning, or general mayhem, you had to have an organization in the area to be considered an A-player. It was kind of like a United Nations for the underworld."

Terri absentmindedly toyed with a flathead screwdriver lying on the bench, digesting his statement for a bit before responding. "We knew this was going on? I mean, America knew they were all down there and didn't do anything about it? Why didn't we ever hear anything about this on the news?"

Bishop chuckled and explained, "Our government was doing a lot more in the region than anyone knew. The DEA had infiltration teams all over the place. A lot of Special Forces were there as well. I'm sure the CIA and every other clandestine U.S. organization had boots on the ground at one point in time or another."

Terri pushed for an answer that made sense. "What about the local governments? Why didn't they do something?"

"The area is quite isolated, and hundreds of years of border disputes bred a society of corruption that was several generations old. I'm sure if you didn't embrace the established method of doing business, you ended up as monkey bait out in the jungle somewhere…or worse."

Terri settled down on the homemade workbench, making herself comfortable while Bishop finished his tale. He turned to look at her before continuing. "Have you ever heard of a city called Ciudad Del Este in Paraguay?"

Terri shook her head no.

"It's a shitty-looking berg, mostly slums. Yet it ranked third in the world in the size and number of cash transactions. Miami and Hong Kong are the only places where more dough changed hands."

Early in their relationship, she would have asked how he came to know such things. Instead, Terri mused, "Sometimes you scare me with the things you know, Bishop."

Bishop shrugged his shoulders. "There was a meeting of HBR's advanced security team. Again, I was still kind of new to the job and trying to figure out how everything flowed at the company. I'll never forget that first briefing. About a dozen of the security team and I were sitting around a large conference table when the door flew open, and the Colonel stormed in."

Bishop paused and smiled at the memory. "I doubt any human being has walked more erect since homo sapien DNA aligned itself in its current configuration. I know you never met him, but the Colonel was about 5'10" and built like the proverbial fireplug. It was difficult to judge his age, but everyone guessed he was in his mid-50s. His hair was closely cut, like a burr. I think it was turning grey, but there wasn't enough to really tell. His shoulders were always squared, and his gut was flat. He was definitely not just a desk jockey."

Bishop moved away from the bench and did his best imitation of the Colonel's stride. "He walked like he was going to throw his weight against a door with every next step. He wore a West Point ring on his finger, but it was unnecessary – any fool could see he was a military man down to the very core. We all immediately stood at attention when he entered the room. I'll tell you Terri, the man had a presence. I'd swear a couple of the guys twitched, subconsciously wanting to throw him a salute."

Terri chuckled and teased, "I've noticed some women come to attention when you've walked into the room, baby." She threw Bishop a couple of exaggerated winks followed by a blown kiss.

Bishop sheepishly grinned and pulled more equipment off of the wall. "That day, the Colonel stood at the head of the conference table, and without any preliminaries, began briefing us on the upcoming assignment. I really, really didn't want to mess up my first big job in charge, so I sat there soaking it all in like a sponge."

In his deepest growl, Bishop repeated the Colonel's briefing that day. "If you ladies have had your fill of the free coffee and doughnuts, take a seat and listen up. We've been given a new assignment, and I want to make this perfectly clear – this is a deluxe shit sandwich on toast. Management has contracted with the government of Paraguay to explore a remote region for natural gas. This job might as well be on the moon as far as we are concerned. The site is so isolated from any civilization or infrastructure we're going to have to build everything up from scratch. In addition, my sources at the Department of State tell me this region is hot, *very hot*."

Bishop scowled and lowered the volume of his voice, barely keeping a straight face as Terri squared her shoulders and tried to look like a soldier. He somehow managed to continue. "The borders have been in dispute for over 200 years. There is practically no government presence, and tribal conflicts have raged back and forth for decades. Due to the remote nature of the area, DEA informs us that several well-established Columbian based cartels use this strip of land both for recruiting

9

additional 'entrepreneurs' as well as the movement of certain cash crops. *They* are actually some of the nicer of the region's businessmen. HBR is going to have to build a small city on the site, and our job is to be the new sheriff in town. There will eventually be over 200 HBR personnel on location along with tens of millions of dollars of equipment. Let me make this perfectly clear to all of you. The criminal element operating in the area has already sent numerous messages to HBR's executives. We, gentlemen, are going to be like a rash in a whorehouse – unwelcome and bad for business."

Terri snapped to full attention and barked, "Sir, I *am* a rash. Sir!"

Both Bishop and Terri laughed out loud, and then he continued. "And so the briefing continued for another two hours. Satellite images, topographical maps, and every possible piece of intelligence was distributed and covered. I was scared shitless."

Terri moved to an old chair next to the wall and sat down to improve her view of Bishop's work. She propped her chin on her hand, making it clear she wanted to hear the rest of the story.

Bishop started to wave her off, but she wouldn't have it. "Bishop, you've never told me much about your work. I still haven't heard about this Moss-whoever-he-was guy. Go ahead…please."

Terri's tone indicated she would not be easily dismissed today. Bishop cleared his throat and resumed working on his gear. He had that "far off look" in his eyes that let Terri know his mind was wrapped up tight in the vivid memory of long ago. Bishop was silent for a minute more as he gathered his thoughts. "In less than a week, we were on a helicopter flying over dense jungle. Pressure was high to get down there quickly. Those first few days are a blur to me now. Packing gear, requisitioning supplies, arranging transport…god…it all flew by so quickly. I didn't get any sleep at all. Anyway, we were on our way to the site - Peg One was what someone had named it. I'll never forget that cool wind from the open side of that old H1 Huey blowing through the cabin. We arrived at the hottest time of the year, and that breeze blowing through was more than welcome. There were five of us in the lead chopper: Elvis, Reaper, Carlos, myself and Mr. Franklin P. Mossback."

Terri interrupted him. "Elvis? Reaper? Carlos? Sounds like a rock n' roll band reunion."

Bishop laughed again and shook his head. "All of the security guys used code names. Kidnapping was big business in a lot of the places we operated. We assumed the bad guys had radios and could listen in on us at any time. We were cautioned against using our given names. The fear was that if the local criminal element knew our identities, they might leverage that information against us somehow, I guess. In reality, using code names made things simpler. You see, we didn't have permanent teams; everyone switched around on different assignments. It was hard enough to memorize everyone's specialties, let alone their real names. Besides, being called Reaper sounded way more macho than Franklin."

Terri thought about that for a minute while Bishop critically examined his rifle rack. He seemed to be having trouble picking the right gun to take with him. He finally selected one and immediately checked to see if it were loaded. He moved quickly back to the bench, picked up a small pouch of tools and began cleaning the weapon.

Terri prompted him to continue the mission's account. "Bishop, what was your code name?"

He showed her a completely deadpan face and responded, "Why, Studly Hungwell, of course."

His unexpected interjection of humor caught her off guard. Terri started laughing immediately and finally covered her mouth in an attempt to stifle the urge to giggle some more. She might have been able to gain control of herself more quickly, but Bishop faked an injured look before asking, "Is that *really* so hard to believe? I don't get it. What's so funny?"

She shook her head, trying to regain her composure, a snicker breaking out again every time she tried to talk. Tiny tears had collected in the corners of her eyes, threatening to stream down her cheeks, when she managed to clear her throat and weakly reply, "Sorry, baby. And no, that's not why I was laughing."

Bishop had turned away from her, pretending to be busy, but she could see his shoulders moving up and down as he tried to keep a straight face. When he finally turned back to her, his own eyes were watering. As he rubbed them, he sniffed. "Sorry, I couldn't resist. To answer your question, I didn't use a code name. I just went by Bishop."

Terri pursued the subject a bit and asked, "What was Franklin's code name?"

Bishop motioned for Terri to come closer as if he were going to whisper a state secret. His eyes narrowed, and his voice was serious. "I told him he had to go as Studly's brother – Hardly Hungwell."

As soon as Bishop's words registered, Terri realized she had been taken in again. She gave him a good-natured jab in the arm, and soon they were both laughing so hard they couldn't talk

11

for several minutes. Bishop couldn't remember the last time he had a good laugh. He decided it was a good thing he had the workbench to lean on. His side was beginning to ache, and Terri was glad she was already seated. Bishop finally got his land legs, moved closer to his bride, and took a knee. They exchanged a quick kiss and Bishop said, "I needed a good laugh. Thanks for listening, babe."

"Oh, no you don't, Bishop! You're going to finish this story," she playfully demanded, pointing her finger at him. "You are *not* going to leave a girl hanging, *Mr. Hungwell*."

Bishop returned to cleaning his rifle and resumed his story. "Elvis and Reaper were part of my security team. Both were veterans of Iraq and Afghanistan. I knew they had a lot more experience than I did, and it showed. They always seemed to walk around with that odd mix of boredom and pent up anticipation. I think the Colonel assigned them to the job just in case I messed up badly. Now Carlos, I had just met. He was our translator."

Bishop paused, but Terri made a rolling motion with her hand – *go on*.

"The fifth passenger that day was my biggest worry. Mr. Mossback was a company geologist and clearly not cut out for the assignment. Business at HBR was good at the time, and that meant human resources were stretched pretty thin. Apparently, all of the geologists with field experience were on other assignments. While no one ever briefed me on Mr. Mossback's history, I think it's a pretty good guess this was his first time away from his corner office."

Bishop stopped talking as he snapped the final component of the rifle back together and worked the action several times.

Terri watched him and then tilted her head to one side. "Bishop, don't you always clean your rifles *before* you put them in the rack?"

"Yup."

"Well, then why did you just clean that one again? Are you okay?" Even though she tried to hide it, the genuine concern in her words betrayed her uneasiness.

Bishop didn't even try to justify his habits. "Terri, telling you this stuff brings back so much... I dunno... Hell, I might clean it again before I leave." Bishop punctuated his reply with a forced grin in an attempt to elevate the mood.

But Bishop's tone seemed uncharacteristically serious to Terri. "All right, Bishop. You don't have to tell me the rest of the story if it's *that* bad. But now, I *am* curious as to how this all ties into checklists, timetables and cleaning your rifle multiple times though."

Bishop started laying out equipment on the floor. As he arranged his load, he looked at her and continued. "At first, the security team really had tried to work with the man. But it quickly became clear that Mr. Mossback had little respect for us *Neanderthals*. He stormed out of the initial security briefing, mumbling the word "ridiculous" over and over. I tried; I really did. I even scheduled a one-on-one meeting with Frank, hoping to use professionalism and diplomacy to work together. We got off to a rocky start that day. Can you believe that little shit looked me square in the eye and informed me that his name was Franklin or Mr. Mossback, and to please address him as so. The relationship kind of went downhill from there."

Terri was clearly puzzled by this world in which she had no experience. She interrupted Bishop's story once more. "Why didn't you go to the Colonel?"

Bishop's words were marked by the sound of exasperation. "Oh I did, but he was no help. When I aired my concerns, he didn't even glance up from his paperwork. I believe his exact words were, 'Earn your fucking pay, or I will find someone who can.'"

A grimace crossed Terri's face. "Ouch."

"Anyway, the whole deal was screwed up from the beginning. We didn't get the normal amount of lead-time to prepare for a job like that. I never did find out why. Our cargo plane landed in Brazil, and the two leased helicopters were there waiting on us. The problem was they couldn't fly at night, so there was only time for one trip that first day. This caused another confrontation with Mr. Mossback. He refused to leave his equipment behind, and there wasn't enough room in the birds for my team, our gear, and Mr. Mossback's equipment. In a way, I don't blame him. He was responsible for some pretty expensive seismic gear, and none of us felt comfortable leaving our stuff unattended overnight. I decided to leave two of my guys behind to guard the equipment. I figured they could join us on the first flight the next morning."

Terri sighed. "So you went into a dangerous area without your entire team and had to leave equipment behind? I can see where this is going. I'm starting to get the picture why you keep such detailed lists."

"Oh, it got worse. When we arrived, the chopper hovered over the area where Peg 1 was supposed to be located. That spot just wasn't going to work. The terrain looked prone to flooding, already muddy as hell, and completely exposed on all four sides. That's what you get for trusting satellite images, I guess. The mineral rights we had obtained included a region where the jungle rose up into some foothills. I had the pilot fly about a kilometer toward the nearest hill and found a pretty good location. He radioed that Peg 1's coordinates had changed, and then we put down at the new spot. That change probably saved our lives."

Terri replayed her husband's last statement in her head, but it didn't help her follow his meaning. "Bishop, what do you mean? I don't understand."

Bishop realized he had skipped around a bit and needed to backfill his story. "There were all kinds of shady-looking characters hanging around the airport. It was part of the reason why we were so uncomfortable leaving any gear behind. I remembered later that one of these hard cases came over and talked to our pilot. I can't prove it, but I would bet the ranch he bribed the pilot to find out where we were going."

Bishop suddenly stopped talking, and his eyes glazed over. Terri sat still just watching him, waiting for him to continue. He turned away from her again, and she noticed that his fists were clenching, the knuckles almost pure white. After a minute or so, he exhaled and took several deep breaths. The words came out much faster now. "As Reaper put it, the whole thing was a 'first class rolling cluster fuck.' We started unpacking equipment and didn't have half of what we needed with us. We had some ammo for our mid-ranged rifles and almost none for Reaper's long-range weapon. The battery was missing from our satellite phone, so we had no way of calling for help. We had tents, but no pegs. It was just ridiculous. Somehow, the food was left behind as well, but that really didn't matter much in the long run."

Bishop's voice then became very soft, almost a whisper. "They hit us at dusk."

Terri wanted to ask what he meant, what was he talking about, but decided to give him time.

Bishop composed himself by staring down at the equipment scattered around the Bat Cave's floor. He tried to be mater-of-fact, but Terri knew her husband well enough to realize it was an act. "The first hour or so, they just probed us. We were hunkered down in knee-high grass and had formed a perimeter in the shape of a triangle. Reaper, Elvis, and I were at each point with Carlos and Mr. Mossback in the middle. We had stacked the equipment cases trying to give those two some cover. The Colonel told me later the attackers were Hezbollah, straight out of Lebanon. I know after what they did to us, they had to be some pretty hardcore dudes."

Terri couldn't help herself and spouted, "Hezbollah in South America? Are you sure?"

14

"Oh yes, I'm sure. There is a town close by in Brazil called Foz do Iguaçu. We were briefed that Arabic was more commonly spoken there than Brazilian Portuguese. It seems that our neighbors to the south encouraged a lot of immigration during the 1990s from the Middle East. The porous borders had allowed an almost unchecked inflow ever since." Bishop's voice trailed off as the memory became intense again.

Terri gently prodded him to finish the tale. "I'm sorry I interrupted you, Bishop, please go on. What happened that night?"

"They started making a lot of noise and popping off a few shots at us from the east. Nothing serious, just trying to get us to shoot back so they could tell exactly where we were. It's a technique called *reconnaissance by fire*. The south was next, and then the west. I guess they finally figured out we weren't going to fall for it, so they tried to rush us. That was a mistake on their part. About 20 of them came out of the tree line simultaneously. Reaper was the closest to them, and when he decided it wasn't just another probe, he opened up. We had night vision and they didn't, and that's probably the other reason why I'm still here today. Reaper tore into them hard. They had to cross about 150 meters of open terrain, and he had a big caliber rifle designed for five times that distance. He didn't miss and broke up their attack single-handedly. Elvis and I couldn't help him much – we had to keep an eye to our front in case they tried to envelop us."

Bishop held up his hand to let Terri know he needed to refocus for a minute. He took a piece of paper and made checkmarks as he placed various pieces of equipment into his backpack. He doubled-checked all of the gear and then sat down on the floor and looked away. When he began again, his voice was a flat monotone.

"The first attempt to rush us was quickly followed by another. The second one was a little better lead, and they got within 50 meters or so of my position. They didn't come in a skirmish line like the first time. They used some pretty good techniques, but I somehow managed to stop the advance on my side." Bishop paused briefly, as something seemed to overwhelm him. His voice quivered just slightly. "After that attempt, the sounds of the wounded were…unsettling."

Terri could see Bishop was back there now. His eyes were watery and glazed over, almost like he was in a trance. She was about to say something when he started speaking again.

"They really wised up after that and rushed us from all three sides at once. I knew Reaper was low on ammo, and I kind of freaked out when I heard his pistol start shooting. That was

15

either a sign he was out of rifle rounds or the threat was *very* close. The night vision doesn't do you much good when they get close. It all becomes shadows…ghosts…movement. I don't know how to describe it really. I'm not sure how they got into the middle of us. I realized they had overrun our position when someone shot at me from behind."

He paused and looked at Terri with such a matter-of-fact expression, she thought at first he was through with the story. "Isn't the human brain amazing sometimes? There were dozens of AK's, M4's, pistols, and who knows what else all firing at once. Lead was flying everywhere from all directions. I could feel the rounds passing over my chest. Dirt and grass spraying and stinging like a swarm of bees when it hit skin. Smoke so thick you could barely see, much less breathe. And so many men screaming - oh god, Terri - the screams. My brain should have been completely overloaded, yet somehow, I knew someone had shot at me from behind."

He shuddered and then had to stand again, his body far too tense to remain seated. "I half crawled and half ran back to try and protect Mr. Mossback and Carlos. On the way, some big Arab dude and I cracked heads and both of us went down, rolling around on the ground."

Bishop bent down, retrieved his fighting knife, and held it close to his chest - like a preacher would hold a Bible. He didn't take it out of the scabbard, but seemed to just want it close to him. Terri watched as every sinew, cord and vein bulged in the arm holding the knife. She got a cold chill when she tried to imagine anyone facing Bishop and that blade.

Terri suddenly remembered her determined pursuit of the perfect Christmas gift for Bishop when the two were still dating. His knife seemed to be one of his favorite things as he was always oiling, sharpening, or messing with it. Without his knowing, she dug it out of his gear and took it to a custom knife maker, whose website was inundated by page after page of 5-star customer reviews, raving about his skill and attention to detail. She had commissioned a blade of similar size for a tidy sum. The knife maker had been polite, but completely unimpressed with Bishop's choice. "It's just an off-the-shelf infantry model. Don't get me wrong, your husband has a good knife here, but it's nothing special." When the job was complete, she had been super impressed with the work of art the man created. She couldn't wait for Christmas morning. When Bishop opened the gift, he smiled and was very grateful, but his reaction was not what she had expected. He never carried the new knife. *Now I know why.*

Slowly, his grip on the sheath relaxed, and he started talking again. His voice was completely emotionless.

"By the time I had taken big man out of the fight, it was all over. To this day, I don't know why they stopped. They had completely overrun us, and we were all but out of ammo. Maybe they had just had enough, I don't know. All of a sudden, nobody was shooting at us anymore. Elvis was wounded badly and bleeding out. He had taken two rounds to his right leg, and one had hit an artery. Reaper was gone - just disappeared. Carlos was missing as well, and Mr. Mossback was buried under a pile of equipment cases and gear, but unhurt."

Terri waited for a minute for him to continue, but he didn't. *This is a critical time for him*, she thought, *he needs to get this out*. "Bishop, where was Reaper?"

"At the time, I didn't know. Big Arab dude managed to hit me in the head with his rifle butt, and the fog hadn't cleared yet. I remember running to Reaper's position and being amazed at the bodies that littered the ground. I remember that because I was checking to see if any of the dead were Reaper. The bodies were kind of piled up. I figured he either had changed position and would show up in a bit or had decided to give chase for a while. Not much made sense right about then."

Terri gave him a questioning look, but Bishop didn't seem to notice. When he started speaking again, the pain in his voice was obvious.

"I ran back to take care of Elvis. He was bleeding badly and fumbling around, trying to wrap a tourniquet on his leg. We somehow managed to get it on as well as some pressure bandages. Right in the middle of all this…this…mayhem, we found out where Reaper was.

Bishop looked up at Terri. She had never seen him look so helpless. She tried to think of something to say, but he started talking again. "They had him, and he was still alive. I'll never forget those howling screams – I didn't know a human being could make sounds like that. It was another hour before dawn and another two before the choppers would be there. Those three hours were the worst I can ever remember. Reaper somehow managed to survive for one of the three. Even so, it was a couple of days later before two Brazilian policemen found his body. Those Hezbollah animals had tied him to a tree and done who knows what to him. I don't know if they were trying to get information out of him, or if it were just revenge. All I know for sure is he didn't die quickly. God rest his soul. That's no way for a soldier to go out. I'll tell you this – he took about 20 of those sons-of-bitches with him. I bet he's still chasing them through hell."

Terri shook her head, now questioning if it had been a good idea to guide Bishop into all of this. What had begun as a simple enough question about his checklists and habits had somehow become a journey in this deep, dark part of his memory. Perhaps Bishop would have been in a better place if that part of his life had stayed buried deep in his mind. She was about to change the subject, when Bishop resumed his tale.

"Terri, there we were, in the dark, listening to our co-worker's agonizing screams and unable to do shit about it. Elvis was bleeding badly, and I couldn't leave him. I've never felt so incapable of controlling a situation. Mr. Mossback was curled up with his head buried in his arms and whimpering. Elvis was still talking, but his words came sporadically as he faded in and out of consciousness. You know, I was the team leader and in charge of the blow-out bag – our medical kit. The simplest little thing might have saved his leg – tampons. We always kept them in the kit because they were just about perfect to stuff in a bullet wound and stop the bleeding. In the time before help arrived, I dumped that kit out and checked the contents ten times. I remember saying, 'I'm sorry man. I'm so sorry, but they just aren't here. I'm so sorry.' We kept torqueing the tourniquet, and both of us knew it was too tight. It was his leg or his life. And to tell the truth, in the end, it really didn't make a hell of a lot of difference."

Terri sat silently, knowing an explanation was coming and sure it wasn't going to be uplifting. "First, let me tell you about Elvis," he continued. "This was a tall, lanky guy from Tennessee. I didn't know much about his military background, but he held all of the records for shooting at the company. Nobody could get close to his times on the courses. He was very quiet, but death incarnate with that rifle strapped across his chest. The only thing he really ever talked about were his kids back home. He had pictures of them all over his locker and was always pulling out his wallet to show off his family."

Bishop's voice became almost a whisper and then grew incrementally louder. "He lost the leg. I know HBR took care of him financially, but I guess he never adjusted to it. The Colonel got a call about seven months later – Elvis had put a barrel in his mouth and ended it all. Several of us flew to Memphis for the funeral. I spent the next day with his wife and kids. Elvis had told his wife I was his really good friend. She went on and on about how he always liked working with me because my smartass remarks helped him relax. She told me he believed I saved his life that day. Ironic, huh?"

Bishop stopped again and shook his head from side to side. The room was eerily quiet except for the sound of his heavy sigh. A minute later, he surprised Terri by looking up and smiling at her.

"Soooo very pretty girl, you wanted to know why I have all these checklists and timetables. Well, now you know. Female hygiene products are the root cause of all of my anal-retentive habits. Tampons. They might have saved a life one time, but I didn't have them with me like I should have. I swore never to let that happen again. I swore never to feel so helpless and stupid."

Terri got up and walked over to him. They hugged each other very close and held on for a long time. After a bit, she felt Bishop's body tense and then several small convulsions raked his frame. He was crying, but she pretended not to notice. She held him tightly and soothed the back of his head.

"Bishop, you can't feel guilty over that. It was an oversight – an accident. It sounds like you did everything you could."

After a time, he sniffed, released his embrace, and then held her at arm's length, looking deeply into her eyes. "Baby, the guilt I feel over the equipment is just part of the story. My demon is that I survived. I'm still alive, and the others aren't. They were more experienced – they were better at fighting. When you go into…situations…yeah, situations like we did, you want to believe surviving is more than just luck. You want to have faith in your skill, or knowledge, or God…or whatever. You want to count on anything, anything at all, but dumb, random luck. Well, I'll tell you something – sometimes skill has nothing to do with it. Sometimes all the training in the world doesn't make any difference. If it did, I would've died that day with those men. I didn't deserve to walk away. You can't control luck. I've burned more than my share of luck in this life. Working in places like where we lost Reaper and Elvis, and walking out alive. Acting like an invincible fool on the trip out here. Now I'm thinking I shouldn't press it anymore. Now I wonder if going to check on that plane is going to suck me back into a shit storm I don't want or need."

Terri thought about his concern for a moment and replied. "Bishop, we didn't go looking for trouble today. That plane came to us. Sometimes you can't control what life throws at you. We've made it through because of what we are and how we have handled it. I trust your instincts and your judgment. I'm with you all the way. Cowering all scared and timid in our little canyon might work – or it might make things worse. It's your call."

He pulled her back close to him, holding her tightly for a while. He announced his decision by looking at his watch and proclaiming, "I've got to get going. I have an airplane to find and a mystery to solve. Help me get into all this gear; would ya, babe?"

Chapter 2

The President of the United States stood looking at a large wall map of his country, his hands folded behind his back. To the casual observer, the jacket he wore looked like a quality lightweight fall coat, with the Presidential seal above his heart and the acronym POTUS (President of the United States) in gold embroidery across his back. In reality, the simple windbreaker was a multi-thousand dollar piece of equipment, which the Secret Service now demanded he wear at all times.

While it was perhaps a few ounces heavier than an identical style purchased off the shelf at a fine men's store, the jacket provided the same protection as level IIIA body armor. Able to defeat any handgun and all but the largest rifle calibers, the material used in the lining was a state secret.

The embroidery on both the front and back had a security role as well. The thread had been treated with a special chemical that emitted heat at a specific frequency. When viewed through the service's forward-looking infrared goggles, anyone wearing the jacket would stand out like a neon sign glowing in a dark night.

The drawstring at the waist was an antenna connected to two micro-transmitters sewn into the collar. Along the zipper, hidden in a slightly wider than normal seam, was a battery pack designed to power these tiny radio stations for five years. These transmitters allowed the Air Force Space Command's satellites to pinpoint the location of the jacket to within one meter, anywhere on earth. The president's bodyguards were equipped with handheld devices that would show the location of the president up to five miles away.

Special Agent Powell was thinking about all of this while he watched the president from his normal station by the door. The two men were alone in the room, and as was his custom lately, the president used anyone nearby as a sounding board. "Agent Powell, I just can't believe we have to rebuild our country like we did Iraq and Afghanistan. When I was sworn into office, if you had told me the United States of America would be in the same condition - no, worse, than Iraq in 2005, I would have thought you were insane."

"I wouldn't have blamed you, sir."

The president seemed to ignore his bodyguard's remark. "I remember those days. I was in the senate, and privately we struggled to comprehend how the Iraqis could behave like they did. How could a civilized people turn on each other and tear each other to shreds? Couldn't they see that their long-term security was more important than any ancient religious squabbles? Why slaughter each other by the thousands over something that was *supposed* to have happened over 1,000 years ago? Deep down, I think we all got pretty smug about the whole affair. We felt ourselves superior, more advanced. Americans would never do that, no matter what the situation. That's what we told ourselves back then anyway. Now, I don't feel so superior. It's happening right before my very eyes."

The president turned back to the map and studied it again, apparently hoping a solution would magically appear. None did.

The map was actually a large flat screen monitor mounted flush in the wall. Feeding the big screen was a state of the art computer system housed in an adjoining facility. The president reached for a remote control and clicked a button.

The image of the U.S. map remained, but three different colors now overlaid the states. The blue tinted areas were those under control of the government. The green areas were known to be organized, but not under the government's control, at least not at the federal level. The third color was red, depicting areas that had a status of "unknown." The vast majority of the map was red.

The POTUS shook his head. It seemed like the blue areas continued to shrink every day. He turned to Agent Powell, ready to make another remark, when there was a knock on the door, and the president's secretary came in.

"Mr. President, the Chairman of the Joint Chiefs is here. Should I show him in, sir?"

"Please, show him in, Martha."

A few moments later, General Truman P. Wilson was shown into the conference room. After the expected social pleasantries were exchanged, the general made his way to the large conference table and opened his briefcase. He pulled out a stack of papers, a pad of paper, and a pen. He stood at attention and waited for his commander to sit, but the president seemed not to notice, instead indicating General Wilson should join him beside the large display.

"General, I see that Indianapolis has turned from blue to red. Do you have an update?"

"Sir, I do. The Marion County area, or greater Indianapolis, was being held by the 38th Infantry Division, mostly Indiana guardsmen. As you know sir, there was an incident three weeks ago when several Marion county sheriff deputies attempted to leave the city limits. The forty or so men claimed their families were starving and were not being protected by the Army. The commander on the ground, who has now been replaced, overreacted, and several of the deputies were killed or injured in the ensuing firefight. The aftermath has resulted in an increasing cycle of civil unrest. The 38th has experienced a higher percentage of attempted resignations by its officer corps and hundreds of soldiers abandoning their posts. But yesterday, we lost all contact. We don't know if the commanding general has decided to go rogue, if a mutiny has occurred, or some other type of control is now being exercised."

"Damn it! That is four cities in the last week."

"Five, Sir. We lost contact with Miami as of two hours ago. The map will be updated soon."

The president shook his head, thinking back to the comment made a few minutes ago to Agent Powell. He turned to the officer and questioned, "General, I know we are having a staff meeting later, but given your news this morning, could you provide me with a fresh status of our plan's progress?"

The general returned to the conference table and shuffled through the first few pages. "I'm sorry, Mr. President. I don't have the latest information with me. I can have it brought over, sir? "

The president nodded and drifted off in thought.

Almost two months had passed since the terrorists had killed hundreds of thousands of Americans using nerve gas. The combination of the Second Great Depression and those attacks had resulted in anarchy. The president, living in the bubble that was unavoidably associated with his office, had been isolated and unaware of the pain and suffering of his people. That bubble was soon to burst.

The National Mall in Washington had been the scene of almost daily demonstrations for months. Some of these gatherings involved 200,000 or more people. As the economy worsened, the demonstrations gradually become protests. In the last months before the terror attacks, confrontation with the D.C. police became common. After the terrorist's attacks and the subsequent withdraw of the United States from the United Nations, things got downright violent.

The Secret Service and the Pentagon tried to get the president to move all executive branch operations to either a military installation or Camp David. The response was always the same. "I *am not* going to be the first President of the United States to run from my own people."

It was a Saturday morning when the Secret Services' worst nightmare became reality. There was a rally sponsored by several national labor unions on the mall. Intended to send a message to the White House about unemployment, over 210,000 angry workers and 1,000 hired agitators jammed into the public area between the Washington Monument and the U.S. Capital building. No one really knew what started the rock and bottle throwing. The Marine Corps garrison had sent over additional manpower to supplement the D.C. police. The Secret Service uniform division was out in full force as well. There were over 2,000 armed men forming a human barrier between the protestors and the White House grounds. They were overwhelmed in less than four minutes once things turned ugly. Some in the crowd believed the police and Marines had initiated the shooting to break up the demonstration. Others were so frustrated with the federal government they relished any opportunity to fight back. As the first line of police officers fell to the barrage of rocks, bottles and other projectiles, participants picked up the weapons and used them against the remaining guards.

Even though protests were a daily event, the news media still covered every demonstration. It was a quick thinking engineer, several blocks away in a satellite truck, who realized there was something different about what was happening at the White House today. He initiated an interruption of normal programming with the now, ever so common breaking news alert.

American viewers were shown an image of thousands of people climbing the fence surrounding the White House. Secret Service agents with sub-machine guns were spraying automatic fire into the crowd, some of whom were shooting back. Seconds later, the view switched to an aerial shot from a helicopter. A wall of people was pictured pushing against the heavy steel fence surrounding the White House. Suddenly, a post gave way, and the throng poured onto the south lawn. The Secret Service snipers on the roof of the White House could only stop a small percentage of the rushing mob.

World response was instantaneous, as if the global human population were collectively holding its breath in disbelief. Millions of people literally stopped whatever they were doing, glued to the developing scene on their television screens. The United States was in complete revolt. At first, many people hoped they were watching yet another Hollywood disaster movie, but it soon became clear that this was real - and live.

About the only people who didn't watch the ransacking of 1600 Pennsylvania Avenue were those who lived in cities that were without electricity. Houston, Atlanta, and Cleveland were already burning and had lost power days before.

The president had been in the Oval Office that morning when two agents burst in without warning. The largest, an ex-college football lineman, had physically lifted the POTUS over his shoulder and carried him to Marine One. The iconic image of that historical day was of Marine One lifting off the ground with two protesters hanging onto the skids. A Secret Service agent was leaning out the door with his handgun aimed at the two men, both of whom were killed when they fell over 40 feet onto the east lawn. Newspapers all over the world printed that single frame, taken from a city webcam used to promote tourism for the nation's capital. Within an hour, the White House was a looted, empty shell with thousands of bodies littering the grounds.

The reaction across America was mostly one of shock, coupled with a "hunker down" mentality. Some people interpreted the newscasts as a sign that complete anarchy had taken hold and began looting rampages. Others simply stayed at home and refused to report to work or duty. America was exhausted by years of economic hardship, massive unemployment and most recently, terrorist attacks. Those attacks had disabled part of her infrastructure and left so many dead in Chicago, Boston, and Los Angeles, those cities were still struggling just to bury their dead.

The "hunker down" mentality soon was replaced by "every man for himself." Within a day, bedlam erupted in thousands of cities and towns all across the country. No one knew if the president had escaped alive. Even though Marine One had safely transported the president to Andrews Air Force base, the Secret Service would not let him go public with even a simple statement until they were confident he was secure. It was only after Air Force One landed at Fort Knox, Kentucky several hours later, that a statement was made clarifying that the president was alive and well. So shaken was the Service by the close call, that ever since, the chief executive was surrounded by dozens of M1 Abrams Main Battle Tanks and a large contingent of the 101st Airborne. By the time the news networks verified the source and content of the president's statement, it was too late. Almost every major American city was out of control.

Gas stations, corner pharmacies, and grocery stores were immediately swamped by an unprecedented number of customers frustrated with the shortage of available merchandise and unbearably long checkout lines. The situation escalated as stockers and cashiers deserted their posts in order to take care of their own families. Impatient shoppers quickly lost hope in the ability of stores to keep control when thugs elected to snatch and grab, rather than wait and pay. Folks that had never even so much as rolled through a stop sign turned into desperate looters. Fistfights escalated into gun battles, and hundreds lay bleeding or dead within a few hours. Banks in almost every major American city experienced riots. The branches had no choice but to lock their doors when the run on cash began. As the long lines of already frightened customers saw the banks' doors being locked, frantic customers became violent, desperate people.

It wasn't all complete chaos. Churches, synagogues, and communities initially banned together and attempted to organize. Labor unions, biker clubs, and even businesses held meetings in an attempt to establish order. Some were successful, given they already had a leadership structure in place and a few resources at their disposal. Small town mayors and city councils all over the country tried their best to keep order, and many achieved promising results. In the first few weeks after the White House had been overrun, it wasn't uncommon for some people to believe they were better off. The late mortgage payment was no longer a concern, past due taxes were scoffed at, and a court date for that speeding ticket was forgotten.

Rural communities fared the best. Folks residing outside of the major metropolitan areas already knew how to live self-sufficiently before the breakdown transpired. Tending gardens, canning seasonal vegetables, hunting and bartering had all become common ways to "get by" during the rough economic times that the country had been experiencing. Additionally, their lower population density prevented substantial drain on resources, such as firewood, orchards, local livestock, and most importantly, water.

Because the downfall occurred in early autumn, the eventual winter weather was devastating. Areas that typically coped well with snow and sub-freezing temperatures no longer commanded the basic resources for survival. When the interconnected electrical grid failed along the east coast, keeping warm became a daily struggle for millions of people. The combination of cold, hunger, fear and a vacuum of leadership left the metro areas even more chaotic and often violent.

Initially, the Pentagon recommended an old cold war era plan that had been dusted off and hastily modified. Originally created in the 1950s and kept current until the late 1970s, the overall strategy was to order various military commands to take control of key cities. The president approved the plan, and in retrospect, this had been a mistake. The military was almost one million personnel smaller, and the population was 70 million people larger than when the plan had been created. Additionally, the military was not ready for a nationwide deployment. National Guardsmen were called away from home right at a time when their families needed them the most. Even regular Army units usually take weeks to prepare for deployment, and the logistics of a mass, impromptu mission were a nightmare. All of the military depended on civilian suppliers and many of those businesses were no longer functioning. Food, fuel, and critical spare parts deliveries were either delayed, or never arrived at all.

Despite a heroic effort by all involved, it was still eight days before the first military convoys began to parade into the 40 largest American cities. By then, the police and fire departments were tattered at best, and non-existent in several areas. One veteran Army officer, assigned to the Denver area, was overheard comparing the Mile High City to Baghdad after the fall of Sadam. "We expected the police, city services, and fire departments to all be functioning. But it was just like Iraq when we rolled in there. Every cop, fireman, utility worker, and city manager had just vanished into thin air."

In some cities, the local government kept control and maintained order by establishing coalitions with local churches and businesses. In Salt Lake City, for example, the Mormon Church banned together with the city and state governments. Governor Pratt of Utah was quick to call out the National Guard and integrate their resources into the command and control structure of local police and other first responders. By the time the Army began to enter the city ten days after Washington D.C. had become a combat zone, they were neither needed, nor welcomed. When the general in command of the Army division assigned to that region met Governor Pratt and the mayor of Salt Lake City on the courthouse steps, the exchange was heated to say the least. The general handed over his orders for the establishment of martial law to the two leaders. In that document was a provision stating, "The right of free assembly is hereby suspended. No assembly of more than five people will be allowed without express permission and military presence." When Salt Lake's mayor asked for clarification, specifically if that rule included worship services, he was informed that indeed it did. The mayor asked the general to please remove his forces from the city limits, and Governor Pratt expanded the request to include the entire state. Unfortunately, the general had his orders and wasn't about to give in. Civil war practically broke out right then and there.

Every city was different, and the success or failure of the imposed martial law depended partially on the inherent skills of the officers in charge and how they interacted with the community. The commanders on the ground who were mature and flexible often achieved better results than those who went strictly by the book.

Another factor was the population, diversity, and culture of the city being occupied. A social scientist could have made an entire career of studying how Americans regrouped after the collapse. Miami had a large Cuban-American population, and

27

when things got bad, the city divided into racial segments. In Orlando, it was by age, with the retirement communities banding together. Dallas broke down into east siders versus north siders. San Francisco divided into three sections, gay, Asian and none of the above. Many cities and towns in the south returned to racial divides of black and white; although one officer in Mobile, Alabama noted this was because of geographic separations and didn't appear racial in nature.

As the military personnel started arriving, there began a series of unintended consequences. Young soldiers, suddenly pulled from the relatively isolated confines of their bases, were shocked to see the state of their countrymen. Of course, this led to many of them wondering how their own wives, parents and families were doing back home. As the situation deteriorated, the National Guardsmen were the first to begin deserting in waves. Their families were usually geographically close by and sometimes even within the city where they were constantly reminded of their directive to maintain order – at any cost. Desertion was not tolerated by the American military. As more and more personnel were consumed by court martials covering everything from dereliction of duty to sedition, overwhelmed officers began implementing harsher and harsher punishments. A young Nebraskan reservist was the first to be executed by firing squad, only two weeks after his unit occupied Oklahoma City. His crime was sneaking food to his cousin's family. Nothing degrades a military unit's morale more than having to execute their own. Many soldiers commented they had joined up to defend America – not kill her citizens and each other.

This is why the map on the wall of the V.I.P. quarters at Fort Knox continued to turn any other color but the blue that indicated federal government control.

Shortly after it became apparent the military wasn't going to be able to reestablish order, what remained of his cabinet had approached the president with a new plan. The problem seemed simple enough: food and energy. While the forces under the president's control had made every effort to jumpstart American food and fuel production, ultimately the original plan was failing. The inter-dependency of a complex, free market economy, combined with the geographic disbursement of resources, seemed to handicap any effort. No single location had all of the tools, spare parts, electrical energy, and know-how to reorganize effectively. The lack of communication capability was the primary cause of failure for many of the attempts. Almost every communication outlet in the United States was electrically operated. Without television, radio, email or newsprint, calling in

28

workers, repairmen or even finding the location of a spare part was next to impossible.

A case in point was when the commander of Portland was approached by two captains of Brazilian freighters tied up at the city's dock. They had several tons of refrigerated beef onboard, originally destined for Japan. The captains couldn't requisition the diesel fuel necessary to make the trip and offered their cargo if it could be unloaded before it spoiled. The commander agreed and ordered military personnel to go house-to-house and retrieve the crane operators and other workers to unload the ships. This seemingly simple task took a significant amount of time because the payroll records, and thus the home addresses of the workers, were stored on computers housed in a different city. A time consuming house-to-house search throughout the city of Portland was the only way to identify and contact dockworkers. Even if the military had commandeered the local television stations, powered them up, and broadcast the order for the crane operators to report to work, the audience would be mostly comprised of upper middle class people who owned generators. Electricity was not generally available to white-collar workers. By the time the beef was being unloaded, most of it had spoiled.

The president listened intently as his staff outlined what had been named Operation Heartland. It was clear that the resources available were insufficient to start any sort of recovery nationwide. The plan was to begin with a small, limited area of the country containing all of the basic components required to initiate the recovery. Once this had been accomplished, they would use that region as a base of operations and expand outward from there. As the assets required to accomplish this plan were outlined to the Commander-in-Chief, he had to agree that it all made sense. The first requirement was electrical power, and it was decided that nuclear power plants were the best option. The second requirement was for the refinement of diesel and gasoline fuels. The third, and most important aspect, was large quantities of foodstuffs.

The POTUS was shown a map that outlined the only region of North America known to possess all three of these requirements. The area identified by the White House and Pentagon experts was the Mississippi River delta from New Orleans, north to a parallel with Chicago. The territory for 150 miles east and west of the river would be the focus of the vast majority of the government efforts. Every available government resource from the Army Corps of Engineers to the Department of Agriculture would concentrate their efforts on securing this section of the heartland. The great river systems would provide the primary transportation artery. The nuclear power plants in Illinois and Louisiana would be restarted to provide energy. The vast stores of grain held in co-ops and along the river ports would be utilized to start producing food. When the spring planting season arrived, the Great Plains would once again feed the hungry nation. A large percentage of the nation's beef and poultry producers had prospered in this same geographic region as well. The Gulf Coast, the region's southern border, possessed numerous refineries and could also contribute seafood harvested from the Gulf of Mexico.

There were two major risks associated with Operation Heartland. The first was that the military had all but ignored this area during the initial deployment of forces. New Orleans, Baton Rouge, Memphis, and St. Louis were the only cities in the region that had received troops. The status of Memphis was currently unknown. The second risk was sacrificing the stability and recovery of the rest of the nation. What would happen to areas on the east and west of this initiative when resources were reallocated to accomplish the plan? Currently, most of the cities being helped by the military were barely maintaining some level of law and order, and if the number of troops were reduced, no one could predict the consequences.

But the most prevalent complication was the lack of good communication. Beaumont, Texas, central to an area rich in refineries required for Operation Heartland, was used as an example. No one knew how this medium-sized city had coped or organized after the collapse had occurred. Without at least minimum information, the level of resources required to initialize production of fuel was a complete unknown.

The president absorbed all of the information being presented, followed by the inevitable unending debates, due largely in part to lack of solid information. Debate without resolution was to be expected in a situation where no clear answer was apparent. After listening to point and counterpoint for over five hours, the chief executive cleared his throat and stood. The conference room became silent as he paced in front of the assorted maps and charts scattered around the room. Finally, he announced, "When all of this started, I agreed to our initial actions without knowing the facts. I'm not going to do that again. Whatever our next step is, ladies and gentlemen, it is our last. We have one shot left, and it needs to be the right move. We simply don't have enough information to make a good decision here. Can we - what do you call it, General - perform a reconnaissance of these critical areas, and then make informed decisions?"

Eventually, it was determined that a variety of experts, both military and civilian, would execute fact-finding missions. The president sensed what was at stake and wanted input from people he trusted. It was thought that the majority of senators and congressmen were in hiding or had not made it out of Washington D.C. alive. The few who had reported in to military commands had used their influence to be transported back to their home states and districts, and most had not been heard from since. It was finally determined that the president's staff would reconvene the next day with a list of recommendations concerning who would be assigned these all-important duties.

The following day had been a long and difficult one. For all of its former power and glory, the United States government was virtually incapacitated. A year ago, the president's staff would have been inundated with a practically endless list of available academic, business, and government professionals clamoring to fulfill the jobs. Some would have volunteered to expand their influence and power, while others were simply patriots. In the end, choices were made. Many of the people selected had a personal history with the president. For the first time in his life, the POTUS made his selections based purely on qualifications and his belief that he could trust the people who would bring him their recommendations. Influence, political favors and party influence had no bearing on his decisions.

Orders were drawn up and transmitted to the military commands surrounding the area defined for Operation Heartland. The POTUS hoped this plan would stir the phoenix to rise from the ashes of the United States. Those orders had been issued some time ago, and the information that had drifted in since was mixed at best. He was waiting on one final report before making the decision regarding the operation.

When the general returned a few minutes later, his report was the same as the day before – no new information.

Chapter 3

Bishop was lying prone between two large rock outcroppings. The small area of hardpan soil between the rocks provided some cushion, but really, he had picked the spot for concealment and the vantage. He had left the camper almost two hours before and slowly worked his way to this position. He was overlooking Highway 98, using a high-powered riflescope. He had found the mystery aircraft and was now spying on it from his perch some 200 feet above and 600 yards to the west of its position. The sun was past its zenith and behind him, but the day was still hot for this time of year. The brim of his hat was soaked, and he had to use his shirtsleeve to keep the sweat from running into his eyes.

It looked as though his initial assumption had been correct - the pilot had attempted to land on the highway. It hadn't taken any great knowledge or mystic powers to reach that conclusion - there wasn't another paved surface for over 50 miles in any direction. Bishop remembered the sputtering sound that had come from the plane's engine and guessed it had been without power during descent. While it was difficult to be sure from this distance, it appeared as though the plane had skidded off of the highway and into a small ditch along the side of the road. One wing was sticking up in the air, and the other was broken off, lying some 50 feet away. From this vantage, the plane looked like a plastic toy that had angered a small child and been thrown to the ground in frustration.

He had been watching the crash site for about ten minutes before he detected any movement. The low spot where the plane rested, combined with the protruding wing obscured most of his view. He did see someone moving down there, and suddenly realized there might be more than one survivor. *I didn't even think about that. How many people can a small plane like that hold? Two, four, six? Shit…there might be six injured people down there.*

After about 20 minutes, the realization set in that he had to get closer or find a better angle to observe the wreckage. Bishop was torn between the safety and survival of his family versus the feeling that he should somehow help those people on the road. *I should just walk away. They are no threat to Terri and me. Just set a few more tripwires between here and there in case they wander toward the camper. I should leave them to their fate.*

After scanning all around, he couldn't see a better spot. The terrain just wasn't going to cooperate. He had decided to pull back and head home, when he heard the second unusual noise of the day. It was another engine.

Highway 98 ran practically straight north and south through the barren west Texas landscape. Starting at the small town of Alpha to the north and ending at Big Bend National Park to the south, it transverses one of the most isolated, uninhabited areas of North America. Even before civilization collapsed, the roadway was lightly used. There were no gas stations, crossroads, or even utility poles for mile after dusty mile. It was one of the few state highways in the United States that had no posted speed limit. Drivers were welcome to motor along as fast as they felt comfortable. Besides, there wasn't any place for a police officer to set a speed trap anyway. About the only sign of civilization along the route was the Border Patrol Inspection Station just north of Big Bend. The men assigned to this remote outpost were often caught napping by the occasional ranch truck passing through. The running joke was that these agents were the best card players in all of Homeland Security given the amount of practice time they logged.

It took Bishop about 10 seconds to find the source of the new noise. Coming out of the heat waves rising from the blacktop, still two miles to the south, a Hummer raced toward the crashed plane. It wasn't a military vehicle, but a shiny, black civilian model with lots of chrome glistening in the remaining sunlight. *What the hell?*

Not only was it odd to see any car after the collapse, it was very strange to see a clean one. Bishop thought about his truck, safely covered in camouflage nets back at the trailer, and how dirty it was. *Who would waste water in these times to wash a car?*

The pristine black Hummer stopped right in the middle of the road about 100 meters away from the plane. Bishop was fascinated as he watched the doors fly open and five men exit. Through the riflescope, he could clearly see four of the men were armed with what looked like sub-machine guns or short-barreled assault rifles. *Well, so much for my sneaking down there for a joy ride in that pretty Hummer.*

Two of the men walked slowly toward the plane, yelling menacingly as they got closer. Someone answered them back, but Bishop couldn't make out any of the conversation. The exchange lasted for a few minutes. The other three men from the Hummer soon joined their comrades, and all of them slowly crept closer to the plane. There was talking, followed by carefully calculated movement, as they edged a few steps closer. Then the pattern repeated itself. *They are working their way toward that plane cautiously. I wonder why they aren't rushing up to help the survivors.* As they got closer, their weapons slowly moved to a ready position, and they spread out. *They aren't stupid; I'll give them that.*

Bishop jumped when the first shot rang out. It had to have come from the airplane because he had been watching the newcomers closely, and none of them had raised their weapons. He expected the exposed men on the road to scatter or move, but they just looked at each other and then to the guy who was clearly their leader. *They knew that was just a warning shot. It worked because they aren't moving any closer.*

The leader, unarmed, ventured forward a few steps with his arms spread wide. Bishop could discern enough of the body language to figure he was trying to talk "nicely" to the plane crash survivors. It didn't work…another shot rang out, this time causing the men to scatter.

Bishop switched his view to the airplane wreckage and could now see at least one of the passengers was a woman. He couldn't see her face clearly, but estimated she was late middle-aged. She was holding up a revolver, pointing it in the direction where the men had been standing. *Now hold on a minute, a woman? I didn't know there was a woman down there. Who are those guys anyway?*

Automatic weapons fire rattled from the other side of the road causing a lot of movement around the crash site. Bishop could no longer see the woman, but now two teenage children came into clear view. Bishop was sure it was a boy and a girl, and the boy was trying to cover the girl with his body. *Now just a damned minute…kids? They're shooting at kids?*

Now that he knew the color of the woman's clothing, he picked her out easily, hiding under the tail of the aircraft. And there was something else. She was bent over someone lying on the ground. Another person was lying under the body of the plane. He couldn't see the head, but from the dark spot on the clothing, it appeared as though someone were injured and bleeding badly. The picture was finally becoming clearer to him. At least four people had been in the plane and survived.

The visitors decided at that moment to rush the plane, and Bishop followed their movement through the riflescope as best he could. He watched, as moments later the two teenagers were forced from their hiding spot with their hands on top of their heads. The woman got off one more shot, but missed. She soon joined the two teens on her knees beside the road.

Two of the men dragged the injured fellow out from under the plane, and he was dumped in front of his friends. *What I would give for a little better vantage point. Sure seems like an odd rescue. If the victims didn't want to be rescued, why didn't the Hummer crew just leave? Why take the chance of being shot?*

Watching from such a distance and limited line of vision was frustrating. Bishop just couldn't figure it out. *How did the Hummer know the plane had crashed there?* It couldn't have been just a random discovery. *How did the crash victims know the Hummer crew was hostile? Why had they shot at them?* This just didn't make any sense. As he watched, the leader lit a cigar and sauntered forward, engaging the injured man on the ground. The leader would speak to the man, stop to listen, and then point at the children and woman.

After a few of these exchanges, the leader was becoming increasingly frustrated. His gestures came faster, and his voice was louder. Bishop could hear little bits and pieces now, but couldn't make out any words. Finally, the boss gave a commanding gesture to one of his team members, who walked over to the woman, jerked her up by the hair, and marched her around to the front of the captive audience. The guard pushed her back down to her knees in front of everyone, produced a pistol from his belt, and held it to the back of her head. *Ohhhh, fuck!*

Bishop wasn't prepared to shoot from this position. He started digging around in his load vest for his notebook that contained all of the ballistics data on this rifle and the ammunition he had loaded. He tried to keep an eye on the action below while at the same time getting out the DOPE he needed to take a shot. The leader was really pissed now and was stomping around on the road. *Don't do it man. Oh, God, please don't do it.*

It was all going downhill on the roadway. The young girl tried to stand up to help the woman when one of the goons hit her in the back of the head with the barrel of his rifle, knocking her to the ground. Bishop decided he had to chance a shot from memory and quickly did the calculations in his head. When he thought he had a solution for aiming, he aligned the crosshairs of the big riflescope and then froze. Since he was higher than the target, he was going to have to pull the trigger with the aim point right at the back of the boy's head. The plane crash family was between Bishop and the bad guys, and he was in a "hold under" position. What if his aim were off just a few inches? He couldn't do it. He finally found his pencil and began figuring the math as quickly as he could.

Bishop had been right with his initial calculation and put the crosshairs right at the back of the young man's head. If he were correct, the bullet would clear the top of the kid's skull by about 10 inches and hit the guard holding the pistol on the woman. If he were wrong, well, he didn't have time to worry about that now. He flicked off the safety, took a deep breath, and steadied his aim. But he was too late. The boss man turned to the executioner and nodded. The woman's lifeless body slumped to the asphalt in a bloody heap. Bishop turned his head to the side, sickened. He had seen more than his share of death, but to see someone killed like that made him feel ill. He finally forced himself to refocus, and what he saw this time was even worse. The young girl was now being hauled up to the roadway by two of the henchmen. Bishop knew with five targets, he wasn't going to get them all. If they scattered toward the wreckage, there would be hell to pay rooting them out. Their weapons were not the sort to be a threat right now, given his distance, but he wouldn't put it past them to try and hunt him down. *Terri. What if they started searching the area and found the camper? What would happen to Terri and the baby?*

Bishop put his cheek on the rifle stock and found his weld. He decided to kill the man who was holding the young girl. *You sick fuckers. So you are going to kill the girl in front of her family? Not today.*

But he didn't have a shot. One of the guards was now holding the boy who was fighting like hell to help the girl. He didn't have much of a chance, but was putting up a struggle regardless. The boss was bent over talking to the injured guy on the ground, much too close to shoot. The girl was screaming hysterically and flailing about - so much so that Bishop could not get a clear shot at her guards without the risk of hitting her instead. Finally, one of the guards got control of her and she went back to her knees on the blacktop. That was the window Bishop needed. *Send it.*

The bark of the .308 surprised even Bishop. The 180-grain TAP round, a specially designed flesh- destroying hollow-point, left the barrel at 2800 feet per second. The bullet was traveling much faster than the speed of sound and hit the thug before anyone on the road even heard the shot. The plastic covered tip of the bullet struck the man right at the base of the neck, almost decapitating him. Bishop realized his aim was a touch high and adjusted as the cloud of red mist and gristle began falling toward earth. Before the body crumpled to the pavement, Bishop fired a second shot.

This time the projectile hit the other executioner dead center, square in the breastbone. Simple physics took over from there. The base of the bullet was heavier than the point, and when the tip was slowed by the impact, the base had to go elsewhere. At that velocity, it had no other option but to tumble, and entered the body, flipping end over end. While the bullet entered at the chest, the round exited out the back of his upper thigh, tearing flesh and tissue the entire journey. All of this took less than a hundredth of a second, and resulted in another lifeless body falling to the blacktop.

The remaining two guards and their chief were now reacting to the first shot. One guard immediately let go of the boy and started running toward the Hummer. The boss rolled to the side and scrambled across the road where a ditch gave him some cover. The third guard made a mistake. He scurried to the body of the plane for cover, but decided to stick his head up to see if he could spot the shooter. Bishop didn't even bother with trying to time a headshot as the guy bobbed up and down. The thin skin of the aircraft was hardly good cover. A third shot was soon on its way. When the round hit the aluminum sheet covering the airframe, it performed as designed and expanded. By the time it exited the other side, the bullet had broken into several projectiles, taking bits and pieces of the hull along with it. In the end, the guard's body was struck by dozens of small fragments of shrapnel, and he lingered only moments.

Bishop now had two remaining rogues to deal with, but he couldn't see either one of them. He suspected the first had made it back to the Hummer and was taking cover behind it. He knew their commander was still close to the wreckage, but couldn't see the man. The boy had managed to pull himself together, and along with the girl, was trying to drag the injured man back to their side of the road. *Has to be family – nothing else would elicit such a response.*

Bishop was now wondering how to resolve this little standoff and kept shifting his gaze back and forth between the Hummer and the boss. He didn't want the remaining goon to sneak up on his position, but also didn't want the boss taking one of the children as a hostage. It was the noise of the Hummer's motor starting that distracted him. Before he could react, the vehicle started moving, and at the same time, the boss deftly leapt from the ditch and pulled the girl back to his side of the road. *Shit!*

The Hummer acted as an effective shield, as it squealed to a halt in front of the boss. Bishop couldn't fire out of fear of hitting the girl. In a few seconds, the vehicle spun around in the desert and hightailed it south, a surreal scene in its wake.

The roadway was littered with bodies and pools of blood. The aircraft wreckage still sheltered two living souls, and Bishop had to react quickly before the Hummer crew returned with reinforcements. As he made his way down the hillside, he was trying to think about what to do with the remaining two survivors. He and Terri barely kept enough food on the table as it was. Unless that airplane were full of food, there was no way they could feed two more mouths. He decided he would take the two back to Meraton as the older man looked to need serious medical care. He and Terri should go there anyway, as they wanted the town's doctor to check out Terri's pregnancy.

After he had cautiously approached within 100 feet of the wreckage, he called out, "Hey, you at the crash site. I'm the guy who just helped you. I'm coming in. Please don't shoot."

It took a little bit, but a young voice eventually yelled back. "Don't try it. I've got grandpa's pistol, and I'll shoot if you come close." *Kid's got balls; I'll give him that.*

"Son, I don't have time for this shit. It's going to be dark soon, and your friends will probably be back. I know your grandfather is hurt badly, so let me come in, and I'll help you out."

Another voice, older but weaker, yelled back. "Bishop? Is that you?"

Bishop froze. *How the hell do they know my name? That voice - where have I heard that voice?*

It took him almost a full minute to recover from the shock. When he did, he called back, "Yes, my name is Bishop. Who are you?"

He could hear mumbling coming from the airplane for a bit. Eventually, the response was from the kid again. "If you are Bishop, what's your wife's name?"

Bishop's patience was wearing thin. "My wife's name is Terri. I don't have time to play 20 fucking questions. Identify yourselves or I'm out of here, and you're on your own."

The kid's voice sounded almost embarrassed, "Come on in, Bishop. I won't shoot."

39

Chapter 4

Senator Moreland was delighted by the sound of the birds singing outside his West Virginia home. It was so rare to hear their chorus this time of year. As he stood looking through the enormous glass windows surrounding the great room, he was tempted to venture outside and enjoy the melting snow and bright sunshine with the little flock. The afternoon had delivered a clear blue heaven, and the sun was working hard to melt the icicles hanging from the roof. After two consecutive days of angry clouds and blowing snow, the front had passed, allowing one of those wonderfully crisp days that were clearly welcomed by the few remaining birds who hadn't made the journey south some months ago.

The senator needed a day like this. For over two years, it seemed like everything in life had been grey. Never black nor white, always grey, like the rolling clouds and darkened sky the last few days. Perhaps this was a sign of the times ahead for his country and his people. Perhaps a new, wonderfully bright day was about to warm the troubled land - a land weary of its long struggle under an overcast of decline.

Another sip from the hot cup of tea cradled in his hand warmed his insides. Maybe his ice would melt as well. He gazed down into the valley that spread out below the Appalachia estate. Patches of earth were becoming visible, seeming to rise out of the sea of white snow. It reminded him of the diagram he had just been studying. It was a map of his country that showed patches of the territory he and his interests now controlled. They had been struggling to uncover as much of America as they could, thawing a small town or city, here or there, from the blanket of anarchy and confusion that fallen on the land like a deep snow. Now some of the larger cities were joining their cause, and just like the sun would eventually thaw the frozen land, he felt their leadership would shine bright enough to free the rest of the nation.

Moreland wasn't sure who had coined the name "the Independents." It was a fact that independent voters in America had been growing in numbers for several years. While his movement's ideology reflected many of the views associated with that constituency, more so than either Republican or Democrat, it was more than political alignment that drove his cause. It was a growing realization that the two party system, Electoral College and many other aspects of government were antiquated and cumbersome in light of today's tangled, mass of bureaucracy.

The tax code, the Federal Reserve, the justice system and many, many other core components of the United States had either outlived their usefulness or had been gamed by small groups of powerful men. The Independents sought to rebuild government as it was envisioned by the founding fathers. One of the senator's staffers had even compared the organization of the Independents to a Second American Revolution.

Moreland could understand the association. This revolution was to have been different in so many ways though. Rather than muskets and cannons, the internet and media were to be the primary weapons. There was no foreign king to overthrow, nor was there any foreign military occupation on U.S. soil. Over a year ago, when they had first began to seriously organize and recruit new members, he remembered talking to a group of senior military commanders about the movement. One of the attendees observed that a foreign military occupation would make their cause more palatable and could thus serve as a catalyst for their recruitment efforts. Rebelling against an outside presence required no soul-searching or evaluation for the average citizen. Little did Moreland or anyone else know how prophetic that observation had been. No one could have predicted that within a year so many citizens of the United States would live under military control and martial law.

An illegal martial law brought about by an illegal order to execute a nuclear strike against a foreign power. That's what the honorable gentleman from West Virginia kept telling himself. So many of their actions in the last few months had been justified by that belief. No honorable man, no patriot, no one who loves his country could sanction what the Independents had accomplished in the last few months without such a justification. To undermine the elected authority of the people, the President of the United States, during a time of such dire national crisis couldn't be reconciled by any other means. The president had broken the law with those two orders. If the country hadn't fallen into the abyss, no doubt he would have been impeached. His executive powers were no longer legitimate.

The senator turned and walked back toward the kitchen. His loyal aide of over 35 years was busy preparing dinner, flashing his boss a quick smile. "More tea, sir?"

Moreland paused for a moment before responding, "No, Wayne. One is enough for me today. The sunshine is thawing these old bones, no need for a second cup of warmth."

Wayne inquired, "Our guests will be arriving within the hour, sir. Do you require anything of me before your meeting?"

The senator was reassured by Wayne's concern, "Just the usual fine food you always manage to prepare, Wayne."

"Of course, Senator. Your words are too kind. We are blessed to still have the materials for me to work with."

Wayne was a little surprised when Moreland stayed in the kitchen. He normally didn't spend much time here, and it seemed like his old friend had something on his mind.

He came immediately to the point. "Wayne, am I a traitor?"

Wayne didn't even look up from the potatoes he was slicing. "What is a traitor, sir? One man's freedom fighter is another man's traitor. One man's revolutionary is another man's rebel."

The older man chuckled. "Okay, so we're going to debate definitions here, are we? You know what I mean Wayne. You know me better than anyone on this earth. Is there any chance history will look at me with the critical eye of sedition?"

Despite his culinary duties, Wayne didn't even hesitate. "Senator, perhaps you should rest before your meeting. You aren't thinking clearly, sir. History will be written by the victor. You, of all people, should know that. If our cause fails, you will be remembered as the man who stalled the recovery of the United States of America. It will be written as though you had glorious visions of power and rule. You will be painted as a man who would be dictator in order to enslave the freedoms of the people. If the movement succeeds, you will be celebrated as a visionary and patriot. Ticker tape parades and bank holidays will mark your birthday for years to come. You know the consequences, Senator; you've always known. "

The senator smiled broadly at his assistant. "You old smartass. I should've known better than to start this conversation with you today. I could tell you were in a foul mood by how strong my tea was."

Wayne stopped slicing and looked directly into his old friend's eyes. "You are always welcome to openly display your self-doubt and anxieties to me. I wouldn't reveal those inner feelings to anyone else though. It's too late for real indecision; you've come too far, and there's no turning back."

The senator laughed and responded using his deepest southern drawl. "Self-doubt? Anxieties? How dare you, suh! Why if I were a younger man, I'd slap you with a white glove and demand you defend your honor, sur."

Wayne tilted his head backwards and smiled. "Now that would be funny, Senator. Two old goats like us heading out to the veranda with dueling pistols. Wouldn't the Washington Post give anything for a picture of that?"

Both men chuckled at the thought, and Wayne continued preparations for the evening meal.

"Seriously Wayne, do you ever wonder if Abraham Lincoln questioned if he were somehow misguided in his quest to keep the union whole?"

Wayne pondered the senator's question for a few moments and chose the words of his response carefully before speaking. "And I quote President Lincoln, 'Always bear in mind that your own resolution to succeed is more important than any one thing.'"

The Senator smiled at Wayne's choice of quotation, but countered with one of his own. "Nearly all men can stand adversity, but if you want to test a man's character, give him power."

Wayne replied, "Touché. Senator, you didn't begin this movement to overthrow the government. You never once proposed treason. I remind you, sir, that this all started as a purely political movement to stop the insanity in Washington."

"While I respect your view of the truth old friend, if we fail, I don't believe history will agree with you. We were very clandestine in our affairs. Even our communications were secretive and protected."

Both men thought about that for a bit. When Senator Moreland first began his efforts, he realized the need for some method of communication that couldn't be traced, intercepted, or discovered. This requirement allowed them not only to operate under the radar of the press, but federal and military agencies as well. Coincidentally, one of the men joining their cause was a professor at M.I.T. preparing to market a rather clever invention to several of the predominant cell phone providers. His contraption converted a regular cell phone into a satellite communications device. The professor originally began the research for the military, who wanted a small transceiver that would work anywhere in the world without any land-based support. The simplicity of its use was quite impressive, and its encrypted signal rendered it practically impossible to trace. You merely dialed the cell number of the person you wanted to reach. Simple, secure, and inexpensive - the senator had financed the manufacture of almost a thousand of the diminutive units without hesitation.

At first, their secret communications network was used to avoid the ever-prying eyes of the press and competitive political organizations. The senator knew that U.S. intelligence agencies were occasionally used by the party in power to scout the competition. The professor's device would circumvent any chance of discovery, even by the most capable agencies. When the grid failed, their satellite phones were probably the most sophisticated non-military communications in the world. It had

44

allowed them to organize and execute activities that would have otherwise been impossible.

After the White House had been overrun by protestors, the Independents had initially tried to support the federal government in maintaining control. And when the president declared martial law without congressional approval, many in the movement voiced concern, but cooperated. As the situation deteriorated, Senator Moreland had asked his followers to take control and organize only the areas that had been ignored by the military. More than ninety percent of the country had been left to fend for itself, and without critical infrastructure, the help the Independents promised was welcomed.

When his people approached town councils and churches, explained their plan and movement, it had been easy to gain almost everyone's buy-in. Those who hesitated were shown documentation of what was happening in the large cities being "controlled" by the president. No one wanted *that* loss of freedom combined with extreme hardship in their own backyards.

What had really surprised the senator's organization was the ease at which military officers switched sides. As one Army Captain explained, he had sworn an oath to support and defend the Constitution of the United States against all enemies, foreign and domestic. A core element of the Independent's message was a strict adherence to the U.S. Constitution. The infamous Patriot Act of 2004 allowed the president broad powers in declaring martial law, with one important restriction – The president had to "advise Congress in a timely matter." This critical provision had never been executed. The president made no effort to either assemble congress or contact any of its members. The president had broken the law.

There were other motivating factors. The demoralizing duties being heaped upon the typical military field officer were unprecedented. The American people, and often members of their own command, were treated as the enemy. Many of the troops who joined the Independents were looking for any excuse, any logical reason to make a change. It was easy to convince these men that it wasn't the people who were the domestic enemy, but rather a president who had run from the fight and had now taken over as a dictator.

When a staffer at Fort Mead passed along information about the new plan called Operation Heartland, all of the Independent's leadership was suspicious that a spy existed in the organization. An almost identical plan had been initiated weeks ago in the Independent camp, and the similarities were hard to dismiss as coincidence. This led them to accelerate their efforts, especially the recruitment of military personnel. Assets, once loyal to the president, were being drawn to the Independents in growing numbers.

The discovery that both the Independents and the executive branch were targeting the same exact territory prompted Senator Moreland to gather the brain trust of his organization. A critical decision had to be made. And as is required in a republic, he was careful not to make that decision alone.

Chapter 5

By the time he was finally approaching the crash site, Bishop realized where he had heard the mystery voice. As he rounded the front of the fuselage, he discovered the Colonel lying on his side and a young man pointing a pistol at him with shaking hands. Bishop slung his rifle to the rear and moved immediately toward the injured man. On the way past the kid, his hand shot out like a striking snake and snatched the pistol away from the frightened youth. He ejected the rounds from the weapon and tucked it in his belt, and then knelt beside his old boss.

The Colonel's words were strained. "How are you son? I bet you didn't expect visitors today, did ya?"

Bishop hardly recognized the man before him. "Colonel, how badly are you hurt? Let me take a look."

Bishop helped him roll slightly to one side and immediately saw the problem. There were about two inches of metal shaft protruding from the Colonel's body, right above his kidney. The metal had once been part of the aircraft, but now it looked like he had been shot through the side with an arrow. Bishop started to ask him how deep the metal was inside him, but a sudden coughing fit produced a bloody mist that sprayed from his mouth and nose. *Shit.*

Bishop unhooked his rifle from its sling and unloaded it. He turned to the boy and said, "Do you know how to look through a riflescope?" The lad, clearly frightened of Bishop, nodded vigorously.

Bishop tried to soften his voice, but the adrenaline still bled through. "I want you to take this weapon and go about one football field down the road. I want you to watch for anyone heading toward us from that direction. They may not stay on the road, so sweep back and forth. We need as much warning as possible. The rifle is unloaded, so if you see anybody, hightail it back here, yelling all the way. Now go."

The young man hefted the weapon and started to turn, but Bishop grabbed his shoulder and stopped him. "I'll take good care of your grandpa. Just one more thing before you go. Have you had anything to drink since the crash?"

The boy pointed toward a pile of empty water bottles lying nearby.

Bishop held his shoulder tightly, but his eyes showed concern. "Good. Are you Okay? Hurt? Need anything before you go?"

"No, I'm fine. What about my sister?"

"First things first – there's nothing we can do to help her right this minute, so get going. Remember, you see anything odd at all, get your ass back here pronto."

Bishop opened his blow-out-bag and began digging around inside, not sure what he could do with this type of wound. While he was hunting through the contents, he momentarily looked up to check his patient and noticed the Colonel's eyes were intently focused on something, and tears running down his cheeks. Bishop followed his gaze and saw the woman's body lying in the road. Her empty stare was looking straight back at the Colonel.

What a dipshit I am, thought Bishop. He immediately went to the airplane and dug around until he found a plastic tarp, probably used to cover the aircraft during bad weather. He went to the woman's body, and under the watchful eye of his ex-boss, gently wrapped her in the tarp. He then picked her up and moved her from the man's field of view. Something was familiar about her, but Bishop had way too much on his mind at the moment to think about it.

When he returned to the Colonel's side, the man looked up at Bishop with pathetic eyes and mouthed the words "Thank you." Bishop nodded back and then said, "Sir, I can't do much for you here. I have basic pain relief in my kit, but nothing stronger than aspirin. We have to get out of here, and I think we can move you. Is there anything else I can do for you right now? Anything that would make you more comfortable before we head back?"

The older man thought for a moment and then said, "My granddaughter, Bishop…I need you to patch me up so I can find her. But right now, I need you to get my briefcase from the plane. It has some documents in it. And there is food and water in the luggage hold, but not much. There's no gasoline left, we were empty."

Bishop went to the aircraft and soon found the briefcase, along with a couple of cardboard boxes filled with food and water.

"What is your grandson's name, Colonel?"
"David."

Bishop yelled out to David, waving him back. As soon as the boy arrived, Bishop asked him to stay put for a few minutes and keep an eye on his granddad. Bishop reloaded his rifle and slung the weapon while trotting off toward the nearest patch of scrub oak. He proceeded to cut several long branches, each about seven feet long and a little smaller in diameter than his finger. Returning to the wreck site, Bishop retrieved a small bundle of para-cord and a large net from his pack. He spread out the net and began weaving the oak branches around its edges. When he had several of the fishing pole sized sticks in place, he bound them together with the cord and tested his contraption. He had constructed a sturdy, makeshift stretcher.

Bishop handed David two bottles of water from the boxes and told him to put them in his pocket. He filled his camelback water bladder with another and left the rest. After he had gently rolled the Colonel onto the stretcher, he scattered the scavenged food around the patient's head to put the majority of the weight toward the front. Next, he hurriedly collected all of the weapons that were lying around and hid them behind a nearby rock formation. He might want to retrieve them later.

Bishop and David each grabbed one end of the stretcher and lifted. After verifying David was going to be able to handle the load, the two began their journey as the sun set over the now quiet west Texas desert.

Chapter 6

Bishop and David stopped to rest several times on the trip to the ranch. After carefully working their way through all of the tripwires and booby traps surrounding the camper, Bishop instructed David to stay put and keep an eye on their patient.

Bishop walked to within earshot of the camper, picked up a small stone, and threw it onto the metal roof. It was a few seconds before Terri's voice called out, "What's the password?"

Bishop, whose muscles ached a bit from the late afternoon exercise, was fatigued and a little puzzled. "Terri, we didn't set a password."

Terri, in a playful voice responded. "Oh well, just so I know it's you, Bishop, which of my features is your favorite?"

Bishop hesitated, knowing Terri had no idea what had just transpired on the road. "Ummm... errrrrr... your eyes?"

Terri was delighted he had fallen into her trap. "Imposter! My Bishop likes certain other features the best! You better turn around and get outta here, you charlatan! OR...being a fair-minded kind of girl, I will give you a choice. Would you prefer I deliver the slow death by staking your body to a fire ant hill, or would you rather I just put you out of your misery with a high velocity lead treatment?"

Bishop rolled his eyes wondering where she got this shit. *Okay, enough.* "Terri, damnit, I have an injured man with me. We don't have time for this shit, and I *do* like your eyes the best. Coming in – shoot me if you want to."

Bishop and David were soon standing outside the camper, toting the Colonel on the makeshift stretcher. Terri, now embarrassed by her bad timing, met them with the big medical kit, busily working to get everyone situated in the Bat Cave.

Bishop hurriedly introduced Terri to both David and the Colonel. Obviously, the first order of business was to attend to the wounded man. Terri flashed Bishop a perplexed look as she assessed the Colonel's condition. He looked very pale and the "ambulance ride" seemed to have taken its toll. Bishop had applied some compress dressings earlier, but those had only slowed the bleeding. Terri dug out some stronger painkillers and helped the Colonel get them down. He refused anything to eat, but greedily swallowed the water she offered him. Throughout the triage session, Bishop updated Terri on the events that had occurred at the Highway 98 landing strip, diplomatically leaving out certain painful details in light of his guests. Bishop's skeletal account of the afternoon's events continued while Terri fussed over their guests' accommodations as much as their current situation allowed.

While David scarfed down some rabbit meat, Bishop and Terri ventured outside the cave to talk at length.

"Bishop, we have to get the Colonel to a doctor. We can't do anything with that rod sticking through him. Should we leave tonight and head to Meraton?"

Bishop sighed, "Babe, I am exhausted, and I couldn't get the truck ready that fast anyway. He is weaker than before, and it might be because we had to move him. I'm also worried about those guys with the Hummer. I might be full of shit, but I read them as the type to return with numbers. I'd hate to be going down that highway at night and run into them. I think we need to stay here for now and head out tomorrow after I make sure the coast is clear. Besides, there is the girl to think about. I don't want to abandon her."

Terri weighted Bishop's logic and then replied. "You're right. We can take turns tending him and sleeping. Do you have any idea what he's doing out here? It would be way too much of a coincidence for him to just accidentally fly within yards of the ranch. So how did he find us?"

"No, there wasn't time to ask any questions. I'm hoping after he rests for a bit, he can talk. I also want to know what those guys with the Hummer wanted. The whole scenario was just weird."

She reached up and stroked his cheek. "Why don't you get some rest? I'm wide-awake and wouldn't be able to sleep anyway. I'll stay up with them. Besides, I haven't had anyone different to talk to for months."

Bishop snorted at her last remark. "Terri, they are our guests, not prisoners. Please…don't torture them too badly," a comment which earned him a solid punch on the arm.

Terri went back to the cave to take care of their visitors while Bishop sauntered over to the shower room, a clear plastic bag containing ten gallons of water that had been warmed by the afternoon desert sun. The water temperature was tepid at best, but in his post-adrenaline rush state, he just didn't care. He untied the rope that pinched the hose closed and let the cool water pour over him. *What I would give for a handful of shampoo!*

They had attempted to make homemade soap, but were either missing some key ingredient or had messed up the process. The result of their labor was a brownish yellow goo that had neither lathered, nor smelled very good. Terri remarked that the odor seemed to attract a kettle of turkey buzzards she spotted circling above. "Bishop," she had remarked, "I don't believe this is a recipe for soap at all. I think this vile concoction

52

of yours is *designed* to attract these foul creatures so that you don't have to expend the effort hunting them down!" Bishop had endured unfathomable tortures and teasing during this little experiment. He decided if he were going to be accused of this heinous offense, at minimum he would reap the reward of Terri's reaction when he returned with one of the smelly birds. Terri had stopped him when he exited the camper upon retrieving his rifle, no doubt aware of his plan for payback. "Let's not forget that is a protected species hun," she said with a slight smirk on her face. She, however, never teased Bishop about the soap again.

Best to keep a good sense of humor these days - I guess. Bishop grinned to himself as he rinsed the desert off his aching body. Terri often resorted to using a bucket of very fine grain sand she kept close by to clean her skin since, for her, half the joy of showering was the multitude of tiny bubbles with their soapy rainbow colors as well as the girlie scent that accompanied it. Bishop made a mental note to resolve the soap issue when they next visited the Meraton market. He had to smile thinking about walking through the market asking if the soap's fragrance was known to attract scavengers or raptors. Even a decent recipe would do the trick.

Bishop had been looking forward to going back there. Meraton was a small town, only a few hours away. During the trip from Houston, they had seen the absolute worst of mankind and the effects of anarchy. Meraton had restored some of his faith and hope in human beings. The people of Meraton, probably due to the isolation of their tiny village, had retained some of their civilized behavior. There was even an open market where peaceful commerce, old-fashioned bartering, and a wide assortment of goods were available. In the Bat Cave, under an old tarp, was a stack of gold that belonged to the people of Meraton. Bishop and the townspeople had found the booty after a gunfight with a gang of mid-western bank robbers. Gold, given the current state of the economy, was worthless. The town's leaders believed that one day the treasure might have value again and could be used to rebuild. They also understood that the loot might attract others who might not be so civil minded. So when Bishop and Terri left Meraton, the fine citizens of the township entrusted the couple to take the gold with them and store it at some "undisclosed location."

The gold! That was it! Bishop tied off the water and hurriedly dressed. He rushed into the Bat Cave and found the Colonel was sleeping. David and Terri were sitting in the corner quietly talking. Terri looked up, surprised to see her husband. "I thought you were going to rest?"

Bishop was eager to fill her in, "I took a shower, and it dawned on me what those guys in the Hummer were after."

Terri, happy to be one step ahead of him, pointed to the stack of gold under the tarp in the corner.

Bishop replied, "I knew it! Now it makes more sense. But how did they know its location?"

David chimed in, "They kept asking Grandpa about gold. Where was the gold; where was Bishop? Where was Bishop's ranch?"

It all came together at once. The town's leaders had made it known that Bishop was taking the gold with him. They wanted that information spread around so trouble wouldn't come to Meraton seeking the treasure. Their plan had worked, but rather than the town attracting troublemakers, Bishop was now the target. *No good deed goes unpunished.*

"Bishop, I always thought you were a stand-up guy, not a pirate with buried treasure." A scratchy voice startled them from behind. "Could someone please give me something to drink?"

They all turned around to see the Colonel was awake and had been eavesdropping on their conversation.

Terri handed him a cup of water while Bishop pulled over the old chair. When Terri declined his offer for the perch, he took a seat. "How are you feeling, sir?"

After gulping down half of the water, the injured man looked up, nodded, and thanked Terri. He turned his gaze to Bishop and said, "I've been better, but that codeine is helping. God bless you for that."

The Colonel seemed to gather himself and gave Bishop a questioning look. "Bishop, are you the type of man who values gold over life?"

"No, sir."

"I didn't think so, but I'm still relieved to hear you say it. You know those men have my granddaughter, and they want that gold. You know they're going to want to make an exchange."

"I believe you're correct, sir. I've been thinking about that. The gold isn't even mine, and I really don't want that shit here anymore anyway. The people who own that treasure are good folks, and will not value metal over the life of your granddaughter, sir. You can be assured that I'll gladly trade it for your granddaughter. I don't know how or when, but I'm sure they'll be back, and I intend to give them exactly what they want."

Both men remained silent for a few minutes. Terri, sitting on the floor close by, gave Bishop a look of "*Go on, keep him talking*," so Bishop did his best to engage the Colonel on another topic.

"Colonel, we are planning to take you to a nearby town in the morning. A few months back, a doctor moved into town. We'll get you patched up right away, sir."

The Colonel looked at Bishop and then over to David, who seemed to be fascinated with the weapons stored in Bishop's rifle rack. Seeing that brought a fleeting smile to the old man's face. When his focus returned to Bishop, his expression was all business. He whispered, "Bishop, you know that's not going to be how this one plays out. I have three purple hearts. I've had my ass shot up before. This isn't going to end that way, and we both know it."

Bishop started to protest, but stopped. The man was right, he'd be lucky to make it a few more days at best. While they had stopped the external bleeding, it was clear his internal organs were badly damaged. Anyone could see it was taking a toll for him to speak. Bishop looked the dying man straight in the eye and simply nodded.

"Well good. Now that we have all of the emotional bullshit out of the way, I'm sure you have a hundred questions for me, and I have a few for you as well. Since you are more likely to be around to use the information, please go first."

Bishop thought for a moment and then began. "Thank you, sir. So, what brings you to our neighborhood?"

"We were all in Houston when everything fell apart. The grandkids were staying with me while their father, my son, was on assignment with the Air Force. I tried to stay put. I know enough people in the military that I thought I could work with the Army when they took over. Actually, I was kind of pissed at the time. I couldn't believe they waited so long to regain control. Anyway, the Army bulldozed several blocks of homes in order to create a firebreak, and the fires in Houston burned out then. Electricity was even restored for a few days to parts of the city. Things were looking up."

The Colonel paused to cough a few times and take another drink of water. He rested for a few moments and then continued. "When the fires abated, food and fuel became the primary issue. About two weeks after martial law was declared, a convoy of rations on its way to Houston was ambushed near Huntsville. The Army was stretched so thin they hadn't provided proper escort security for all those trucks. I was in the occupation headquarters when a report came in that the transport had been found in a field outside of town. The trucks had been emptied of all supplies and fuel. The guardsmen driving them were either dead or missing. Some people speculated it was an inside job. Others blamed the robbery on the convicts that had to be released from the big prison there when that facility depleted its provisions. I don't think anyone really knew what happened or who was to blame. No way to tell. Those trucks were just a stopgap measure anyway. The real supplies were supposed to be delivered by the Navy via the Port of Houston."

Bishop interrupted him, "*Supposed* to be delivered?"

"I think the Navy had their own share of issues, but I can't be sure about that. For some reason, the ships didn't show up as scheduled. The Army estimated there were 1.7 million people under their control in the city limits. Almost 800,000 were homeless after the fires, or had just shown up to be fed. In round numbers, that meant the government needed to provide 3.4 million pounds of food per day. That is one hell of a lot of food. Logistically speaking, you don't truck in that much weight when fuel is in short supply; you have to use ships. The military commandeered hundreds of civilian semi-trucks, but those were allocated to support the inland cities like Dallas."

Bishop quickly did the math in his head. That much food equaled out to 150 full semi-trucks...*per day*. That didn't count medical supplies and other necessities of life. Without thinking, Bishop whistled out loud.

"I see you grasp the scale of the problem. Everything seemed like it was dependent on something else. Command, or what was left of it, couldn't deal with the interlocking priorities or critical path. The general in charge of stabilizing Houston received orders to get the refineries in Pasadena running as soon as possible. The famous strategic petroleum reserve was stored as crude oil and had to be refined into gasoline and diesel fuel. After a house-to-house search, the Army gathered up a bunch of refinery managers and engineers and hauled them to one of the facilities. Of course, they needed electrical power to start the processing. But the power grid was badly damaged by the fires, and the mobile generators used by the military were not powerful enough to do the job. That led to another search for Houston Power and Light employees to get electrical power reestablished to the refinery. Seemed simple enough at the time, but due to the fire damage, the plan required some spare parts to fix the grid in order to restore power. In normal times, a few keystrokes on a computer would have generated an order that would have been trucked in for receipt in a few days. But these are no longer normal times. The local power plant had been shut down for safety anyway. It burned coal, which was normally hauled in by rail car. There was no diesel fuel left for the trains."

Terri chimed in. "Oh god, and all the while, people are getting hungry and frustrated."

The Colonel nodded at her, "You're absolutely right. Tensions were high, and a few weeks after the Army took over, the first riot occurred. Some kids had broken into a warehouse where the military stored its own rations. The teens were caught red-handed, and a frustrated major ordered their execution after a quick tribunal. He lined them up against a wall right in front of about a thousand people standing in line for their daily rations. Without any public explanation, a firing squad shot what turned out to be the captain of the local football team and about half of the defensive line."

Bishop and Terri both just sat silently, shaking their heads.

"At first, the public reaction was just shock. A local preacher began stirring up trouble soon after word of the incident spread around. The next day, about 5,000 people began to march toward the closest military command post. At first the soldiers tried to defuse the situation, after all, the rioters were other Americans. But one thing led to another, and before it was all over, another 1,800 citizens were lying dead in the streets. The situation only went downhill after that. Command was already stretched so thin trying to get infrastructure functioning, it couldn't deal with civil unrest. I've seen this kind of thing before. Officers did what they always do when overtaxed – they got heavy-handed and tried to force the issue. When the water supply became tainted, I knew that was it. I heard the medical officer brief the general that he could expect 200,000 cases of dysentery because sewage had contaminated the city water system. I started making plans to get my family out of there. I had some personal problems as well, but you get the picture."

Terri was trying to digest it all and asked, "What about the rest of the country? Couldn't someone send help? Not every city was burning like Houston."

"I listened to the situation reports from all over the country. The military took control of the 40 largest cities. They simply didn't have the manpower to handle any more than that. In reality, that number was probably too many, given current resources. Anyway, some commands reported initial success. Others were destined to fail from the start. The president disappeared for a while after a protest on the National Mall turned violent and overran the White House. According to one report I heard, the Commander-in-Chief barely got out alive. The corridor along the east coast was simply out of control. Police forces rebelled against military authority. Every remaining government organization thought they should be in charge and then soon enough, *no one wanted to be in charge.* In New Jersey, the governor took control of the National Guard after the commanding general committed suicide. The New Jersey 2nd fired on a group of New York City police officers who were crossing the river to raid a warehouse. During the confusion, the 307th, trying to control New York City, came to the rescue and a full-fledged battle broke out before anyone realized what was happening. Some of the Army units simply stopped reporting in. No one knows what is going on there."

The Colonel paused for another drink and then closed his eyes, clearly exhausted.

Terri gave Bishop a look that said, "*Let him rest,*" and Bishop had to agree. After looking at his watch, he decided he had better get some sleep himself. It was almost 2 a.m., and tomorrow promised to be a busy day. He kissed Terri good night and went to the camper to lie down.

Chapter 7

While Bishop and David had been carrying the Colonel back to the camper, Estebon Julio Belisario peered out the large picture windows of the Chisos Mountain Hotel. Despite everything that had gone wrong the last few weeks, he was still awed by the view. The lodge had been built at the perfect location to take advantage of the unrivaled beauty of Big Bend National Park. As Estebon watched the last of the sun disappear to the west, he couldn't help but think about the parallels between this place and his current situation.

The initial reaction by first time visitors to Big Bend is, "Why would anyone want a national park here?" After a long drive across the desolate, un-noteworthy Chihuahuan Desert, crossing into the park's well-marked boundaries typically produces disappointment. The landscape is just more of the same. About the only point of interest is a slightly higher than average mountain, located some 19 miles after you pass the park's entrance.

Emory Peak rises to over 7,000 feet above the surrounding desert floor. As one of the tallest points in the Chisos range, it is the very heart and soul of Big Bend. To the south of the rocky crag, over 200 miles of the Rio Grande River serve as both the border with Mexico, and as the boundary of the park.

The winding highway to the park's headquarters begins climbing the steep northern slope of Emory Peak using a series of switchbacks cut through the desolate rocky landscape. About three quarters of the way, attentive observers begin to notice the presence of plant life, and even trees further up the face of the mountain. As the road tops the rim of the mountain, the contrast is breathtaking. An enormous, fertile valley spreads out for miles to the south. With over 1,200 plant species and abundant wildlife, the vista looks completely out of place when compared to the sparse, moon-like landscape just a few hundred yards behind. The vibrant green colors on the path ahead immediately bring to mind the phrase "The Hidden Valley."

He was a man of seeming contradictions. It was this startling contrast with which Estebon found similarities between Big Bend and himself. As he watched the colors change on the exposed purple and red formations to the west, he couldn't help but feel a sort of brotherhood with this land.

Just like the park, Estebon's ruthless, harsh exterior surrounded what he considered to be the inner sanctum of a calm, peaceful man. Fate had determined that he be born into one of the harshest, most violent places on earth. That environment demanded that he develop a lifeless, desert persona in order to survive. Nobody rose to the top of the Colombian M-19 organization at the age of 21 without being respected, and in his world, that was generally equivalent with being feared. It wasn't Estebon's ruthless actions that had allowed him to rise to that esteemed position however, it was his IQ. Colombia was full of desperate, vicious men who would kill or torture - men with no moral compass whatsoever. No, what separated Estebon from all the rest was his intellect. He was known throughout certain Latin American circles as a genius. At times, he could be quite charming as well. Just like the terrain that surrounded him, he visualized himself as having a rich, surprising interior.

Estebon's brainpower was first recognized when he was a young teenager, working as a messenger boy for the Medellin cartel in the slums of Bogotá. He was waiting for his pickup one day at a cartel "count house," a place where receipts were tallied. The man in charge was frustrated because the laptop computer used to convert currency wasn't working. Estebon bailed the guy out by simply calculating the answer in his head. The skeptical boss tested him on a few individual line items, quickly verified with a hand calculator, and decided to trust the kid's math. Estebon had not only been correct to the peso, he had saved the man from a serious beating, sure to be delivered if the report had been late.

At first, the older cartel members used Estebon's gift for entertainment. They would play games or give him puzzles to solve, but never anything serious concerning the business. Still, word spread about the child prodigy and his amazing math skills. Estebon was more than just a walking calculator though. He was extremely observant and his memory was flawless. He remained a quiet youth, always in the background, watching everything and learning from the exposure.

Unlike most men of his age, Estebon constantly observed and analyzed the world around him. As the United States and Colombian governments began systematically breaking apart the cartels, he became even more street-wise. The primary lesson that this conflict had taught him was that direct involvement with illegal activities eventually leads to having a black helicopter hover over your location. He could not help but notice that when the ropes dropped out of the sides, things ended badly.

Estebon figured out that a fringe involvement with illegal activities was acceptable, as long as you maintained the proper political allies. For Colombia, at that time, the best recipe was a touch of cartel involvement, a pinch of money laundering, and just the right amount of opposition political activity. The latter helped maintain the respect of underworld colleagues. The M-19 organization was considered by most intelligence agencies to be a second tier, badly funded rebel organization. Their violent history was primarily associated with overrunning remote villages and ambushing random Army patrols. On occasion, the group had gotten lucky and scored some local headlines, but overall, they were a bumbling group of incompetents.

Estebon found out that the group was all but disbanded due to a lack of funding and leadership. He also calculated that the current government needed to appear as though they were working to achieve a coalition of sorts. Estebon, through his cartel connections, made contact with a few of the primitive M-19 cells and made them an offer – give him two months as their acknowledged leader and he would give them legitimacy as well as fund the organization's inevitable growth. With a little pressure from his cartel friends, they agreed.

His second step was to contact the Colombian government and offer to rein in the rebels in exchange for their being given a fair share of representation in the assembly. The general public grew weary of the constant barrage of bickering and escalating violence. When the newspaper headline "Reconciliation Talks in Progress" appeared, the president's popularity with the people immediately soared, as the citizenry breathed a collective sigh of relief.

Over the next few months, Estebon maneuvered both sides perfectly, and he soon rose as a legitimate political figure in Colombia. The common man viewed him as a champion of the people while the cartel winked and nodded, knowing he was really their guy. The Colombian military really didn't care to know who or what he was as long as he delivered on bringing M-19 to heel. When Estebon provided the American DEA with the location of certain M-19 cells, he received even more power and respect. When he aligned himself with the anti-cartel task force, delivering intelligence on certain cartel activities, he became untouchable.

Everything had been going very well for Estebon until the terrorist attacks crippled the United States. For years, the prevailing wisdom was that if America caught an economic cold, Latin America got the flu. When America started sliding over the edge of the abyss, it was clear that most of Latin America would quickly follow, perhaps even arriving at the bottom before the great power to the north. Again, Estebon's foresight had been on target. A few weeks before everything had completely collapsed, he had gathered several of his most trusted men and left Colombia for a "Trade Exploration Mission" of northern Mexico and the southern United States. He had carefully studied the region looking for a defendable, remote location that would provide for the needs of his rather large entourage. He sought a retreat that was isolated enough to be protected, yet provided for a reasonable existence.

His wife and daughter loved American National Parks. Estebon's position and wealth had already positioned them to tour many of the popular U.S. tourist attractions. They had been to Yosemite, Redwood, the Grand Canyon and many more.

Estebon couldn't predict how long the injured beast that once was America would hold on. He also had to maintain some level of credibility with his cover story. The answer to all of his problems was Big Bend. He knew that all U.S. National Parks were somewhat self-sustaining, due to the Americans' silly preoccupation with being "green." In addition to many of the buildings and infrastructure being solar powered, there was food and fuel stored in vast quantities. The laws governing federal jurisdiction meant there would only be the lightly armed park rangers as potential obstacles to his relocating his operation there. He estimated that the terrorist attacks combined with martial law would leave the park practically abandoned. He was again, correct.

Under the guise of his official Colombian trade mission credentials, his family and 30 of his most trusted men had been visitors at Big Bend when everything fell apart. They had pretended to be frightened, stranded guests until the right moment, when they had killed the rangers and taken over the park. Their diplomatic immunity had made it easy to bring in weapons, disguised as trade samples.

Estebon had been clueless about the gold until a few weeks later. One of his men reported an odd encounter with a low-level member of the Mexican cartel. The chance meeting had occurred in the Mexican village of Chilua, right across the river from the park. It seemed that rumors were flying all along the border about a hoard of gold in the town of Meraton. The cartel messenger had initially been ordered to meet with a Yankee gang who wanted safe passage to the coast. They had offered to pay with gold - lots of gold. Apparently, when the shit had hit the fan, the cartel's man had never received further instructions and had been waiting ever since.

Estebon could care less about the gold. He knew it had little value now that things had gone to hell. Perhaps one day it might, but right now, a loaf of bread was worth more than a pound of gold. What disturbed him about the meeting was that the cartel believed Estebon already had the booty. His man was plied with free drinks at the village's cantina in an attempt to dislodge the location of the treasure. When that hadn't produced results, threats were made and a shootout had seemed imminent. His employee, an ex-Colombian Special Forces captain, was reliable. The good captain had reported that his new Mexican friend asked over and over again, "Why else would you be here? Why else would you pick this spot if not to take the gold, eh?"

His beloved Carmen and little Isabella disappeared the next day. They had become bored and begged to go for a hike in one of the park's remote areas. Estebon had finally given in, ordering two bodyguards to accompany them on their trip. Six hours later, a rock sailed through the front window of the hotel. Tied to the rock was a note wrapped around Carmen's ring finger. Still attached to the bloody stub was the wedding ring he had given her ten years before.

The note demanded a meeting at the river. It recommended he bring the gold with him. There was to be an exchange for his loved ones. Estebon didn't have the treasure, but, of course, went to the meeting anyway.

He didn't know the Mexican who came across the river in a small rowboat. The man was clearly nervous, and obviously just a messenger. When Estebon told the hombre that he didn't have the gold, the messenger had handed him a hand-written letter and paddled away very quickly.

Estebon read the letter and was stunned. He was given three weeks to find the gold and deliver it to the Santa Rosa church in Cuidad. If he failed in his mission, Isabella would be sold into slavery and Carmen would lose much more than a finger.

He had immediately called his men together and implemented a plan to send teams into all of the surrounding towns to gather all of the intelligence they could. It was to be a subtle effort with each team pretending to be travelers simply passing through. Estebon's second order was to search the desolate countryside outside of the park. Using two vehicles, a grid-based examination was initiated to discover any local people and again, gather all of the data they could.

The two spies sent into Meraton came back to the park quickly with information that was useful to Estebon. The couple recounted a story of bank robbers, the gold and a mysterious stranger named "Bishop." Clearly, the legend of this gringo had grown over time, or so Estebon believed. According to the sources in Meraton, this Bishop person had taken on an entire gang of vigilantes single-handedly and slaughtered them all. Estebon thought the story was one of those tales that had become embellished with each telling. Losing three men this morning, to an exaggerated legend, had Estebon reconsidering exactly who he was up against. Bishop was said to have a ranch west of Meraton. The gold was rumored to have been taken to that location.

Estebon had immediately changed the mission of his roving search teams. The new priority was to find Mr. Bishop's ranch. It was one of these search teams that had seen the Colonel's airplane that very day.

Estebon did the math, and the odds were not good. There were thousands of square miles of inaccessible territory, and even if the rumors about this Bishop character were completely blown out of proportion, he might still be capable of hiding any sign of a buried treasure.

Estebon believed he had finally found Bishop, or more accurately, Bishop had found him. He glanced over at the young girl asleep on a nearby couch and smiled. He would soon meet this so-called living legend face-to-face. Estebon returned his gaze to the steep walls of the mountain and the exposed formations of igneous rock. He couldn't help but compare himself to the rugged landscape and realized a sense of confidence. He identified with the mountain – strong and indifferent to surrounding events.

In truth, the parallel never existed. The mountain was a manifestation of strength and a presence of resolve. Its honor was an unquestionable majesty, fully exposed and laid bare to time itself. Air, wind, and water were true tests of character. Endurance measured in eons of sun from above and magma from below earned confidence. Nature's magnum opus rarely has much in common with "fool's gold."

Chapter 8

Bishop's watch alarm was set for 4:00 a.m. It managed two beeps before his finger squashed the tiny reset button. He groggily rubbed his eyes and rolled out of the narrow camper berth that had become his bed. He stretched and then immediately checked for Terri, who was not in her normal place beside him. He reached for the nearby pistol before everything came rushing back. He relaxed a bit, believing her to be with the Colonel and David, hopefully catching a few precious winks in the Bat Cave. He pondered if he would ever wake up like a normal person again. He looked out all of the windows of the camper, listening for any sign of something being wrong or out of place. Everything seemed fine.

He pulled on his best pair of faded blue jeans, found a clean pair of socks, and then laced up his boots. The socks smelled like sun-dried laundry, and that was one of the positive things about their lifestyle. They had used the last of their toothpaste supply last week, so this morning he brushed his teeth using baking soda. He double-checked the pistol's safety and then slowly made his way to the cave. He entered the rock walled room and found Terri asleep in one of the hammocks. The Colonel and David were both resting on the floor. Bishop checked the Colonel's breathing and found it labored and slower than before. He was unsure if that were the effect of the codeine or a sign of the man's physical deterioration.

A bright flash of light outside startled him. It was followed quickly by the sound of thunder crashing against the exposed rock walls of the box canyon. *Oh great, just what I need - a thunderstorm.* While this area of Texas received little annual rainfall, the occasional winter tempest did roll through. Normally, Bishop would have welcomed the rare squall. Today, given his plans, a storm was going to complicate an already difficult situation.

Using a lighter, Bishop started a fire in a miniature cook pit he had built inside the cave. After the shootout with the bank robbers in Meraton, Bishop had found their loot in a hotel room. While he had no use for the gold and other stolen valuables, he did find something that he treasured even more than precious metals. Somewhere, somehow, the thugs had managed to pick up two 10-pound bags of coffee beans. Since they were all dead, it was impossible to know where the gang had come across this roasted prize. The grateful people of Meraton had gladly rewarded Bishop with the beans.

While 20 pounds of coffee was not an infinite supply, Bishop figured his back stock would last about six months if it were rationed carefully. He had joked with Terri that he was going to mount an invasion of Colombia after his stores were depleted. Knowing Bishop's weakness for his morning caffeine, she hadn't been so sure he was kidding. *She didn't like my joke about having a new career as a bean counter, either.*

While the coffee water was heating, Bishop ran his checklists and packed equipment. His attention was diverted from his work when he heard the now uncommon sporadic sound of fat raindrops falling on the desert floor and watched as another flash of lightning ripped the night sky.

"Is that thunder?"

He spun around to see a sleepy looking Terri sitting on the edge of the hammock, her legs dangling over the edge.

"Good morning, sleepyhead; and yes, that was thunder."

Terri looked down at their sleeping guests and whispered, "Oh wow. Bishop, it hasn't rained since we've been here. You never told me there were thunderstorms in this part of Texas."

Bishop's eyebrows went up and down. "Baby, you haven't experienced the best part of a desert storm. Just wait."

Terri walked over to the cave's doorway and peered outside while Bishop made his coffee. He was about to take his first sip when a gravelly voice asked, "Is that coffee?" Bishop glanced to see the Colonel's head turned toward him.

Bishop whispered, "Sure is, sir. Would you like a cup?"

"My god, son. That is about the dumbest question I have heard in a month of Sundays. My dying wish would be for a hot cup of hot Joe." The injured man managed a small laugh. "I guess that's not so funny anymore –'dying wish,' that is."

Bishop grinned and began exploring the cave for another mug. He opened a couple of plastic containers and poked around, but couldn't find any cups. Terri walked directly to the right box, pulled out a set of two matching mugs, and silently gave Bishop a triumphant look that clearly said, "*You couldn't find your head if it weren't attached.*"

Bishop became teasingly sarcastic. "Terri, would you like coffee as well?"

She grinned and replied, "While you're at it, yes, please. I feel like celebrating because of the storm."

On cue, the rain began coming down in sheets, and they could hear the wind whistling through the rocks surrounding the camp. Bishop handed Terri her drink and motioned for her to follow him to the doorway. When they were standing side by side, he whispered in her ear. "Take a deep breath through your nose, baby."

Terri allowed the air to fill her lungs before stopping. She repeated his instructions a second and then a third time.

"Oh my god! What is that wonderful smell?"

"I'm not sure, but it does that every time it rains here. I don't know if it's the soil, or the plants or the rocks. Maybe it's everything."

"How long does this last?" she asked, inhaling deeply again.

Bishop scratched behind his ear. "It varies, but at least another ten minutes or so. You will notice the same scent again when the storm stops, but it doesn't seem to linger as long then."

Bishop looked at his watch and really needed to get moving, but decided some things were more important than timelines. He put his arm around Terri, and they stood together drinking coffee, watching the lightning, and enjoying the aroma of the desert. *One of these days, I hope this is the most important thing we have to do together. Dear Lord in Heaven, please make that day come soon.*

Estebon was busy giving instructions to his men. It wasn't raining at Big Bend, 70 miles to the south of Bishop's ranch. He could hear the thunder in the distance and wanted to get on the road north as soon as possible. He had initially thought about placing some of his personal thugs in the area to trail Bishop back to his ranch, but had quickly dismissed the idea. He couldn't be positive Bishop would even take the bait. The girl he had taken hostage knew nothing. According to her story, she had slept through most of the plane ride, having been exhausted after her family's escape from Houston. She claimed to have awakened as the engine sputtered out of gas, and then they crashed on the highway. She'd never heard of Bishop or any gold. She knew her grandfather worked for a large oil company and had been in the Army. She also was worried that her granddad was going to die from the injuries sustained during the crash landing. The woman Estebon had executed was a good friend of her grandfather's, but the girl knew little more than that.

Estebon had interrogated his share of people and believed she was telling the truth. While her lack of knowledge didn't help his confidence in the plan, he still believed Bishop would show up at the site of the plane wreck. He was counting on the relationship between Bishop and the old man. He would not be disappointed.

Bishop left the camp in the rain. He was wearing a poncho that covered his pack and most of his body. He knew from experience that his legs would be soaked in a short time, but his core would remain dry and warm. He had changed weapons, preferring his favorite M4 Carbine to the heavier, longer-range rifle he selected for the first expedition in search of the Cessna. While this rifle didn't have the range or a scope that was nearly as powerful, it was more effective at close range. It was his "go to gun," as he had trained and fought more with this weapon than any other.

As he made his way through the maze of tripwires and booby traps surrounding the camper, he was concerned that either the rain or wind might set off one of his devices, or make it inoperable. He made a note to check each one after the storm passed.

He was also troubled about the lightning and the visibility it would provide for anyone searching for his camp. He was using a night vision device, or NVD, and knew it would give him an advantage over any foe. Now, his advantage was somewhat diminished, given the light created by the occasional flashes of the storm.

As he made his way toward the road, he was careful to take his time, moving slowly, staying behind cover as much as possible. He could have taken a shortcut and arrived at the crash site much sooner, but that involved covering several hundred meters of open ground. Wisely, he kept to the rock formations and small patches of scrub that dotted the area.

When he finally reached a good observation point from which to view the wreckage, he took his time and scanned the entire area several times. Nothing appeared to have changed, with the dead bodies still strewn about exactly as he remembered. His next move was to identify and note every location nearby where he would personally choose to set up for an ambush. He pinpointed seven such locations; and that was simply too many spots to check and verify no one had arrived before him. Bishop decided to change the game somewhat, and proceeded toward the south for several hundred meters. As he moved through the rocks paralleling the road, he eventually came to an area that contained only two good hiding positions. *There's no reason why our meeting has to be at the plane. I'll just move the location.*

Estebon finally had his men loaded into the Hummer, and they were slowly winding around the switchbacks on the trip down the ridge. He knew the plane was about 140 kilometers to the north, a little over an hour's drive. He settled back in his seat and watched the brilliant explosions of light illuminate the northern sky.

Bishop picked his spot on the highway and set to work immediately. The rain had slackened to little more than an annoyance as he began slicing branches from the nearest scrub patch. He pulled out his net and began weaving the foliage through the mesh. It took him almost 20 minutes to complete his homemade "ghillie suit," and he wished there were some way to check how well it blended in with the landscape. He really didn't need it to pass any detailed scrutiny, only to hide him for a short period of time.

While he continued to watch the roadway to the south for any sign of movement or lights, he sprinted back to the wrecked Cessna, and using a steel rod, pried one of the seats out of the back. He quickly carried the empty seat back to his selected spot on the highway, placing it square in the middle of the road on a painted white stripe.

Running back to the aircraft, he secured his rope around one of the dead men and dragged the cadaver back to the seat he had relocated. The body was already stiff from rigor mortis, but Bishop was feeling little respect for the dead after being reminded of the earlier execution. It was slow work, pulling the heavy body behind him, and his legs began to burn, but he finally made it. He propped the corpse against the airplane seat and savagely kicked the backs of both legs, breaking the bones. He then picked up the body and sat it in the seat. It looked like the dead man had decided to take a break right in the middle of the highway. Bishop wished he had one of the Colonel's cigars. It would have been funny as hell to put a smoking stogie in the cadaver's mouth. *That should be a pretty effective stop sign.*

He checked the roadway to the south and wasn't surprised to see headlights off in the distance. He finished just in time. Bishop moved to the side of the road where he had dropped his net, now a makeshift ghillie suit. He covered his head and back with the net, then knelt beside the road, hoping he would blend in with the small patch of scrub nearby. It wasn't perfect, but it didn't have to be.

He chambered a round in his rifle, double-checked the safety, and then remained absolutely still as the area around him began to grow brighter from the glow of the Hummer's headlights.

69

Estebon was focusing on the lightning off to the east when he felt the Hummer slow drastically. His attention snapped to the view directly in front of their speeding vehicle. Ahead, something was in the road, just coming into sight. The wipers cleared the big windshield of the few drops of lingering moisture, and the driver pushed the brakes hard.

Estebon's first thought was that Juan had *not* been killed by the sniper a few hours ago. He and his men had left in a hurry and not checked the bodies, and the man was still alive. After studying the figure sitting in the chair, a second possibility flashed through Estebon's mind - that Juan had survived long enough to begin walking home, but had died on the way.

As the Hummer crept closer, the color and details of Juan's body became clearer, and the driver crossed himself before coming to a full stop.

Estebon realized what was going on within a second or so of their stopping. He chuckled and turned to the passenger in the back seat, "Our friend Bishop is already here. He must have decided he didn't want to meet at the airplane, and this was his way of telling us. I'm thinking I would like this man…perhaps in another place and time."

The driver, still staring at his comrade's corpse, took a moment to digest his boss's words. "He's here? Ambush?"

The driver reached for the gearshift to put the car in reverse, but Estebon stopped him. "Yes, he's here; but no, not an ambush. If he wanted to ambush us, we would already be dead."

The passenger in the backseat instructed the driver to slowly navigate the Hummer around, using the beams to scan the landscape for their prey. Eventually, they were pointed back the way they had come, without having detected Bishop.

"Turn off the motor, leave the lights on; everyone get out slowly and stand in the beams. Make no sudden moves, and leave all of the weapons in here," Estebon instructed.

He noted the driver gave him a questioning look, but then reached for the ignition key to turn off the engine. The three men slowly exited the vehicle, walked about twenty feet, and stood in the open road, each facing a different direction.

When the lights had passed over Bishop and continued their search, he had exhaled and thrown off the net. He waited until he was sure they weren't coming back for another pass and then trotted to the side of the road. He was now walking up from behind the Hummer, checking to make sure no one remained inside.

He stepped through the beam of the driver's side headlight, his shadow causing all three men to snap their attention back toward their ride. A voice rang out.

"Senor Bishop, my name is Estebon. You will forgive my skipping the pleasantries, but I believe we have business to conduct."

Bishop wanted to get to the point as well. "I'm listening."

Estebon tilted his head slightly to one side and used his hand as a shade against the bright beams. "It would help our discussion if I could see you without discomfort."

Bishop's voice relayed impatience. "I'm just peachy right here. Go ahead with your proposal."

Estebon didn't understand the word "peachy," and that gave him a bit of a pause. *No matter*, he thought, *the meaning is clear.*

More from habit than any tactical advantage, Estebon took a step toward the man he was about to address. The sound of Bishop clicking off his safety froze him in mid-step. Estebon's two companions visibly stiffened, but neither moved. Estebon shook his head and then held his arms out wide. "You are making it difficult to establish our partnership."

Bishop was becoming annoyed. "I don't partner with scum. State your business. I'm a busy man."

Estebon shrugged off the insult and continued. "I have the girl, and you have the gold. We each have something the other needs. I propose a contract to resolve the situation to each other's mutual benefit."

Bishop didn't hesitate. "I will exchange the gold for the girl."

Estebon smiled and replied, "No, Senor Bishop. An exchange is unfortunately not enough. You see, because you greedily hoarded this treasure, my wife and daughter have been kidnapped. I am afraid you are going to have to deliver the gold and retrieve my family. I will then trade my guest for my wife and daughter."

This revelation took Bishop by surprise. He had anticipated a simple swap, conducted under his terms. He needed to buy some time to digest this new information. "I have an alternative proposal. How about I shoot the three of you right here in the road, take the Hummer, and drive down to Big Bend. Once I get there, I will slaughter the rest of your group and bring the girl back home."

Estebon smiled easily and replied. "I anticipated you might consider that plan. There is a, what do your Hollywood movies call it? Oh, yes, a 'secret signal' is expected when we return to the park. Senor, you would be one man against many,

71

and while your skills are impressive, your visit would be expected this time. Besides, you would never find the girl. As I'm sure you are aware, the park is a very big place."

Bishop decided to play a mental game of chess with the man while he figured out what to do. "I'm one step ahead of you, Estebon. I thought you might set up a secret signal and wanted you to confirm that. Thank you. Now I'll shoot your two friends and then convince you to tell me both the secret code and the location of the girl. I can be *very* convincing."

Estebon sounded genuinely disappointed. "Senor, I would only tell lies under torture. Please, senor, you know that. Let us both quit being dramatic and talk seriously."

Bishop had to admit, the man was no fool. He didn't like this new turn of events one single bit. He had anticipated a simple but dangerous trade, gold for a girl. Now he was being drawn into a far more complex situation. "Let's just say I'm willing to consider your proposal for a moment. When and where is the exchange for your family to take place?"

Estebon exhaled, relieved that Bishop valued the life of his hostage enough to at least consider his offer. This had been the one unknown variable in his calculations. "The deadline is eleven days away. The exchange is to take place at a church on the outskirts of Juarez."

Bishop shook his head and whistled, "Juarez?"

Estebon didn't understand, "Senor?"

"I wouldn't have gone in to Juarez *before* everything fell apart. You must know that was the most violent place on the planet outside of declared war zones. I think the casualty rate was even higher than most of Afghanistan. I heard not long ago that an open war had broken out between the people of El Paso and the good citizens of Juarez. You're telling me that you want me to deliver 300 pounds of gold, by myself, into the most violent city on earth? Not only that, you want me to safely retrieve two women who are in God knows what condition and probably don't even speak English? Mister, I think you are loco. I don't know that I would attempt that mission, even if I had an entire armored battalion."

Estebon had anticipated this reaction. "First of all, Senor Bishop, there is no need to take all of the gold. Do you really believe the bank robbers told the truth about how much gold they had in their possession? The ransom note I received did not demand an actual amount. Secondly, no one said you would be going alone. I am going to send my best man with you. He is a very skilled individual such as you, Senor. And finally, there is no need to travel through El Paso. The church selected for the meeting is on the outskirts of the city. You would pass through very little of Juarez."

Bishop considered the options. "Why don't I just trade you all of the gold for the girl? You and your men can take whatever amount you want to Juarez. It sounds like you have good people. Why do you need me?"

Estebon replied, "I have considered this option. I know that we are being watched, perhaps there is even an informant among us. I believe we run the risk of being ambushed within an hour of leaving the park with the gold. Secondly, my men are brave, but they are urban fighters, not experienced in the field or with military backgrounds. There is one exception, the man I spoke of before. You see, Senor Bishop, not only is he a former captain in the Columbian Special Forces, he's also my brother-in-law. It is his sister and only niece that are being held."

Bishop hesitated, not knowing what to do. He didn't want anything to do with this, but he couldn't let Estebon kill the Colonel's granddaughter either. The gold stored in the Bat Cave had become the proverbial "hot potato," and Bishop wanted it out of his life. *What has this world come to when I can't even give away 300 pounds of pure gold?* On the other hand, there was Terri and the baby. If he walked away right this moment, where would this all end? The plan to spread the news about the treasure being taken out of Meraton had worked – too well. Every desperado and thug within 150 miles would come looking for "Bishop's Gold." He recalled the legends of the "Lost Dutchman's Mine" and several others. Many treasure hunters had spent their whole lives looking for those rumored riches. Why should this pile of metal be any different?

Estebon had, again, anticipated Bishop's dilemma. "Senor, why don't you go home and think it over. The sun is rising on a new day. Meet me here in two days at the same time, and I will bring the good captain along with me. The two of you can sit quietly and talk. His English is excellent. Perhaps that will assist you in making your decision. As an act of good faith, my men and I are going to face the south and enjoy a good cigar. When we are finished, I plan to walk back to our car and return to the park. The girl in my care will be unharmed until 11 days from now. Is this agreeable, Senor?"

"Yes, I'll see you in two days at this spot, at this time. If I'm not here, the answer is no. If I am here, it only means I am considering it, or have decided to kill you and whoever you bring in order to better my odds."

Estebon nodded toward Bishop as his men turned their backs to the Hummer. True to his word, each man pulled out a cigar and began smoking.

Bishop watched them for a few moments and then disappeared into the pre-dawn desert, or so it seemed to the three men enjoying their tobacco.

Chapter 9

As the Hummer sped south toward Big Bend, Bishop was hanging on for dear life underneath the oversized SUV's gas tank. He had considered regrouping at the ranch, but decided against that. He needed more information and elected to hitch a ride. He rolled underneath the back of the vehicle and quickly used a carabineer hook to secure his load vest straps to the tow hitch and tucked his feet in the leaf springs. His pack barely cleared the surface of the road, and he knew it would drag if the driver hit any potholes along the way. Bishop also understood if he fell while traveling at full speed, those potholes would be the least of his worries.

As they sped south, Estebon was very content with his plan. This Bishop character was brave, and no doubt was experienced, but he wasn't any different than the dozens of such men he had manipulated throughout his life. The boss turned to the passenger in the backseat and questioned. "So, brother-in-law, what do you think of your future comrade in arms?"

The man in the back was very serious. "I was unimpressed. I'll tell you Estebon, we don't need this man. I could command a handful of our men to make the exchange and retrieve my sister. I have worked with these American types for years. Their ego and macho attitude will be trouble. They believe themselves invincible."

Estebon pondered the captain's words for a moment. "I think this man is more timid that you give him credit. Perhaps he is cautious because of these times in which we live, or maybe he has had recent experiences that have reduced his ego. I think he will do exactly as we ask and increase the odds of our family being returned to us. We have already lost so many men, why risk sacrificing more? My friend, trust me on this – it is all about the odds. The numbers do not lie."

"I will do as you ask Estebon, but I still remain skeptical. Bringing in this stranger, this unknown…I just don't like working with unknowns."

Bishop was starting to cramp and realized the heat from the exhaust was becoming a problem. He also was worried that the suspension would flex and crush his ankles. *This was a bad idea. Why do I get myself into these situations?*

A few minutes later, the speed of the Hummer decreased substantially, and Bishop felt the angle of the SUV start to change as it began to climb the mountain.

Bishop knew Big Bend well. With the park being one of the few attractions in the area, he had spent more than his fair share of his teenage years hiking and camping at the facility. When he had been in high school, he had earned a chance at a summer internship sponsored by the park rangers.

The hairpin turns of the switchbacks demanded the driver slow the vehicle's speed to less than five mph. Bishop counted the turns and knew that everyone in the passenger compartment would be focused on the road due to the steep drops and remarkable vistas. It was now daylight, and Bishop had to get out from underneath the Hummer before there were lots of eyes watching the boss return.

Bishop reached up and unhooked the steel clamp that held him to the frame. He counted, waited, and then pulled his legs out from between the leaf springs and let the heel of his boot drag on the pavement. He waited until the driver was coming out of a very tight turn and let loose.

Even at such slow speeds, the force that took control of his body was shocking. He tumbled over and over on the asphalt surface, every rotation causing his back to flex over his pack. His arms, covering his head as much as possible, were scraped, cut, and no doubt bruised. As he rolled, his rifle took a beating and its stock jabbed into his body armor.

Bishop had intended to scramble to the side of the road immediately after releasing his grip on the underside of the car. The impact to his body left him lying in the road, trying to catch his breath, and making sure nothing critical was broken.

After a few moments, he finally made it to his knees and quickly checked that none of his gear had been knocked off during his tumble. *Now I know what it's like to be a pair of sneakers in a dryer.* Only his hat was lying on the asphalt surface a few feet back.

Bishop limped off of the road and vanished into the surrounding forest.

The Hummer pulled into the circular drive in front of the lodge. All three men quickly exited and proceeded immediately inside. The driver, always hungry, headed directly to the kitchen to see if he could rustle up some breakfast.

Estebon checked in with the guard to verify all was well with his hostage. After being told the teenager had slept through the night undisturbed, he wanted to shower and get some sleep. His mind was too exhausted to think through the next phase of his plan without some rest. As he entered his empty room, he was reminded of how much he missed his family. After a quick shower, he fell into a fitful sleep, his mind still engaged in the uncertainty of the condition of his wife Carmen and their daughter, Isabella.

Bishop cautiously made his way toward the main lodge. From his elevated perch, he had watched the Hummer navigate through the valley below and eventually heard its motor shut off. The lodge was somewhat isolated from the other buildings at the park, so he was pretty sure that is where his adversary had stopped.

This slope on Emory Mountain was steep and treacherous. Bishop had to be very careful not to fall from the 50 to 100 foot drops. He slowly made his way to a location that afforded him a bird's eye view of the lodge and surrounding terrain. Sure enough, the Hummer was parked out front in the semi-circular driveway. He identified a strategic spot to hide and observe the vigilantes and settled in to wait for nightfall.

Terri was worried sick about Bishop. While he had warned her there was no way of knowing when the hoods would show up to talk, she still couldn't help but be concerned. *He's a big boy and very capable; he'll be okay.*

The Colonel's breathing was more labored, and she knew they had to get him to a doctor. She didn't buy into this macho thing about it being predetermined the injured man was going to die. Bishop and she had agreed that if he weren't back by a couple of hours after dawn, David and she should load the Colonel into the truck and head to Meraton.

While David was busy cleaning the breakfast dishes and checking on Grandpa, Terri went to the back side of the camper where the pickup truck was underneath a camouflage net. The once-beautiful truck was covered with months of dust and road grime collected during their trip from Houston. While the spring provided plenty of water, Bishop had decided not to wash the vehicle, giving the truck "its own Ghillie suit."

As Terri pulled away the netting, she remembered how proud Bishop had been the day he had taken delivery of the new pickup. It had been a difficult decision for them as the economy had been so weak, and the young couple had barely qualified for a mortgage. A new car was a luxury few people could afford. But one morning, when Bishop's old truck wouldn't start, he had been reprimanded by HBR and informed in no uncertain terms that promptness was essential to keep his job. That threat had frightened them both, so squeezing a new truck into their budget was the decided course of action.

Terri shook her head, marveling at the difference between that once shiny, wonderful smelling, factory- fresh vehicle and the machine before her. A small scrap of duct tape could be seen sticking out from under the hood, an emergency patch for when a bullet had punctured a radiator hose. There was a crease and small hole in the fender where the bullet had entered the engine compartment. The front bumper was scratched and slightly dented where she had used the truck as a battering ram, pushing in a door. There was another small hole in the backseat passenger window where a second bullet had almost killed her husband. When she opened the door, the slight odor of blood could still be detected. Bishop and she had scrubbed the interior several times trying to remove the smell, a remnant of when he had almost bled to death in the backseat.

David scrutinized the truck. "We are going to try and make it to the town in *this*?"

Terri snorted. "This old beast has carried Bishop and me through hell. Don't judge a book by its cover, young man." She got behind the wheel, inserted the key in the ignition, and the motor started immediately - purring like a well-oiled machine.

Terri turned back to David and explained, "This truck is our lifeline. Bishop takes very good care of it. It's the only transportation we have and, well, you never know when we might have to bug out again or rush to Meraton for help. Walk around and check that all the tires are full, would ya?"

David nodded and proceeded to circle the truck, kicking each tire. Terri didn't have the heart to tell him that wouldn't do any good, but at least his mind was off of his grandpa for a bit. She couldn't help herself and reached for the buttons that controlled the radio. She tried the AM band, hitting the seek button and letting the device search for a station. Only static came out of the speakers as the blue numerals cycled through their range two times, never finding a broadcast. She tried the FM band and then all of the satellite channels. The radio detected nothing but empty airwaves and static. Sighing, she hit the power button and turned it off. *Well, it was worth a try.*

As David and she walked back toward the Bat Cave, she wondered why she had felt so compelled to check for signs of life on the radio waves. Bishop and she were doing pretty well considering the circumstances – probably better than most. So why did she feel the need to look for signs of civilization so suddenly? Bishop started the engine of the truck regularly to keep the battery charged. She had had dozens of opportunities to spin that radio dial before and yet never had. That's when Terri realized the Colonel's tale of his own escape from Houston had gotten to her more than she wanted to admit. *Just come back to me Bishop. Everything will be okay if you just come back.*

This wasn't the first time she had been at the campsite without him. Bishop had gone hunting several times since their arrival. Those times had been different, however. Back then, he wasn't heading straight into a dangerous situation where someone might try and kill him. And before he had told her the story about Elvis and Reaper, she had always assumed his business trips were mundane and routine. He always brought her back souvenirs from his travels and often called her on the company's satellite phone. Once she realized the true nature of his work, she was a little pissed off that he had never divulged how dangerous his job was. Now that she was walking around worrying about him, she was thankful he hadn't. She couldn't imagine how she would have coped with all those trips had she known the truth. *How do the wives and families of military men cope with this? I would go nuts if I knew my husband was away fighting a war for months at a time. Just come back to me, Bishop. Everything will be okay, if you just come back.*

They had to move the Colonel to the truck. Despite his weak protests that their actions were in vain, Terri and David didn't have Bishop's net and needed to figure out a way to load him into the back of the bed under the camper shell. The net covering the truck was thin and wouldn't hold his weight. The answer was simple enough, or so they thought. He was lying on some cushions to soften the earthen floor. Terri had covered the old foam with one of their few sheets. David and she planned to pick up each end of the sheet and move their patient to the truck. That attempt resulted in pain for the Colonel. They couldn't hold onto the corners of the fabric, and they weren't strong enough to lift the heavy man. Terri finally figured it out by using the same stick bundles Bishop had used in his net. She found them out by the firewood pile, still tied together. David and she cut several small slits in the old bed sheet and wove the sticks through each side. They picked up the patient and dragged him to the back of the truck after Terri pulled it closer. After propping one end on the open tailgate, they went to the foot of the litter and lifted it in.

David volunteered to ride in the bed with his grandpa. Terri opened the small window in the back windshield so they could talk on the way. She made one last check they had everything they needed, including her rifle and several magazines full of ammo. She left the weapon sitting in the passenger seat beside her. She double-checked that all the doors were locked, before inching the truck forward, gently gaining momentum on their trip to Meraton. *Just come back to me Bishop. Everything will be okay if you just come back.*

Bishop managed to eat a little bit of the salted deer meat he kept in his kit. He found some wild carrots and enjoyed the roots, which tasted like lemons. His water bladder was full, and he even managed to sleep for about an hour. He had found a good observation spot between a large, car-sized boulder and a pine tree. His rifle had a four power magnification scope, so he had a pretty clear view of the activities below at the hotel. He was shocked at how many men, women, and children were there. At first, he was concerned this wasn't the right spot, and he was looking down on normal tourists, not a gang of Columbian hoods. One of the men with Estebon this morning eventually walked outside eating a plate of food and waved at two small children playing nearby. They both ran over to give him a hug, and he patted them on their heads and sent them back to their game. When Bishop realized these men had brought along their families, he had to rethink the entire situation. He had had thoughts of busting into the hotel, gun blazing and somehow breaking the hostage out. With women and children all around the place, he decided that plan was no longer realistic.

As the sun moved across the sky, Bishop began to worry he had taken this risk for nothing. He never saw Estebon or the Colonel's granddaughter. He couldn't even be sure she was at this location. Estebon had been right; he was one against many, and the park was a very big place.

It was going to be dark in about four hours, and he decided he had better do something. He had to make the other side take some sort of action. Bishop scouted around with his scope, trying to remember the area from summers he spent here as a youth. Beside the updates to the hotel and what appeared to be a new headquarters, not much else had changed in the last 20 years. As he swept the terrain, he noticed the roof of the head ranger's residence, about a quarter of a mile away. He was focusing on the area around the home when movement a few hundred feet directly below caught his attention. A Mexican black bear was lifting a fallen log, foraging for food. Bishop remembered there was a small population of these magnificent creatures living in the park. This big fella was moving slowly due to the extra girth of his frame in preparation for winter hibernation.

While the population of bears at the park was thought to be less than 20 adults, the government was serious about keeping them away from the tourists. Bishop had seen the pictures of an automobile in the park's main parking lot with one of its doors torn off its hinges, the result of a hungry bear. A red and white wicker picnic basket piled with fried chicken had been left in the front passenger-side seat. The animal had smelled the grub and decided to get a closer look by pulling off the door for a meal. Ever since that incident, the park had replaced every trashcan, dumpster, and food storage bin with "bear-proof" containers.

Bishop stalked down the side of the mountain carefully, fearful that his movement would draw the human eye. He stayed behind cover as often as possible, and when he was visible from the hotel below, he crept along very slowly. He was also on the alert for the local wildlife. Besides the bears, there were a few documented mountain lions inhabiting the park. A chance encounter with one of these 500-pound cats could ruin your day. The deer meat in his pouch made him wonder how many lions were still living here.

Bishop circled around the hotel giving it a wide berth. He remembered there was a worn, gravel path between the ranger's residence and the hotel, which he found without any trouble. He didn't know if anyone were still staying at the residence and approached it carefully. *I might even get lucky – they may be keeping the girl here.*

The residence wouldn't have looked out of place in any suburban neighborhood. A single story, ranch style abode, the government had wanted its employees living in comfort, not luxury. The partially grassed yard hadn't been mowed in several weeks, and knee high weeds surrounded the rusted swing set in the backyard. Bishop stayed back behind a large pine and scouted the home with his riflescope. It soon became apparent why everyone was staying in the hotel.

The modest structure had been the site of a gun battle and had taken heavy fire. Bishop could see the remains of two bodies, one on the back stoop and the other hanging out of a window. Scavengers, probably of the bird variety, had worked over the dead, leaving yellowish white bones scattered around the area. The wooden clapboards, windows, and doors were riddled with bullet holes. Bishop slowly edged closer to investigate. After observing no movement from the area's residents, he slipped up to the back porch and peeked inside one of the hazy windows. The interior had been completely ransacked, and there was evidence of a fire. *Probably the incoming bullets ignited the curtains.* A splash of color lying next to the closest skeleton caught his attention. The golden colored badge read, "United States Park Ranger."

Bishop began checking the inside, not really sure what he was looking for. Within minutes, he was rushing back outside to the edge of the yard, tearing off his baklava mask and trying to suck the clean air into his lungs. His efforts were unsuccessful. Beads of sweat lined his forehead, and he vomited the deer meat snack he finished a short time ago. He took a seat in the grass, propping himself against a large above ground propane tank that helped to cool his skin.

It was pretty clear what had happened here. The children had been gathered around the wooden picnic table, still partially covered by a faded, plastic covering that featured round, rainbow-colored balloons and the words "Happy Birthday." Still sitting on the table were a few gifts wrapped in foil paper, clearly intended for a younger child. In a childlike scrawl, the message "I love you, Janie," had been preserved in crayon on the now faded card. What really bothered Bishop was what he had discovered inside the building. Huddled together in a back bedroom were the bodies of two women and several small children. Empty shell casings littered the floor at the doorway. The caliber matched the weapons he had taken from the dead men at the plane crash. The attackers had waited until the entire park staff had gathered here for a birthday party. When the violence had begun, the women had gathered up the little ones and herded them into the back room. After all of the rangers were down, the murderers had entered the building and executed everyone hiding inside.

It took Bishop several minutes to get his legs. He finally managed to stand, bracing himself against the steel tank. He was not a stranger to the sight of death and horror. Every time he believed he couldn't see anything worse from his fellow man, he was proven wrong. After catching his breath and rinsing the foul taste from his mouth, his mood altered, quickly building into a boiling rage. He had come here to scout, gather information, and perhaps steal a vehicle and go back to the ranch. Now, he was consumed with wrath, and he wanted to kill these men. His heart, mind, and very soul wanted to walk down the path and deliver death to these sub-human scum. His common sense was being compromised by his anger, and he tried desperately to regain control. He kept visualizing those two women trying to cover the children with their bodies as the bullets were ripping through the house. They would have heard the agony of their men outside dying. The children would have been screaming and crying. *Will someone ever do this to my child?* He imagined the bedroom door being kicked in, and the gun barrel hovering over the threshold. He doubled his fist and punched the metal tank out of pure frustration.

The pain in his hand snapped him back to reality. As he flexed his now throbbing limb to verify he hadn't broken any bones, an idea occurred to him. Perhaps it was providence he had come here; perhaps the ghosts inside of the home had guided him here for a reason. He would make sure these murderers would never harm another child. *I hereby appoint myself judge, jury, and executioner. The sentence is death,* Bishop resolved.

Terri slowly maneuvered the truck through the boulder field that cluttered the open end of their box canyon. She kept the speed very slow so as not to raise any dust. This really didn't require much effort since the large rocks barely left enough room for the truck to pass anyway. Bishop had set up three tripwires along the route, and she had to stop and disable each one. Once she had passed by an early warning device, she again had to stop and rearm the wire.

This was only the second time she had been out of the canyon since they had arrived. The first time, Bishop and she had decided they needed a vacation before she got too pregnant to hike easily. So they had loaded up their packs and left for an extended food-gathering excursion.

That trip had been wonderful. Bishop remembered a secluded mountain waterfall on a neighboring property, and the two had set off to camp at the site for a few nights. When they had first arrived at the ranch, she had set about converting the camper from a seldom-used hunting retreat to a home. In one of the small storage nooks, she found a couple of yellowed old books. The subject matter of one was edible desert plants, and it had made a big difference in their lives. Terri had packed the book to take with them. While Bishop knew a lot about the land, he'd never been in a situation where he needed to live off of it. As they had hiked, Terri pulled out the book and referenced any unusual plants to determine their value. At that time, they still had supplies carried with them from Houston and gathered along the way. Both of them were beginning to realize those staples would not last forever. That trip had proven to them that they could survive off the natural resources of the ranch. Terri had gathered a small bag of seeds from a tree on the way back home. She had dried them and then ground them into flour. While it was only enough to make a few dumplings, it hadn't tasted bad, and they had not gotten sick.

As Terri and David maneuvered toward the highway, she couldn't help but make mental note of the plants she could remember from the book. Depending on what she found available at the Meraton market, she might be out here hunting and gathering soon.

Bishop returned to the house and kicked in the side door of the garage. He found the previous owner's toolbox and was quite impressed with the man's collection and organization. If the situation had been different, he might have considered borrowing a few of the tools to take back to the ranch. He located what he needed and returned to the yard.

Next to the picnic table was a small, half-full propane tank that supplied the barbeque grill. Bishop removed the tank and the brightly colored, plastic tablecloth. His final stop was a water spigot that had about 50 feet of garden hose attached. After Bishop removed the hose, he wound his way thru the pines, working his way ever closer to the hotel.

Terri stopped the truck as soon as she reached the paved highway. She checked with David that the Colonel was handling the bumpy ride okay, and he responded that his grandfather had only grimaced a few times. Even before the current economic disaster, traffic on the public road had been almost non-existent. Still, Terri double-checked to make sure there were no chance travelers observing their journey, grabbed her rifle and walked around the vehicle, clearing the tire tracks left from their passing.

After she had covered the evidence of their passing, she headed toward Meraton. She had not driven in months, but that didn't seem to be a problem. The truck was running fine, and she had almost a full tank of fuel. What did bother her a little was how far back she had to move the driver's seat. She was almost four months pregnant and thought she was only now beginning to show. The room required by her belly to fit behind the steering wheel made her question that thought. She hadn't driven more than 20 minutes when she had to stop the truck, go behind a bush, and relieve herself. David, sitting in the back, decided to lighten the mood with a little humor. "How long will it take us if we have to stop every 20 minutes for you to pee?"

Terri delivered her best evil laugh, and then her voice became serious. "You would say that to a pregnant woman holding an M4 rifle, young man? Hmmm? Either you are not very bright or you have been talking to Bishop too much." David still didn't have a read on the hormone-driven woman navigating the truck and decided it was probably best to quietly pretend to busy himself with his grandpa. Terri let the teen suffer for about a minute before giving the kid a break. "Just kidding…you'll have to tell Bishop that one. He will *really* think it's funny."

Bishop approached the backside of the hotel. It was easy to determine where the kitchen was located due to the big exhaust fans on the roof and the smelly dumpster close by. After checking that he was alone, he removed his pack, tying it to the canister of LP gas with one end of his para-cord. He then scooted the dumpster against the side of the building and climbed up. His perch on the dumpster was the perfect height; enabling him to jump, get a handhold, and pull himself up to the rooftop. He had not seen any sentries on the flat roof of the single story hotel while looking at it from the mountain above and hoped he hadn't missed any guards who might have a view of the area. He would be trapped up here if discovered. He pulled the pack and LP tank up with the para-cord rope before taking a breather. It was only about two hours before dark and the timing of his actions was critical.

Bishop understood that Estebon was a highly intelligent man. And after stumbling upon the birthday party massacre, he further counted him as absolutely ruthless and without honor. Bishop's evaluation of his adversary had figured prominently in his plan. He had two goals. The first was to get Samantha out into the open. While she was inside of the hotel, he had little chance of accomplishing anything other than getting them both killed. His second goal was transportation. There were over 80 miles of harsh, rugged terrain between Big Bend and the ranch. While he was confident he could make it, he wasn't so sure about the young girl. He had no idea of her condition or capabilities. Given the girl's key role in the scheme to retrieve Carmen and Isabella, Bishop didn't believe Estebon would let Samantha get far from his sight. If Bishop could draw the captors into the open by forcing them to move the girl, he would create an opportunity to rescue her. Certainly, his chances of pulling this off were better than taking gold to Juarez. He needed a catalyst. He considered several different diversions, but worried Estebon would easily identify the ruse and perhaps even harm the girl.

Bishop waited until about an hour before the sun would slip behind the mountains to the west. During this time, he managed to get down some pine nuts and jerky. It wasn't much, but his stomach was still not settled. He pulled the top off of the exhaust fan cover and peered inside. The tube was about ten inches in diameter and lined with a thick coating of grease, fat, and carbon. At the bottom, he could see the blades of a small fan spinning. Beyond the fan, he could see what appeared to be a gas burner on a stovetop.

Bishop listened for any sound coming from the tube. He knew that as the hour grew late, the chances of activity in the kitchen increased. His last glance at the front of the hotel had shown the children were still outside playing a game of tag. Several adults relaxed on the porch and the lawn, enjoying the splendor of the setting west Texas sun. He still didn't see Estebon or the girl.

Bishop slowly lowered one end of the garden hose down the exhaust pipe until a ticking noise indicated it had reached the fan blade. He fed another few inches down the tube until the end of the hose jammed the fan. He paused, listening for any sign that the sound had been noticed, before he cut the garden hose so that it was just long enough to reach the propane tank sitting beside him on the roof.

Bishop double-checked that the valve was closed and then proceeded to unscrew the snap-on safety connector used by all outdoor grills. Once the connector was removed, he took a small hose clamp, scavenged from the Ranger's garage, and secured the end of the garden hose as tightly as possible. The propane was stored at about 175 pounds of pressure. He knew the hose was rated at about 50 pounds max and hoped it would hold long enough for the tank to empty. Propane is heavier than air, but dissipates quickly. Bishop wanted a nice cloud of the explosive gas covering the kitchen floor below. Hopefully, a pilot light would do the trick, but he was ready even if it didn't explode on its own. Little by little, he loosened the valve and released the volatile gas into the hotel's kitchen.

Bishop had no idea how long it would take to empty the tank or for it to ignite. He moved quickly away from the exhaust chimney to the other side of the roof, keeping his profile very low. He checked his watch, opting to give the gas exactly one minute to ignite. If there were no blast within the next 60 seconds, he would go back and "help it along."

It took about 30 seconds for the half-filled tank to empty, releasing a cloud of explosive vapor that spread across the kitchen floor. Somehow, the sinking gas missed the pilot light on the gas stove. It was one of Estebon's men who pushed open the swinging kitchen door that caused the gas to ignite. The motion of the door being pushed open fanned a wave of the gas toward the pilot flame on the kitchen's hot water heater.

Bishop expected a loud blast and a fire. He was completely taken by surprise when the roof of the kitchen buckled upwards and the entire hotel shook underneath him. The noise of the explosion was followed almost immediately by the hotel's fire alarm. Bishop started making his way to the front of the building.

Estebon had been deep asleep when the explosion occurred. He awoke with a start and bolted upright in his bed. Disoriented, he initially thought he was back in Colombia and under attack. It was the claxon of the fire alarm that caused him to snap back to reality. He was reaching for his pants when the sprinkler system came on. It sputtered, ran for a few seconds, and then sputtered again. With only the solar backup system there wasn't enough water pressure to make a difference.

Bishop was peeking over the roofline of the hotel's entrance. Confused people poured out the front door. He watched carefully for the Colonel's granddaughter or Estebon to exit, but so far, he couldn't pick them out of the crowd.

Estebon threw open the door to his room only to be met with a hallway full of smoke and two of his guards breathing thru handkerchiefs over their faces. His first reaction was to reach for his pistol because he thought the masked men were there to kill him. Once he realized who they were, he barked an order for them to get everyone out of the hotel. He pushed the evacuees out of his way, as he headed down the hallway, toward the sentry outside the hostage's room. "Get her out, and take her to the Hummer," he commanded. The guard nodded and opened the door to retrieve the girl, who was now struggling to catch her breath. Estebon continued running for the front door.

Bishop watched as people continued to pour out of the burning building. He headed back toward the kitchen area, carefully avoiding the weakened roof. He slipped over the edge, jumped down onto the dumpster and then dropped to the ground. After checking to make sure he hadn't been noticed, he began pushing the heavy trash container toward the front of the hotel.

The Hummer was parked in the handicapped spot closest to the lobby. Estebon exited the main entrance to the lodge, and immediately three of his men rushed over for orders. His first response was not an order, but a question. "Are we under attack? What is going on?"

"There was an explosion in the kitchen. Other than that, we've seen no sign of any attack," a guard responded. Estebon scoured the surrounding area, looking for clues about the cause of the explosion, when his hostage, followed by the coughing guard, reached the driveway. He motioned for the guard to get Samantha into the Hummer and for another of his men to follow. Estebon turned back to the hotel, and like everyone else, was mesmerized by the spreading fire - the flames now clearly visible through the windows. No one noticed the large steel dumpster sluggishly roll around the corner.

Bishop knew the parking lot slanted downward and away from the hotel. He gave the dumpster one last good shove. The thing was three times as heavy as normal because it was "bear proof." The walls, hinges, and doors were all heavy, thick steel and the wheels were oversized to allow movement and emptying. Bishop walked along behind the rolling shield as gravity steered it directly at the parked Hummer.

Estebon saw the dumpster rolling toward his position and didn't know what to make of it. He motioned for one of his men, but no words came out of his mouth. He turned to look for the hostage and saw the guard unlocking the Hummer door with the girl in tow.

It suddenly became clear to Estebon something was wrong. A warning was rising in this throat, when Bishop popped around the corner of the dumpster and began firing.

While he was outnumbered 30 to 1, Bishop had the element of surprise and the distraction of the fire. He placed the red dot of his riflescope on the chest of the guard opening the Hummer door and fired twice. Before the empty shell cases had even hit the ground, he pivoted and fired at the man next to Estebon who was trying to raise his MP5 sub-machine gun. The dumpster came to rest against the front fender of the Hummer, and Bishop swept up the young girl and threw her inside with the smelly trash. He pulled the keys from the dead guard's hands and stuffed them in his dump pouch.

The already anxious crowd gathered outside the hotel turned into a scrambling, screaming mob almost instantly. Most of the men were armed only with pistols and Bishop ignored them. Automatic fire pinged off the dumpster as Bishop took cover behind it. Sparks flew as the Colombian's shots ricocheted off of the heavy, steel trash container. Mothers who had been merely panicked over missing children in the fire escalated to desperation with the increasing gunfire. Two screaming women sprinted directly in the line of fire being aimed at Bishop. The shooter instinctively raised his weapon in order to avoid spraying the women. Bishop killed the man before he could bring his barrel back down to aim again. That shot prompted the rest of the Colombians to realize they were completely exposed. The hotel had been their headquarters, their bunker, and a burning building could not shield them. As two of the men looked for cover, Bishop appeared over the top of the dumpster and took them both out of the fight.

It was only a short time before the advantage of surprise expired, and Estebon's men started to regroup. Bishop did his best to ensure they did so under the worst of circumstances. Estebon had somehow managed to run and take refuge behind the large stone pillars supporting the awning at the front of the hotel. Bishop saw the man snap around the pillar and fire two shots with his pistol. A hail of 5.56 NATO bullets tore into the limestone pillars. Dust, shards of stone and bits of rock were flying all around Estebon's hiding spot. It seemed as though Bishop intended to saw through the pillar using his bullets as a blade.

Bishop wanted the man badly, and it was almost his undoing. His focus on the boss allowed two of the guards to move into a flanking position, hoping to catch Bishop from behind. Bishop was saved by his rifle locking back empty. When he reached for a full magazine, the movement of the two men caught his eye. Bishop slammed the full magazine into his rifle, slapped the release, and shot the two men on the run.

Seeing that Bishop was distracted, Estebon ran, zigzagging in retreat, around the corner of the hotel.

Only light, random fire was now coming in Bishop's direction. He knew it wouldn't be long before Estebon reorganized his forces and came back at him. Bishop reached into the dumpster, pulled the shaking girl out by the shirt, and literally threw her into the backseat of the Hummer screaming; "Stay on the floor!" as he slammed the door. He pulled the keys out of his pouch and ran to the driver's side, randomly shooting at anything that moved. He threw his rifle into the front passenger seat and pulled his pistol. He managed to get the keys into the ignition and start the motor when Estebon and five of his men rounded the corner of the hotel.

Bishop put the big SUV in reverse and slowly let the Hummer roll backwards. The dumpster followed it down the hill. Bishop stuck his left arm out the window and fired a few wild shots from his pistol just to give the pursuers something to think about. Bullets continued to thump into the dumpster protecting the front of the Hummer. When he had rolled about 50 feet down the parking lot hill, he gave the engine some gas and pulled away from the rolling trash bin. He backed up as quickly as possible and once they had travelled a reasonable distance, he yelled, "Hold on!" and cut the wheel hard.

The front end of the SUV swung hard right, with the tires smoking on the pavement. Bishop slammed the transmission into first gear and floored the accelerator, cutting the wheel all the way. The back glass of the Hummer exploded inward, and Bishop automatically ducked, although he knew it wouldn't do any good. He watched as small holes appeared in the glove box door, each one seeming to get closer to his body. Everything was moving in slow motion, and it felt like the Hummer was taking all year to get up any speed. Another round from the pursuers hit the passenger side glass. Bishop was trying to drive on the narrow park road while barely keeping his head above the dashboard. Foam from a seat somewhere was now floating through the interior and the screen of the expensive navigation system exploded right in front of Bishop's face.

All of a sudden, it was quiet, and the Hummer sped away. Bishop rose up just in time to avoid hitting a tree and jerked the wheel to point them back to the center of the road. Without looking, he asked the girl if she were hurt. The response almost made him laugh. "Yes, I am fine, but I think I wet my pants."

Bishop could only reply with, "That makes two of us."

Estebon was furious as he stood in the hotel parking lot. His men were scrambling to find the keys to the tour busses and other cars they had arrived in, but he knew they were probably in the burning hotel. Others were trying to bandage the wounded and account for their wives and children. Estebon stood on the edge of the ridge, watching the Hummer as it wound its way up the side of the mountain road above him. He was joined by his brother-in-law who stood watching in silence as well. As soon as the Hummer was out of sight, the former Special Forces Captain turned to his boss and asked calmly, "What is your plan now? You realize my sister is a dead woman and my beautiful young niece will spend the rest of her days under fat, smelly Mexican men in a whorehouse, don't you? What does your superior intellect have to say about that, senor? How will your super brain reconcile that?"

Estebon turned and looked the man up and down and responded with a crisp, "Fuck you," and walked away.

Bishop exited the park as fast as he thought the Hummer could handle. After checking the rearview mirror several times, he finally decided it was okay for the girl to get up off of the floor. She quickly sat in the seat and looked around outside. Bishop could see her face was dirty and smudged by streaks of tears, but she made eye contact with him in the mirror and smiled.

"You must be Bishop. My name is Samantha, but everyone calls me Sam."

"You're correct Samantha; my name is Bishop. I'm taking you to see your brother and grandfather."

"Is grandpa okay? I know he was hurt badly."

Bishop thought before responding, "He was still alive when I left early this morning. My wife, Terri, should be taking him to a doctor by now. We are going to try and meet them there."

"Do you have any clothes? These stink from when you threw me in the trash. I have junk in my hair, and I think I need clean underwear. My smell isn't bothering you, is it? Please don't let David see me like this. He will tease me forever."

Bishop laughed and smiled at the girl, "No, young lady, I don't have any clothes, and your smell isn't bothering me at all. You sit back and relax; and when we get to town, I am sure Terri will find you some clean clothes and a bath."

"Mister Bishop, I forgot to thank you for getting me away from those men. I listened to them talking through the door of my room. I think they were going to kill you and then me after you brought back the scary one's wife and daughter."

"You're welcome. I would do almost anything for your grandpa. He's a good man, and he helped me once when I really needed it."

"Mister Bishop, shouldn't you fasten your seatbelt?"

Bishop smiled again at the girl in the mirror. *Little Miss Samantha and I are going to be fast friends, I can just tell.*

The green and white sign said "Meraton 5," and Terri was excited to be coming back. She slowed the truck and as it crested a small rise, she saw two pickups blocking the road. *What now?*

She stopped about 100 yards short of the roadblock, grabbed her rifle, and told David to stay put. She got out of the truck and started walking as two men got out and stood in the road.

She hadn't traveled more than ten feet when the challenge was issued. "That's close enough, lady. Meraton is closed for the night. You are welcome to come back in the morning. We don't let strangers pass after dusk."

Terri answered in her best distressed female voice. "I have a badly injured man in the back. Please let me pass, he needs medical attention."

"I'm sorry, but the rules are the rules. We've had more than our share of trouble at night and everyone voted. Meraton closes at dusk to everyone but residents."

Since that didn't work, she switched to her best pissed female voice. "Look buddy, why don't one of you go into town and tell Pete that Terri is out here waiting." *Maybe name-dropping will work.*

The two men looked at each other and Terri could hear them mumbling. Finally, one of them said, "No way. We're not allowed to leave our post. How do you know Pete anyway?"

Terri had to pee again and was exhausted from the ordeal of the last few days. Her voice was angry now, "Look asshole, I don't have time for this bullshit. If that man in the back of my truck dies while I am arguing with you, my husband will not be a happy man. You'll be lucky if he doesn't come right down here and kick your sorry ass. Now get in the fucking truck and go tell Pete I'm here. That's Terri. T, E, R, R, I."

The men laughed and looked at each other for a second. One of them yelled back, "Lady, I don't give a shit about your husband. Send him on down. I can't and won't let you by until the sun rises, and that's that."

Terri took a few steps forward, and one of the men chambered a round in his rifle. She froze, but it only made her madder. "You stupid shit, when Bishop hears about this, he is going to be *so* pissed off. Especially when he hears you threatened his pregnant wife with a rifle."

"Bishop? Did you say 'Bishop?'"

"Hell yes, I said 'Bishop.' Who do you think my husband is, dipshit? He is going to be here shortly; I'll let you take this up with him."

"You're *that* Terri? Oh my god, ma'am, I didn't know you were *that* Terri." The man quickly turned to his partner and said, "Well, what are you waiting for? Escort Miss Terri into town."

The man who had loaded his rifle took off his hat and tipped it towards Terri, mumbling something like, "Sorry ma'am, I didn't know, really I didn't know," as he backed up a few steps, then turned, and ran back to his vehicle.

Terri exhaled deeply and spun around heading back to her truck. She laid her rifle in the passenger seat and slammed the door. David poked his head through the back window and said, "What was up with all that?"

Terri put the truck in gear and looked back at him, "I guess it pays to have a trigger happy husband sometimes."

As the two-car convoy entered Meraton, the escort driver pulled in front of *Pete's Place* and honked his horn twice. *Pete's* was the local watering hole and the owner had become good friends with Terri and Bishop during their last pass through town. Pete had become the Mayor of Meraton by default, even though he never asked for the job. A few cowboys came outside to see what all of the ruckus was about, followed closely by Pete toting his shotgun.

When Terri's truck pulled up, Pete looked at it and tilted his head. "No, say it ain't so…is that…" Terri opened the door and hopped out. Pete smiled and shouted, "Terri! Oh my god, Terri!" They hugged and patted each other for a few moments, and then Pete looked around and questioned, "Where's Bishop? Is he okay?"

Terri smiled, "He's fine as far as I know. He should be here soon. Pete, it's a long story, but I have a badly injured man in the back. He needs help now."

Pete didn't even hesitate and turned to one of the men standing close by, "Go get the doc." Pete and the other man hurried to the back of Terri's truck and were met by David. He jumped out of the bed and helped the men carry his grandpa into the saloon. Everyone inside Pete's moved out of the way while space was cleared on the bar for the injured man. Several people that she didn't even know came up and hugged Terri. She felt embarrassed at all the attention.

After he was sure the patient was as comfortable as they could make him, Pete turned to the man who had escorted her into town and told him he had better get back to the roadblock. As the man started to leave, Terri grabbed his arm and said, "Bishop is supposed to meet me here soon. He may be hurt or have another injured person with him. I don't know if he'll be on foot or what he might be driving. Please don't shoot my husband."

The man nodded, tipped his hat again, and left to warn his partner that Bishop was coming to town.

Bishop and Samantha were making good time heading north from Big Bend. They were almost to the crash site when Bishop saw an odd shape in the middle of the road. He took his foot off the accelerator and asked his passenger to please get down on the floor and not look out. The Hummer slowed as it passed the remains of Estebon's man Bishop had left in the plane seat. Bishop pulled up even with the airplane and stopped.

He grabbed his rifle and scouted around for a bit, making sure no one else had been attracted to the wreckage. Everything seemed to be exactly where he had left it with the exception of the smell of the dead bodies.

Bishop returned to the Hummer and told Sam she could get out. She opened the door and immediately pinched her nose between her thumb and forefinger. Bishop said, "Sam, I know it doesn't smell very nice out here, but there's some water by the plane in that box. You can wash yourself off with it. If you had a suitcase or bag in the plane, I suggest you go get it. I have a couple of things to pick up behind those rocks. I'll be right back."

"Okay. Thank you, sir."

Bishop watched as the girl headed toward the plane and began rummaging around. As soon as she pulled up a small suitcase, he gave her thumbs up and headed into the desert. It took him just a few moments to locate the weapons he had collected from the dead men and retrieve his net. He hurried back to the wreckage, only to be stopped by Sam's voice. "Mister Bishop, I am changing clothes. May I have some privacy, please?"

Bishop smiled to himself and turned away to give the lady her space. He opened the back of the Hummer and unloaded the weapons there. As soon as he had finished, he went to the back of the plane where he had left the remains of the Colonel's traveling companion. He quickly scanned the area and picked a low spot at the base of a large rock formation.

Bishop pulled the tarp containing the female body to the gravesite and dug out as much of the soft earth as his fingers could loosen. He gently laid her in the shallow trench, and then covered her with as much soil as possible. He stacked the random rocks that dotted the area on top of the thin layer of dirt. After several minutes, he had the Colonel's friend covered as best he could and hoped to come back later for a more formal burial and to mark her final resting place.

A few moments after he had finished, Sam emerged from behind the wreckage, brushing her hair. "I feel like a new person. Thank you. Can we leave to go find my grandpa now?"

Bishop nodded and held the door open for the lady. He ran around the front of the Hummer like a hired chauffer, smiling all the way.

It was about two hours later when Bishop brought the Hummer to a stop at the Meraton roadblock. He picked up his rifle and strode toward the guards. He hadn't managed four steps, when someone shouted out, "Who are you?"

Bishop responded with his name, and was shocked to see the headlights of one of the blocking trucks turn on immediately. "Please follow me into town, sir."

Bishop got back in his truck and turned to Sam. "They must know you here." His comment was met with a blank look.

Just like Terri two hours before, Bishop was escorted to Pete's. This time, the guard didn't even have to honk his horn before everyone was pouring out Pete's front door. Bishop parked along Main Street and turned to his passenger, "We're here."

By the time Bishop unbuckled his seatbelt and opened the door, a small crowd gathered around, waiting for him to get out. He saw Pete and smiled. "How are you, Pete? Damn, it's good to see you." The two men hugged, and then it seemed like everyone wanted to shake Bishop's hand or give him a squeeze. He felt like he was going down the reception line at his wedding, not knowing who most of the people were, but scared to ask in case he should've known.

At least ten of the men and two of the women asked to buy him a beer. He had seen his truck parked nearby, and assumed Terri had made it to town safely. As he made his way to Pete's, he almost forgot about Samantha, but she pushed her way through the crowd and was right by his side. He looked at Pete. "I have someone I want you to meet. This is Samantha. She is a brave little lady."

Pete smiled from ear to ear and held out his hand. "Any friend of Bishop's is a friend of mine." Sam shook his hand and nodded. "Pleased to meet you, sir. Where are my grandfather and brother?"

It took Pete a second to connect the dots. "Oh, that is your grandpa? Miss Terri and some of the men took him over to The Manor. Would you like to see them?"

"Yes sir, please."

Pete looked around the crowd and nodded to a woman standing close by. She came forward and extended her hand to Sam, but the girl recoiled and grabbed Bishop's arm. She looked up at her rescuer and said, "Please, Mister Bishop, can you take me. I'd like it very much if you would take me."

Bishop smiled down at her and then signaled the woman it was okay. "Of course I will, Sam. I want to see Terri anyway." He looked around the crowd and raised his voice. "I had better go check in with my wife before I start drinking. She carries a gun all the time now, ya know."

Everyone laughed and several of the men nodded their understanding. Their wives were armed as well. Bishop waved to the crowd and promised to return soon. Samantha and he turned and proceeded toward The Manor hotel.

As they walked silently the few blocks to the hotel, Bishop started getting a tight stomach. He hadn't been back here since the shootout that night with the bank robbers. He had thought it was all over then. But Terri, Pete and some of the town's men had saved his life. As Sam and he approached the front steps to the main door, he was in for another surprise. Betty met them with all smiles and hugs.

"Betty, it's damn good to see you! What the heck are you doing here this time of night?"

"Bishop, I run The Manor now. It got too dangerous for me to stay out at the bed and breakfast. We had some trouble after you left, and the townsfolk asked me to move in here and run the place. But enough about me, dear. I bet you want to see your wife. Come right this way."

Betty lead them through the small office area and out into the gardens. The Manor's gardens were known far and wide. Literally an oasis in the middle of the desert, many guests went out of their way to vacation here to simply enjoy the gardens. Bishop struggled to keep from thinking about the night of the gunfight. The bank robbers had been holed up in The Manor, and the battle had been in these very gardens. He had been pinned down, about to receive the coup de grace, when Terri had come to the rescue.

It helped Bishop a little to see that The Manor apparently was being used for something good now. Betty told him that one whole section of the rooms was now being utilized as a hospital ward for the doctor. As Bishop happened past the spot where he had almost been killed, he couldn't help but stare at the earth as if it should say something to him.

Sam spoke up. "Mister Bishop, you're hurting my hand."

Bishop relaxed his grip, clearly embarrassed. "Are you okay, Sam? I'm really sorry, I would never hurt you."

"It's fine, Mister Bishop. If you're scared and need to squeeze someone's hand, take mine. I'm ready for it now. I understand because I feel the same way when my dad takes me to the doctor to get a shot."

Bishop grinned and took her hand, but was careful not to hold on to tightly.

Betty walked up to one of the rooms and quietly tapped on the door. Terri's face appeared and Betty announced, "I have someone here who wants to see you." Terri peered over Betty's shoulder, and exploded out of the door, "Bishop!"

Bishop met her embrace and lifted her into the air, turning in circles and kissing her cheek. After they had assured each other they were fine and that the baby was fine, Bishop told Terri he had someone she needed to meet. He pointed at the young girl standing beside him, "Terri, this is Samantha. Sam, this is my wife, Terri."

Sam stepped forward and held out her hand. Terri smiled and gently shook her hand, "Was Bishop nice to you, sweetie? He isn't around girls very much; are you okay?"

Samantha got a very puzzled look on her face and then scolded Terri. "Mister Bishop was the perfect gentleman except for when he threw me into the dumpster. He saved my life. He even stopped and let me brush my hair and didn't make fun of me when I smelled like garbage."

Terri gave Bishop a puzzled look, only to have him return one of "*It's a long story.*"

Sam was impatient, "Can I see my grandpa now?"

"Yes you may, sweetie, but you have to be very quiet because the doctor is trying to help him."

Betty offered her hand to Samantha, but the girl hesitated and took a step closer to Bishop. Bishop looked down at her and smiled reassuringly, "It's okay, Sam. You can go with Betty; she will take you to your Grandpa."

Sam hesitated and edged closer to Bishop. "Can't you take me, Mister Bishop?"

Bishop smiled at the girl reassuringly. "I won't go far, Sam. I'll be here in the gardens with Terri. We need to talk while you visit The Col…your grandpa."

Samantha hesitated, but then took Betty's hand. As she walked toward the hotel room, she kept looking back at Bishop over her shoulder.

As soon as they were out of sight, Terri put her hands on her hips as if to scold him. "Well, I see there is another woman in your life. You're away for a few hours, and already I'm yesterday's news."

Bishop shook his head. "I didn't anticipate that but it makes sense. She's been through some serious shit the last few days, and I guess I'm the father figure right now."

Terri smiled and rubbed her tummy. "You should get used to that role. I think it's cute by the way. So what happened, Bishop? How bad was it?"

Bishop held Terri's hand, and they strolled through the gardens. He recounted the day's events, beginning with the meeting that morning and continuing right up to his arrival in Meraton. As usual, his wife interrupted him several times to ask questions or to clarify something he said. Almost a half hour had gone by before he finished the tale of his escapade. Terri hugged him again. "Bishop, for a man who doesn't want to take chances anymore, you sure have a funny way of showing it. I'm glad you got Samantha out of there though. And I really do understand why you took the risk. By the way, what color is my new Hummer?"

Bishop laughed and pulled Terri close. He looked her in the eye and leaned in for a kiss. Slyly avoiding his pass, she whispered in his ear, "Baby, I can make it worth your while to give me the keys to that Hummer."

Bishop decided to beat Terri at her own game. "Did I mention the leather interior and a slightly used nav system?"

Terri, not to be outdone, upped the ante. She pressed her body against his and whispered to him in her most sultry voice. "I guarantee you; it will be worth it, baby." She was just moving into seal the deal, when a distant voice interrupted their moment.

Betty was standing a few yards away. "I hate to break up you two lovebirds, but the doctor has finished, and I think you should talk to him."

Chapter 10

Betty led them to an adjoining hotel room where Doctor Richard Hopkins stood washing his hands. Bishop had met the man the day Terri and he were leaving town, finally on their way to the ranch. The harried looking physician had somehow made it out of Houston and navigated to Meraton. Bishop respected him for that reason alone, having barely survived that journey himself.

The doctor dried his hands before shaking Bishop's.

"I'm so frustrated with this frontier medicine," he remarked, pulling off his glasses and cleaning them in the candlelight. "I might be able to save your friend if I had even basic equipment. I've stabilized him for the moment, but it won't last. I can't remove that shaft without x-rays. It's too close to so many vital internal organs, and I would be operating blind. Even with an x-ray, his chances of contracting infection would be very high, and we don't have much more than a bare bones supply of meds here. Of course, he is already beginning to show signs of infection. The longer we leave that foreign object inside of him, the weaker he gets - eventually the bugs will win."

Bishop looked down at the floor and shook his head. He thought he'd already accepted the fact that his ex-boss wasn't going to make it, but now realized he'd been holding out hope.

Terri broke the silence. "What kind of equipment would you need, Doctor?"

"Terri, I don't know. We only have what I brought with me from Houston. The community gathered up all the odd prescription drugs, but it's a hodgepodge mixture at best. I know many of the antibiotics are expired. I guess I would need the contents of a modern operating room, maybe even a field MASH unit."

Bishop asked to see the Colonel, but the doctor said he was sleeping.

Terri decided to see what David and Sam were doing, while Bishop and Doc Hopkins sauntered down to Pete's. They had just stepped out onto Main Street when the doctor put his hand on Bishop's shoulder and stopped him.

"Bishop, we are all going to have to get used to this. Healthcare has taken a big step backwards with the rest of society. Last week, I lost a woman giving birth. It was so frustrating because I could have saved her just a few months ago. The baby didn't make it either. I am doing my best, but I'm so limited. I understand now what my colleagues went through just 100 years ago."

Bishop's pulse quickened. He stared at the man for a moment and then mumbled, "A woman died giving birth?"

The doctor immediately realized his mistake. "Oh, Bishop, I'm sorry. I'm sure Terri and her child will be fine. I didn't mean to…"

Bishop held up his hand, interrupting the doctor's train of thought. "It's okay Doc. I guess I hadn't considered her having trouble, but it could happen. What was the survival rate of childbirth back in the old days?"

Doctor Hopkins turned away, leading the way to the local watering hole, avoiding the question. "I don't know, Bishop. I shouldn't have said that. I just need a drink."

Bishop thought about all the people waiting for him at Pete's. He didn't like his newfound popularity, but didn't know what to do about it. He walked along a few more steps with the doctor when he got an idea. "You need a drink, Doc, and I need a bath. Tell everyone at Pete's I hope to be down shortly, but had some business to attend to. Give them my best."

Doctor Hopkins nodded, patted Bishop on the shoulder, and proceeded on down Main Street.

Bishop turned around and headed back to The Manor. He had noticed the swimming pool looked as clean and fresh as ever. *The filters must be solar powered, and someone is taking care of it.* When he arrived at poolside, he looked around to make sure no one was close by before removing all of his load gear and clothes. He checked his rifle safety, and then laid the weapon on the pool decking. After he was naked, he dove in the cool water and came up for air.

It felt so wonderful to be free of all his gear and clothing. It seemed like he constantly had to wear heavy armor and a load vest these days. The buoyancy of the water, combined with the sensation of skinny dipping, greatly improved his mood. He swam around for a bit, enjoying the experience, and then realized he was going to have to put his dirty clothes back on. He breast-stroked to the side of the pool, next to the discarded pile of smelly laundry, grabbed his t-shirt, jeans and socks and took them for a swim with him. *I hope Betty won't mind if I pollute the pool a little more.*

After soaking and wringing out his garments, Bishop climbed out of the pool and draped his wash over a nearby lounge chair. He knew his clothes would dry quickly in the low humidity desert air. He jumped back in the water and just floated on his back looking up at the stars.

A few moments later, a voice startled him, "No skinny dipping allowed in the pool, can't you read the signs?" He turned just in time to see Terri's naked body dive into the water beside

100

him. She swam alongside him under the water, before surfacing for air and putting her arms around her husband.

"You're a bad, bad boy, Mr. Bishop. Sneaking into the pool at night and going skinny-dipping. What am I going to do with you?"

Bishop played along. "I have a few ideas, now that you're here."

Terri stuck out her lower lip and pouted. "Are you sure you don't mind being seen with a fat, pregnant girl?"
Bishop misread her meaning and got all serious. "You're not fat, and I love you with all my heart. I'm glad you joined me. Isn't it kind of fun, breaking the rules?"

Terri grinned at her husband's remark. "The kids are asleep. Betty fed them, and they crashed almost instantly. I was heading to Pete's to make sure all those women down there kept their hands off of my man. I heard you swimming and thought you might like some company."

Bishop picked her up, and she wrapped her legs around him. They started kissing passionately, holding on to each other tightly.

It was the rare romantic moment for the couple, and they took advantage of it. The famous gardens of The Manor surrounding the pool were illuminated by the soft, warm glow of the landscaping lights. The cloudless sky was graced by a star field that no longer had to contest the electric lights of mankind. They went at each other slow, soft and gentle at first, each enjoying the weightlessness of the water and the softness of the air. The cool water contrasted with the warmth of skin wherever their tightly mingled bodies would allow it to seep in. Eventually passion took over, and things moved faster, more direct.

Bishop was strong and lean. She could feel the cords and sinew flex as he moved against her softness. As he neared the end, his arms held Terri like a pair of steel bands that would never let her escape. She knew it was a savage taking her now. The man she loved was no longer in her arms. He had been replaced by a wild beast that sensed the end, and nothing could stop him. He was going to take what he needed, and she had to let him. She knew his entire focus was on her, and nothing else mattered. The stars had ceased to exist. The water was no longer there. Air itself had disappeared. There were only their souls, touching through flesh. She let herself go. It was easier knowing she didn't have a choice and waves of pleasure shook her body and took away her breath. Terri pulled Bishop over the edge with her. The noise that came from low in his throat was that of a predator taking its prey. The mighty beast reared its head and roared its triumph.

The warm glow of the aftermath was accented by the hushed sounds of the desert night. After recovering, Bishop and Terri climbed out of the pool and found a stack of soft towels nearby. Bishop made a mental note to compliment Betty on her management of the hotel.

They didn't even bother to get dressed. Picking up their clothes and gear, the coupled headed directly to their room. As Bishop closed the pool gate, he glanced at the wet footprints left on the smooth deck surrounding the pool. *Side by side – just like it should be.* They feel asleep spooning in each other's arms.

Bishop had the doctor by the throat. The man's eyes were bulging out of his head, and his face was a reddish purple color. Bishop was screaming at the top of his lungs, "What do you mean, she is dying? Save her! Save my wife, or I *will* kill you!" Bishop squeezed harder and felt the man's windpipe crush in his hands. The doctor's eyes flashed a last, helpless look as his lifeless body slid to the floor.

Bishop bolted upright in bed. He was having a nightmare and was covered in sweat. Every muscle in his body ached and was knotted. Terri rolled over to face him. "What's the matter, baby? Are you okay?"

Bishop shook his head and wiped the beads of perspiration from his forehead. "I'm okay, hun. It was just a bad dream. I'll be fine." He leaned over, gave her a kiss on the forehead, and told her he needed to go for a walk. She yawned, smiled, and then rolled over to go back to sleep.

He got up and dressed, deciding he would only take the rifle. He quietly brushed his teeth with one of the small hotel tubes someone had left in the room. He was surprised at the sensation in his mouth. After lacing up his boots, he gently opened the door and exited into the cool night air.

Some habits just don't go away, and he subconsciously checked the perimeter of the hotel. Meraton was asleep at this early hour, and it would be some time before the sun rose over the hills to the east. Everything was quiet and peaceful except for his troubled mind. He was walking through the gardens when the sound of footfalls made him pause. Bishop moved into the shadows and waited to see who was coming his way.

"Good morning, Doc. I was just thinking about you."

The physician was surprised, but quickly composed himself. "Bishop, what are you doing up at this god awful hour? Is everything all right?"

Bishop sheepishly responded, "Sorry to startle you, sir. I woke up early and was just taking a stroll. My apologies."

The doctor waved him off. "No problem, Bishop. I was just on my way to check on a couple of patients. Betty is up, too. I smelled coffee brewing when I went through the office."

Bishop smiled and thought that was one hell of a good idea. He nodded at the doctor and headed for the main building. As he opened the door, he called out so as not to frighten any more of the good citizens of Meraton. He also knew Betty had an old double-barreled shotgun and kept it handy.

Betty came out of a back room, smiling. "Why you're up early, Bishop. Come on in, coffee?"

"Yes ma'am – black, please."

Betty nodded and turned for the kitchen. "Coming right up."

Bishop walked around to the hotel's lobby. The building was over 100 years old and had aged well. The wooden floors were covered here and there with southwestern throw rugs and oriental carpets, but they still had *that smell* from years of being oiled and waxed. The walls were finished in a thick, rough paneling, darkly stained, and adorned with numerous examples of local hunting trophies. Bishop couldn't identify the wood, but he easily recognized all of the local wildlife. He returned the blank stare of a very large mountain lion fixed onto an oak pedestal. Now a permanent hotel lobby fixture, it had once roamed the Glass Mountains, only a short distance away.

The floor creaked as Bishop milled about. He couldn't help but think about the age when this building had been constructed. The quality of the glass in the large windows distorted the light; and while the windows allowed a view outside, it wasn't nearly as clear and sharp as that of modern glass. He could tell one of the big frames of glass had been repaired, as it was more transparent than the neighboring panes.

As he gazed out onto the sleepy town's main drag, he couldn't help but recall the last time Terri and he had been here. Bishop had expected the worst as they began their journey from Houston. While he had known the trip would be difficult, nothing could have prepared them for the nightmare of gun battles, scavenging and desperate human behavior they had encountered along the way. They had barely survived being chased, shot, and ambushed during the 600-mile journey.

It was only after they arrived here at Meraton that things began to look up. The small, isolated berg was still "civilized" and had even established trade and commerce. Even this small island of "normal" behavior was soon disrupted by a gang of bank robbers who tried to control the town. It seemed to Bishop that no part of the country, regardless how remote, was immune

103

to the wave of human desperation that swept the land. Good had triumphed over evil in Meraton, but it had been a close call.

Despite Terri's pregnancy, they had not returned to the town since. She seemed to be doing fine, but both of them knew it would be wise to come here during the last few weeks of her gestation. Now Bishop was wondering if that would provide any security for the future of his expanding family. Doc Hopkins had accidently blurted out a story about losing a laboring mother and her unborn child. That was cause for concern to any prospective father, let alone one on the brink of raising a family while the entire world seemed to be going insane.

Bishop desperately wanted Meraton to work for so many reasons. The tiny town served many purposes for him personally, and would no doubt become even more important as Bishop's family grew. Betty brought him a steaming cup of coffee, and Bishop blew on the rim of the cup to cool it off. She watched him for a moment and said, "Bishop, you seemed troubled. Is it your friend? I know these are difficult times, but I want you to know I believe the doctor is doing everything in his power. He's a frustrated man most of the time these days."

Bishop anxiously shifted his weight from one foot to another. "He told me about losing a new mother and baby not long ago. While I know I shouldn't, I can't help but think of Terri."

Betty shook her head, "Oh my, Bishop. He shouldn't have done that. He's an excellent doctor, but I think his people management skills leave a little to be desired at times. I'm sorry he's worried you."

Bishop was about to respond when the back door to the office opened, and the doctor came rushing in. "Bishop, the Colonel is awake and wants desperately to talk to you. He said it's urgent. I couldn't settle him down until I agreed to bring you to him."

Bishop left immediately and quickly dashed through the gardens. He knocked lightly on the unlocked hotel room door and then pushed it open.

The Colonel was lying with several pillows propping him on his side, facing the door. He nodded slightly as Bishop entered the room; and with his eyes, motioned for Bishop to take a nearby chair.

"So, you got her back. Thank you, Bishop; I will rest easier knowing she is safe from those crooks or whatever they were. I've been thinking about something…something very important, and have made a decision. I asked the doctor to have you join me, so I can fill you in."

"No problem, sir. How are you feeling?"

The older man's voice softened. "Not good, Bishop, I've been better. I think this sawbones is a good enough physician, but he's bullshitting me, and I wish he'd stop."

The Colonel coughed again, and the motion caused him pain. After a short pause, he continued, "Bishop, about four weeks ago, I was called into the commander's office in Houston. He had a printout of a letter from the President of the United States, addressed to me. It seems that someone has finally gotten their head out of their ass and wanted to try and put the country back together again. That printout was a half-assed cross between an order and a request from an old friend. I read the damn thing three times. I think the general sitting across from me thought I was slow or something. Anyway, I accepted the mission. I figured I had one last dose of ass kicking left in me and it seemed like an important part in trying to rebuild the United States. I love this country son; I truly do. I've spent so much of my life in other places and probably realize more than most what we really have…had here. 'Fuck it,' I said, 'I'm in.' I told the general to confirm that I would indeed accept the assignment."

Bishop was surprised by this revelation and wanted to immediately ask a hundred questions. He decided there would be time for that later and kept his mouth shut waiting for the man to continue.

"That Betty woman told me what you did here, Bishop. How you took a risk for the town and its people. Your wife told me how important it was that this little speck of civilization survived. I always had you figured for a smart operator, probably a little deeper thinker than most. When the doctor told me my granddaughter was back safe thanks to you, it made up my mind. Do you remember what I said to you when you pulled that Marine out of the burning Humvee back in Iraq, son?"

"Yes sir, I do."

"Well, most guys in our profession don't worry too much about anybody but themselves and the other men on their team. You really can't blame them - it's probably how they have survived. You were different then, and after what I've heard lately, you still are. That's why I've decided I can trust you with this…that's why I need to tell you what is going on. Normally, I would take this to my grave rather than violate a trust. Now, I think I'd be committing a worse sin by not filling you in. Can you bring over my briefcase?"

Bishop looked around the room and found the Colonel's briefcase. It was a stainless steel model with heavy-duty combination locks. The Colonel waved him off when Bishop started to hand it over.

"Son, let me tell you the combination, and be very, very careful you get it right. There are two ounces of white phosphorous inside. If you don't enter the combination perfectly, a glass vile will break and everything inside will instantly burn."

After Bishop entered the combination, he gently opened the case and was relieved that the three folders inside were intact. He could see two glass tubes of white powder were indeed attached to the locks.

The Colonel didn't waste any time. "Bishop, I need you to read the content of those three folders. I request you do so in private, and I have to ask you not to share the contents with anyone, not even your lovely wife. I don't want to be dramatic or anything, but the future of our country could be at stake. I'm now convinced that there are powerful people who want to control this land for their own purposes. I have to rest again. Come back after you have digested it all, and I'll answer your questions then."

Chapter 11

As the Colonel closed his eyes, Bishop looked down at the folders in his hands. He owed the dying man a lot, but even deeper than that, he was a patriot. He picked up the heavy steel case and put the folders back inside, but didn't turn the locks. Picking up his coffee, he quietly left the room and walked through the pre-dawn gardens thinking deeply about the events of the last few days. On his way past Terri's room, he checked in on his wife. She was breathing deeply and still hours away from waking.

Bishop needed someplace quiet to concentrate on the three folders. He returned to the main office and let Doc Hopkins and Betty know the Colonel was sleeping again. Betty offered him a refill of the excellent Manor house brew, and he gratefully accepted.

Bishop had a puzzled look on his face. "Betty, what time does Pete normally open the bar?"

"Bishop, don't tell me you need a little nip already? It's only five in the morning. Did your friend upset you that much?"

Bishop laughed and nodded. "Didn't you know I was a lush, Betty? I just pretend to like coffee so I have a chance to flirt with you before Terri gets up and catches us together."

Betty giggled like a schoolgirl and waved Bishop off. "Now I know you're blowing hot air up this old skirt, hun. But Pete is probably up already. He likes to read in the morning before opening for business. If you see candlelight in the window, he's up. By the way, my coffee is a lot better than his."

Bishop laughed and turned toward the front door. *Pete isn't the only one who needs to read this morning.*

As Bishop walked the few blocks down to Pete's place, he looked around Meraton and wondered if he would get a chance to shop the market when it opened. In the distance, he heard a coyote howl and paused for a bit to see if the call were answered. It was not. *Sorry bud, seems like you are on your own this morning. You don't know how lucky you are...be careful what you ask for.*

Sure enough, there was a dim candle burning in Pete's window. Bishop walked to the front of the building as he remembered Pete's shotgun was always close by.

"Hello Pete, it's Bishop. Can I come in?"

Bishop heard the lock being turned, followed immediately by the door being slowly opened. The solar powered streetlights revealed Pete's cautious gaze peering outside. His look of concern was quickly replaced with a big toothy grin as he waved Bishop inside.

"Bishop, what has you up so early this morning? Is everything okay?"

Bishop flashed thumbs up and said, "Pete, I can't explain right now, but I need someplace quiet to read for a bit. It's important."

Pete swept his arm in a grand jester of welcome. "Well, my friend, you have come to the right place. Welcome to Pete's bar and reading room. Can I get you some coffee?"

Bishop nodded to his still full cup and asked for a rain check. Pete brought out a candle from behind the bar and motioned for Bishop to take any table he wanted.

Bishop settled for the small table Terri and he had used the first time they entered Pete's bar. They had been new in town and absolute strangers that night, completely unsure of what they were walking into. Bishop felt the same way now.

It was three hours later when he closed the last folder. He sat back, rubbed his eyes, and finished the third cup of coffee since he had been at Pete's. The sun was up, and the people of Meraton were going about their business. He stood, stretched, and then put the folders back in their steel case. *I should spin the locks and set off the booby trap – make it all burn. What's in there shouldn't see the light of day. How do I get involved in this shit?*

Movement outside on the street caught his attention, and he looked out in time to see Terri walking toward Pete's, smiling and waving at almost everyone passing by. Terri seemed to be enjoying their newfound celebrity status more than he did, but then again, she is probably just being friendly.

The front door burst open and in stormed Terri, pistol drawn. She winked at Pete and then swept the room with her weapon until her gaze landed on Bishop.

"Sooooo, where is she? You've only been in town one night and already yer cheating on me, ya scoundrel. Where's the little tramp? I'mah gonna give her a bad case of lead poisoning!"

When Bishop and Pete both snorted out loud, Terri couldn't keep a straight face and started laughing as she lowered the weapon. Pete came around from behind the bar and gave Terri a hug while offering her a cup of coffee. Terri declined and rubbed her tummy claiming to be cutting back for the baby. Pete nodded knowingly and went into the back room to leave the couple alone.

"Bishop, seriously, I never took you for a guy who closes down a bar. You okay, baby?"

"That was funny as shit, Terri. If I would've had a woman here with me, I'm sure she would have wet her pants."

"If you would've had a woman here, honey, I would have shot you, not her. Always remember that, my love."

Bishop nodded, absolutely believing she would.

"So baby, what's in that case everyone told me you were carrying around after you talked to the Colonel? Top-secret stuff? Spy stuff? Do tell, do tell."

Bishop looked annoyed and then shook his head. "I guess there aren't any secrets in a small town, are there? Terri, I gave my word to the Colonel I wouldn't talk about what's inside."

Terri smiled and walked around to Bishop's side of the table. She bent over him, kissing his cheek, slowly working her way around to his neck below the ear. Her kisses became more and more determined, and Bishop tried to tilt his head to protect his neck. His wife was relentless, nibbling and kissing him all around his face and neck. She whispered in his ear, "Baby, I need you so, so very bad. Why don't you tell me what's in the case so I can concentrate on making your whole universe spin out of control? I think all this secret agent stuff is incredibly hot. Tell me what's going on, and I'll take you out to my new Hummer and rock your world."

Bishop gently brushed her back, both of them grinning. He stood to escape her onslaught and then pulled her close. "You should change your name to Mata Tari."

Pete came out from the back room, pretending to be embarrassed. "You two should get a room."

"We have a room," they both replied in the same voice.

Pete smiled, "Then you should use it. I run a reputable business here. You two keep that up, and it will taint my near perfect image." *I'm going to have to kidnap my own wife and take her back to the ranch so we won't be interrupted.*

Terri kissed Bishop again and smiled at Pete. "If I keep this up, business will be better than ever," causing everyone to laugh again.

They thanked Pete for his hospitability and headed back for the hotel. The townsfolk were beginning to set up the tables for the market, and it reminded Bishop of both good times and bad. He had witnessed a murder here and had practically lost his mind over it. Terri had pulled him back from what would have been a suicidal charge at the bank robbers. He looked down at her and realized what was bothering him the most about this entire affair with the Colonel and the briefcase.

"Terri, is the Colonel awake?"

"I don't know. The kids were eating breakfast with Betty when I left to find you. Samantha was asking where you were by the way. I think you have a new member of the 'Bishop Fan Club.'"

Bishop rolled his eyes, "I need to talk to the Colonel. He is asking me to keep a secret - even from you - and I don't like it. We've made it this far because we were together. I'm not about to go solo. Either we both are in, or I'm out."

Terri thought she understood, but couldn't be for sure. She smiled and said, "You men go do all your silly secret things. I'm going to get something important accomplished today. I'm going shopping. Let me know if I need to learn the secret handshake or buy a new secret decoder ring or anything."

They walked back to the hotel parking area and opened the back of the Hummer. The weapons Bishop had taken from the dead Colombians were in the back. He took out one of the MP5 sub-machine guns and double-checked it was unloaded. He handed the weapon to Terri. "Here's your charge card darling. Take two of the magazines in case you need a higher limit."

Terri looked at the weapon and asked, "You don't have one like this. Don't you want it?"

Bishop shook his head, "Nope. They shoot a pistol round, and out here in the wide-open spaces, they aren't much good. If we lived in the city, I might consider it. It's a fine weapon, just not real practical for out here. A lot of guys will think it's cool though. You should be able to get about anything you want for it."

That thought made Terri smile, and she slung the weapon over her shoulder and shoved a magazine into each back pocket. She turned away and shoved out her butt, "Bishop, does all this ammo make my ass look fat?"

Bishop wagged his finger at her, "You really expect me to tell a woman carrying a sub-machine gun and lots of bullets that her butt looks fat? Do I *look* stupid?"

Terri blew him a kiss and headed off to spend the morning bartering.

As Bishop strode back to the hotel, he couldn't help but think about what was in those three folders. He entered The Manor's gardens via the back door in order to avoid Samantha, as he didn't want a shadow just yet. He went to his room to wash up and grab some of his gear – but really to think.

The first folder had been the Colonel's letter from the president. The second, and thickest of the three, was a journal of the Colonel's ten-day adventure trying to accomplish the president's wishes. The third was a report, intended to be delivered to the Commander-in-Chief.

The Colonel had been asked to perform an in-depth reconnaissance of the Beaumont, Texas area, specifically focusing on the refineries and processing capabilities available there. While Houston had a much larger capacity, Beaumont was considered the best option given its proximity to the Mississippi and the limited resources available to the government to control the area.

The second folder was where things got interesting. The Colonel had commandeered HBR's corporate yacht and approached Beaumont from the sea. When martial law had been declared in Houston, it just so happened HBR was conducting a training class for some out of town security personnel. The Colonel, realizing the men might be stuck in town for a while, had gotten permission for them to stay on the 65- foot corporate sailing yacht, docked on Clear Lake, just south of the hustle and bustle of Houston. The Colonel had used what he thought was an excuse at the time of "securing a valuable corporate asset from potential looting." His excuse quickly became legitimate.

Bishop would have liked to see the look on the first looter's face when they attempted to raid HBR's boat. According to the Colonel's report, there were six ex-Special Forces operators staying onboard. Needless to say, HBR's floating asset was well protected. As a matter of fact, the entire pier was the only one in the marina that didn't experience any vandalism. *Crime doesn't pay.*

What followed in the detailed diary was, in Bishop's opinion, worthy of a Hollywood movie. The Colonel and his team had taken the big sailboat out into the deep water of the gulf and anchored offshore from Beaumont. Using the outboard powered launch and jet skis, the group had split into two teams to find out what was going on.

The primary assignment was Intel regarding the status of the refineries in the port area. What the Colonel found was shocking. In the dead of night, when his team and he had made their approach, there was a military unit already waiting on them. Floodlights bathed their entourage in light, and the small group was met with four Stryker armored personal carriers, each full of infantry. A loudspeaker asked the Colonel, by name, to approach, and a meeting ensued.

The report continued detailing the conversation, during which the Colonel was asked to enlist and pledge his loyalty to a group that called itself the Independents. They claimed to be a well-formed organization that was growing in strength throughout America. The man, whom the Colonel didn't know, alleged that over 20% of the military forces and more than a few local governments had already joined the cause. The Colonel and his men could either join, or die right there.

According to the journal, the spokesman for the Independents was convincing and logical, and the pitch was well considered. This was a political movement that had been organized before the collapse. The representative explained to the Colonel that the group's allegiance was dictated by a strict belief in the Constitution of the United States, and that after they had reorganized the country, they planned to implement a full democratic government. Until that time, they were quietly recruiting various military commands all across the land. Would the Colonel join them?

The Colonel's journal indicated he seriously thought about the offer. What troubled him about the group, and the offer, was the "or die" part. That didn't seem very democratic at all. The journal contained an entry in bold print. "I have taken one oath, and that is all a man is allowed."

An intense firefight, followed by a narrow escape, ended the meeting. The Colonel and only one of his men managed to make it back offshore to the anchored yacht. The second team fared better, and returned to report that Beaumont was practically functioning at pre-collapse levels, including electrical power in some areas. They reported seeing a very heavy military presence, but all of the vehicles and personnel were from assorted units and organizations. It was as if someone had swept up remnants of several different units and was reconstituting a new army. They estimated at least a division-sized presence, including armor and airmobile units. The troops seemed to be preparing for deployment.

When the Colonel returned to Houston, an attempt had been made on his life almost immediately. He had gathered his family and made a hurried escape that included stealing a private plane and barely getting out alive.

The folder containing the summary report was short and to the point. It warned the president that he had one or more spies for the Independents on his staff. Having a mole in the president's inner circle was the only explanation for the Independent's anticipation of the Colonel's arrival and the rendezvous they arranged for him. Additionally, the clandestine insurgents also knew the details of Operation Heartland. Not only did the group have assets embedded within the president's staff, they clearly had infiltrated the military at the highest levels. This was evidenced by the attempt to kill the Colonel upon his return, since only the senior army staff in Houston knew he had made it back.

Furthermore, the Independents appeared to be one step ahead of the government. If the president attempted to execute Operation Heartland, he was walking into a trap, or worse yet, a civil war with a large, well-equipped foe. If the status reports the Colonel had heard were accurate, that adversary was gaining strength every day.

The Colonel had gone on to theorize that the recent "failures" of various military commands to reorganize the country had, perhaps, been sabotaged by this group. While he had had a mere, 30-minute exposure, it only made sense given all that they had discovered.

Bishop wasn't shocked by the Colonel's report at all. Military personnel weren't any different than other Americans. Any man who experienced a daily life of lawlessness, animalistic behavior, and desperation by his peers was bound to question his loyalty to the leadership that put him in that situation. Since America was divided politically before the collapse, why should anyone be surprised those differences had become deeper? A desperate population would be drawn to the Independents. Their organization was demonstrating progress, order, and security with the promise of eventually reorganizing something new and better. The federal government on the other hand was asking for suffering and sacrifice so as to return to the system that had led to the problems to begin with. Bishop knew the Colonel wasn't anyone's fool, and neither were the vast majority of military officers. If they were joining this movement in droves, the message must be pretty compelling. The Colonel had noted in his journal that the representative of the Independents had almost sold him, and Bishop could understand why.

After finishing the journal, Bishop headed to the Colonel's room and quietly cracked the door open. Seeing the man's eyes were open and alert, he went on in and took a seat without saying a word.

The injured man did his best to sound gruff. "I assume you finished reading everything and have a lot of questions."

Bishop was unimpressed by the attempt. "Not really, Colonel. I can only think of one – what is it you want me to do?"

The answer came quickly. "I need you to get those reports to the president, Bishop. He needs to know what is going on."

Bishop couldn't help himself and snorted. "Colonel, I have no idea where the president is. Even if I did, he is probably surrounded by rings of security in some remote underground bunker. It's not like I can just pick up the phone and call the White House."

The Colonel dropped another surprise. "He's coming here, Bishop."

The pitch of Bishop's voice jumped about three octaves. "He's what? He's coming to Meraton?"

The Colonel chuckled and shook his head no. "He's coming to Fort Bliss, son. Look at the last line of his letter to me. It says, 'I look forward to hearing your report. We can meet again in six weeks at the same place where we first met so many years ago.' That's Fort Bliss, Bishop. I met him there when he was a senator almost 15 years ago. He was on a tour of the base, and I was assigned to be his tour guide."

Bishop's voice was questioning, "Fort Bliss? Why the hell would he go there? Are you sure?"

The Colonel had obviously thought this through. "It would make sense for him to tour the various military posts and show his face. Rally the troops, show someone was in control – you know the drill. I'm sure the Secret Service is only going to let him visit major installations in remote locations. Bliss received several billion dollars' worth of improvements under his administration, and he probably knows the base commander. He was a senator from New Mexico after all, it's perfectly logical for him to want to rally his support close to home. That's how I ended up here, Bishop. I was on my way to Bliss when we ran out of fuel and crashed."

Fort Bliss was a major military installation bordering on the northwest side of El Paso, only a few hundred miles away from Meraton. Bishop only visited the base once, and that was to pick up an old friend and go carousing in El Paso.

Bishop stared at the floor and slowly shook his head side to side. His focus finally cleared, and he looked the Colonel directly in the eye. "That big speech you gave me a bit ago...the one about self-sacrifice and loving our country...doing good deeds for others. That wasn't fair Colonel. As a matter of fact, sir, it pisses me off. You were setting me up."

For the first time Bishop could remember, the Colonel averted his eyes. Suddenly, the older man looked weak, sick, and tired. It was a few moments before he looked back at Bishop. "I am sorry, son. I don't often find myself in a situation where I am not in control. With this piece of metal sticking in my body, I feel helpless at a time when so much is depending on me. Please accept my apology."

Bishop's eyebrows arched in surprise. *An apology from the Colonel? God, the guys back at HBR would never believe me. I would be labeled a liar and advised to seek out a shrink for even considering such a thing.*

Bishop nodded, "Apology accepted, sir. I have to tell you though, my first reaction is 'to hell' with the president and his lot. On the way over here, I couldn't help but think that these 'Independents' deserve a shot. They can't be any worse than what we had before. I'm thinking it might be best to let the two fight it out and see how the last man standing does with ruling the nation."

The Colonel paused and then took a deep breath. "I agree. On the boat ride back to Houston, the other men and I discussed it, and we all thought the same way. Were it not for the nukes, I'd say let the strongest survive. The people would suffer badly, but they're going to anyway. We survived brother killing brother once before. The difference now is that nuclear weapons don't allow for reconstruction. They result in permanent destruction. If a hot civil war breaks out, how long before both sides have nuclear weapons? Given the infiltration of the command structure so far, the Independents probably already control some inventory of hydrogen weapons. How long before the losing side gets desperate and sets one off? What would the opposition do – retaliate. Pretty soon there would be nothing left to rebuild."

For the second time in the last few minutes, Bishop's eyebrows sought the top of his head. He hadn't anticipated agreement, nor had he thought about the nuclear angle.

"Sir, I understand what you're saying, but how will filling in the president help? I mean, won't giving him warning just prolong any conflict? Giving him time to prepare might result in making things worse. Both sides could get stronger and do more damage in the long run."

Again, the Colonel surprised Bishop by agreeing. "You are absolutely correct, Bishop. I wasn't going to Bliss to warn him; I was going to convince him to compromise. He has to work out an agreement with the Independents and figure out a way to include them from here on out. Were it not for the subversive nature of their movement, working out a deal with them would be no different than brokering an agreement between Democrats and Republicans. The man who tried to recruit me said they had originally intended to be a new political party, not an armed movement. The president needs to handle them that way, not as an opposing military force. If he doesn't, no one is going to win this fight, and he needs someone with the balls to tell him that straight up. I know the man well, Bishop. While he's not stupid by any measure, he is driven by pride and ego. No one around him, not even the general staff, will have the guts to tell him like it is. He needs to hear it from someone he respects and trusts. That's why I was going to Bliss. That's what has to be done."

Bishop looked at the man beside him in a new light. While he had always respected his boss for his no bullshit leadership skills, he had never thought of him as a deep-thinking political analyst who had the ear of the most powerful man on earth. His expression betrayed his thinking.

The Colonel sensed Bishop's thoughts. "Now, you owe me an apology. Of all people, you would be the last person I'd expect to stereotype anybody. You think just because I commanded men who carried a rifle for a living that I'm nothing but an old warhorse? Do you honestly believe my use of foul language shows I am an uneducated brut? I have a P.H.D. in political science from Yale, Bishop. I was the president's advisor when he was in college. Just because I decided long ago I could do more good in the military doesn't mean you should sell me short, son."

Bishop was, yet again, shocked. He started to stutter out an apology, but the Colonel waved him off. "Don't worry about it. We have more important subjects to cover than my ego or your lack of insight. I don't have long on this earth, and I don't want to waste any more time."

Bishop took the easy way out. "Sir, I understand, but I have to ask how you knew where I was. I don't remember ever telling you about the ranch. While you were flying the plane, how did you find my place?"

The Colonel smiled, "Bishop, there you go again. I wasn't flying the plane, David was. I'm a lot of things, but a pilot isn't one of them. The boy did a great job getting it down without power. As to how I knew where you were, I found the information in your house back in Houston."

Bishop tilted his head in thought, trying desperately to connect the dots. The Colonel coughed again and needed a little time to recover. Finally, he continued. "When they tried to execute me after the Beaumont trip, I gathered up Mrs. Porter and the grandkids and tried to sneak out of town. That wasn't an easy task, given the fact that I was being hunted. Our plan was to head north to Hooks Airport where my son kept a plane. We had to choose an alternate route when the guys chasing me caught up with us, and during the encounter, my car was shot to hell. There we were, stuck on the north side of town with nowhere to go. In desperation, I remembered you lived not far away. We hid in your house for the night. Bishop, it probably saved our lives. Anyway, while I was there, I dug around looking for food and was curious as to what had happened to you and your wife. I found some old tax records for your place out here. It caught my eye because it was so close to where I was heading."

Bishop's eyes lit up. "You were in our house? How was it? It's still there?"

"The weeds and grass were a little out of control, but otherwise it was intact. Don't tell Terri, but it was very dusty. The entire neighborhood was deserted; we didn't see another soul. Oh, and sorry about the back door – I didn't have a key."

Both men chuckled at the Colonel's whimsical apology. It helped relax them for a moment and gave Bishop some time to digest everything. There were still some holes he couldn't fill in.

He struggled with the connection. "Colonel, I'm flattered you remembered my address, but that seems like an odd thing for you to know."

The Colonel smiled again. "Oh, don't be too flattered. Mrs. Porter used to live close by your home. I never wanted anyone at HBR to know we were seeing each other. She noted your address when you bought the house and told me we would have to be careful not to run into you if I were out that way. That's why I remembered your address, Bishop – I was seeing Mrs. Porter. God rest her soul; I expect I will be seeing her in the hereafter soon enough though."

All at once, it clicked for Bishop. He remembered how the Colonel had warned him Mrs. Porter was a friend and to respect her wishes during his hiring process at HBR. Then an odd look came across his face, and he snapped his head toward the man lying beside him. "The woman the Columbians executed at the plane…that was…. Oh lord, Colonel, I'm sorry."

The Colonel waved him off. "No need for all that, son. She was a brave woman and died with honor. I wish there had been time to give her a proper burial, but I understand. Her husband was under my command in the first Gulf War. We met when I came to tell her that he had been killed in action. A few years later, we met again at HBR and started seeing each other. She was a good woman. We were going to get married after I retired in a few years."

Both men remained silent for a few moments. Bishop now had all of the pieces of the puzzle straight in his head. The Colonel spoke next. "Bishop, I'm getting tired again and having trouble thinking clearly. Go digest what you have learned today. I'm sure I'll be able to hold up my end of this conversation again after I've rested for a bit."

Bishop understood, but one last question begged for an answer. "That's a good idea sir, but I have one more thing I need to go over. You've asked me to keep all of this confidential, and I have, but I need to talk this through with my wife. She deserves…no… has earned the right to know what is going on. If

117

you say no, then I am through with the entire affair. I won't do anything without her being in the loop."

The Colonel thought about Bishop's statement and weakly responded. "You're right about that, Bishop. The time and place for everything being a secret is long behind us now. You have my permission to seek any council you feel is necessary. I have to sleep now."

Bishop left the Colonel's room and wandered absent-mindedly through the gardens. His head was reeling from everything he had taken in, and he desperately needed to talk it all through with Terri. As he turned decidedly toward the hotel office, David and Samantha strolled out the back door. The young girl immediately bolted toward Bishop.

"Mr. Bishop, there you are! We were on our way to see Grandpa, and I wondered if you would like to go with us?"

"I just left your grandpa, Sam, and he's sleeping now. He's fine, just needing lots of rest."

Sam seemed a little disappointed, but recovered quickly. "What are you going to do now? Can we go to the market? We were watching all of the people through the window, and it looks interesting. Can we go?"

Bishop thought a distraction might help clear his head, so he agreed to accompany the pair through the market. He turned to David. "I have a rifle I might want to trade today. Would you mind carrying it? I want to keep this one with me, and carrying two would suck."

David nodded, and the three headed to the shot up Hummer in the parking area. Bishop pulled the second MP5 he had taken off of the dead Colombians out of the back, checked to see if it were loaded, and passed it to the tall, thin teenager.

David immediately racked the bolt to see if the weapon were loaded, which surprised Bishop just a little. After scrutinizing the weapon carefully, David remarked, "H&K MP5. Probably made in their Rio plant from the markings. You can tell those guys were from the city. The 9 mm this thing shoots is about worthless at any distance. Dad told me the SAS use these on rescue missions, but have had trouble taking down their opponents with a single shot."

Bishop's raised eyebrows marked his surprise. "So, you know weapons?"

"My dad is Air Force Pararescue. He and I used to go shooting a lot. I only like the long distance stuff and won a couple trophies in the NRA junior leagues. Sam shoots pretty well too, but doesn't like the noise."

Bishop whistled, "Pararescue? Your dad must be one hell of a soldier, David. Those guys are one of the most elite units in the entire military. I've heard about their qualification school."

Sam chimed in. "I hate shooting, but my dad and grandpa made me go. David teased me about how I hold a pistol, and the earphones mess up my hair. My daddy joined so he could save wounded pilots. I bet if he was here, he could help Grandpa."

Sam's comment brought Bishop back to his conversation with the Colonel for a moment. He didn't want to mentally go there just yet, so he told David to sling the MP5 over his back and handed him the remaining two magazines to carry.

As the threesome trekked to Main Street, it was like entering a different world of sights, sounds, and smells. Word had spread quickly to the surrounding ranches and homes about the Meraton market. It was free enterprise in its rawest form because U.S. currency no longer held any value. Everything was barter and trade, which made negotiating interesting, to say the least.

People came to the market using all modes of transportation. There were beat up old farm trucks, ATVs, two motorcycles, hand-pulled carts and even a moped. By far the most popular however, were horses. Bishop pointed out how someone had taken rope and scrap lumber to make rails for tying up horses. Every streetlight and highway sign had been repurposed, and dozens of horses were now hitched around the town. Someone had put sweet grass in wicker baskets, and the buckets in front of every makeshift hitching post were filled with water.

As they entered the market, the smells arising from the street were another clear indication that commerce was underway. Small adobe ovens baked fresh bread on the spot. A local rancher butchered beef right out of the back of his pickup truck. An assortment of homemade candles was lit, their sweet scent competing with all the other odors of the outdoor bazaar.

Anyone was welcome to come into Meraton and participate in the market. Each morning, the full-time merchants along Main Street sat out their display tables of all sorts and sizes. It was first come, first serve, and the best spots were occupied right away. Some people simply walked around with their goods, holding up homemade signs. Bishop saw one man with an old shotgun on his shoulder. Sticking out of the barrel was a hand-lettered sign that read, "Will trade for a healthy hen."

Sam tugged on Bishop's arm. "Mr. Bishop, why is everyone carrying a gun? Aren't there policemen?"

Bishop paused to explain. "There are no policemen here, Sam. If there is trouble, some of the town's men will come, but there are no regular lawmen. All of these folks carry guns because there are some bad people in every crowd, and everyone knows they have to be ready to take care of themselves."

David decided to help. "Sam, it's like those cowboy movies Dad likes to watch. We're out in the Wild West now."

Sam pondered this for a minute, and then looked at Bishop's rifle slung across his chest. "Mr. Bishop, if there's trouble, I'll come looking for you."

Bishop patted her on the head, "Sam, if there's trouble, you won't have to look for me. I'll be right beside you." He meant it.

The teens adjusted quickly to the activity around them, and Bishop let them drift further and further from his side. He was glad they seemed to want to stay together, though he never let them out of his sight.

As they slowly made their way up the street, Bishop couldn't help but notice how much things had changed in just a few short months. The word "finite" kept creeping into his mind. After Terri and he had settled in the camper, they realized that the supplies and equipment they brought from Houston were now "finite." It seemed like every activity, chore or task depleted their limited resources. As was his habit, Bishop was cleaning a weapon one day after returning from a hunting trip. He picked up the small container of gun oil and realized it would be empty one of these days, and he had no idea where to get more or how to make a substitute. Terri had been washing their bed sheets when a corner had caught on a rock and torn. They no longer could run to the mall and buy new linens. Factories were not even making new sheets anymore.

Almost every single item touched, used, or consumed had now become finite. As the group meandered through the market, Bishop found his eye was drawn more and more to items that were homemade or renewable rather than those that had been manufactured in some far off production line before the collapse. He stopped in front of one table that held a few small stacks of cloth. Two ladies, sitting behind their "counter," were explaining to another woman how they had woven the cloth. One of the women had an old spinning wheel in the corner of her house, an heirloom from her grandmother. The antique decoration was now being pressed into service once again.

It wasn't difficult to imagine that knowledge would soon be as valuable as goods. It had always been that way he supposed, but what was going to be in demand now was old ways rather than new. Six months ago, a new car had more value than an old one. Now, a horse and wagon would be worth more than a brand new Mercedes. The latest software was in demand before, now Bishop and Terri would be glad to trade just to find a workable recipe for soap. They wouldn't even consider the latest model laptop with a gazillion mega-whatevers – it was worthless to them now.

As it always had, the market cheered him up in so many small ways. Since he had been here last, he could see that more and more of the goods being offered had actually been made after the collapse. His realization seemed to push that word "finite" toward the back of his mind a little.

They browsed about halfway through the vendors when Bishop noticed a large crowd of people surrounding a table in front of Pete's. Bishop checked on David and Sam, who were busy petting a lamb tied up to the back bumper of a farm truck, and wandered over to see what was so interesting.

Before he could even see through the crowd surrounding the table, he heard Terri's voice. She was manning the table and clearly enjoying it. As he came around behind her, he could see an old igloo cooler and several small bottles were on the table. Some of the bottles had pieces of tape on them, handwritten labels lettered with either "Rye" or "Gin." The cooler was clearly identified as "Ale."

Terri looked up suddenly to see her husband by her side, "Hey babe, do you want a sample too?"

Bishop sized up the crowd before asking, "Terri, what the hell are you doing?"

Terri didn't answer him right away. She was busy keeping track of the customers gathered around her table. There were four men negotiating with her all at once and another five or six who were trying to get a sample. Terri was chatting, observing, joking, and serving little bits of the liquids into cups that were being sampled by the interested parties.

When there was a short pause in the action, she smiled at Bishop. "Pete wanted the rifle you gave me, but he didn't have anything to trade but booze. He's been making moonshine and brewing his own ale. We agreed that I would trade him the rifle for so much white lightening, and then I could trade that for what we really needed. I decided that it would sell better if folks could taste test."

Terri stood on her tiptoes and whispered in Bishop's ear. "These guys get a couple of samples in them, and they don't negotiate so well." She immediately returned to a friendly argument about the exchange rate for gin and relative value of one man's stack of used dishtowels.

Bishop just grinned and shook his head. *Only Terri.*

Bishop backed away from the table and double-checked on the kids. Sam was now feeding the lamb. David's attention was focused on two girls about his age. He seemed to be holding his own, and were it not for the rifle strapped across David's back, it would have looked like a couple of teens exploring a petting zoo.

Terri was wheeling and dealing like crazy. There hadn't been any hard liquor in Meraton in months. Pete had almost run out of beer when he first attempted to make his own brew. The third batch had been almost drinkable. When Pete sampled his fifth brew, he decided the taste wasn't bad at all, and he woke with only the slightest headache the next morning. But he needed a more efficient way to produce his liquid treasure. That led to the still and the bathtub gin. Terri's timing had been just perfect with the machine gun. Pete had been planning an announcement to the community that their thirst was no longer in danger of being out of control. He had wanted Terri's weapon badly enough to let her steal his thunder.

Terri grasped a bottle in one hand, which she was using to fill small plastic bottle caps with samples. The men standing around the table were all trying to get her attention at once. In her other hand, she held a sheet of paper listing everything she needed at the ranch. Bishop hoped toothpaste was on the shopping list. His wife's behavior was similar to a carnival hawker, a lot like a bartender, and a little like an auctioneer. Every now and then, she evidently said something funny because all the men would break out laughing. One thing was clear. Several of the fine gentlemen gathered around her table had had more than one or two samples. *I would give anything to see what's on that list she's holding, but I would probably start a riot if I interrupted.*

Bishop wandered to a spot several feet behind Terri's table where he could watch both his wife and the Colonel's grandkids. They had now gotten bored with the lamb and had moved on to a table full of comic books and magazines. David had the two girls in tow, and everyone seemed to be getting along fine. He glanced back at Terri and froze. One of the men standing beside her table had evidently had far too many samples and was grabbing his wife's ass. Bishop tensed and started to take a step forward when Terri removed the offending hand and wagged her finger in the man's face, clearly issuing a warning. Bishop relaxed just slightly, but the move had gotten his attention. It wasn't but about a minute later that the hand returned. Again, Bishop was about to charge like a bull, when Terri moved the hand and this time issued a sterner warning. The offending gent, probably a ranch hand in his early thirties, just smiled and nodded. It took the cowboy another two minutes or so to work up his courage to reach for Terri's ass a third time. Bishop didn't even get a chance to move before Terri's pistol magically appeared in the man's face. Everyone became suddenly very quiet, and no one moved a muscle. The offender raised his hands in the traditional "don't shoot" position, and his eyes were crossing trying to watch the barrel of Terri's pistol, which was touching his nose.

"I warned you twice, friend," Terri said in a very serious tone. "I'm not going to tell you a third time. You ever touch me again, and I'll split that face of yours wide open. Do you understand?"

The cowboy had trouble finding words, "Ye..ye…yes."

Terri's voice was cold as ice, and Bishop noted her hand wasn't shaking. "Now, I know you're going to walk off and think about this for a little while. Your male ego is going to get the better of you, and you're going to want to come back and teach me a lesson. So maybe I should go ahead and end this right now - save me the trouble later."

Terri clicked off the safety, and Bishop started moving forward, scarcely believing he was going to try and save the guy's life who had just been feeling up his wife. It was Pete's voice that broke the silence, "Terri…Terri…don't do it. Take a deep breath and just calm down. He's had too much to drink Terri, it's not worth it."

Pete was walking slowly toward Terri and the frightened man. He reached carefully and put his hand on Terri's arm.

Terri never took her eyes off the cowboy.

Pete said, "Terri, it's okay. Let him go. It's not worth this."

Bishop was surprised by Terri's response. "Pete, you know he's a dead man anyway. When Bishop finds out about this, he'll take that big knife of his and skin this scum alive. I'd be doing him a favor putting him down now before Bishop gets a hold of him."

The cowboy's eyes got even bigger, "Did she say 'Bu…Bu…Bishop?'"

Pete looked at the man and nodded. "Yes, you dumbass, she said 'Bishop.' You should check whose wife you're messing with first. I don't know where Bishop is, but I would suggest you get the hell out of town before he shows up. We're tired of digging graves around here."

The cowboy nodded as much as Terri's pistol would allow. Terri pulled the weapon back, and the man turned and left immediately. Bishop decided to follow him for a bit, just to make sure he wasn't going to change his mind. The man mounted a good-looking stallion and headed east out of town. He never looked back.

By the time Bishop returned, Pete had taken over the table, and Terri was nowhere to be seen. Bishop found the teenagers, and David informed him that two men wanted to talk about the rifle he was carrying. David had told them Bishop would be around soon.

Terri casually strolled over, like nothing had happened. "Hey guys, are you enjoying the market?"

Bishop looked at her and grinned. "That was quite a show you just put on back there, kiddo. I actually thought you were going to shoot that guy. Nice."

Terri was matter-of-fact. "I thought it was better that I handle it. I knew you were standing behind me, and if you had gotten involved, it wouldn't have ended well. No big deal. Pete's giving me a break, but I don't want him trading away all my supply. I need to get back over there before the crowd thins out too much."

"Terri, you know if you guys keep making me out to be Mr. Super Badass, one of these ol' boys is going to eventually challenge me. You realize that, don't you? I wish you guys would stop."

"Okay, Bishop. Next time I'll just shoot the guy so you don't have to get involved." Terri spun around and headed back to her table, leaving Bishop with his mouth open and no words coming out.

When Bishop recovered, he found Betty standing beside him. "Bishop, the doctor said you should go see him as soon as possible. He's in your friend's room. I'll watch the kiddos."

Bishop thanked her and hurried to the Colonel's side.

Chapter 12

When Bishop rapped lightly on the hotel room door, Doc Hopkins motioned him outside. As the two men crossed the covered porch, the physician's tone was serious. "Bishop, I can't do anything for him, and his fever is getting worse. Infection is going to win, even with the strongest of my antibiotics. The only chance is to remove that foreign object from his body. As I said, I can't do that with the equipment we have here. I'll most certainly kill him during the operation."

Bishop could see the man was tired and frustrated. The two slowly ambled through the gardens, each lost in his own thoughts.

The doctor looked at the ground and moved his head slowly from side to side. "It's a shame, just a crying shame. If this had happened just a few months ago…. I guess I'm going to see a lot of this from now on. The children will be the worst, I suppose."

Bishop kept thinking about Terri. While she seemed healthy, there was no way to know for sure. *You're being selfish, think about Meraton and what they are building here. Think about the Colonel and how important his mission is.*

Bishop put his hand on the doctor's shoulder. "What do you need? I heard you mention equipment that would help. Is it too late to save the Colonel?"

The doctor snorted. "Oh my god, Bishop! What I wouldn't give for a simple x-ray machine and a basic operating room kit. I need something to look inside the body. I need to be able to transfer blood and monitor heart rates, blood pressure, and other vitals."

Bishop was at a loss when it came to medical equipment. "Isn't an x-ray machine huge? Doesn't that equipment take up an entire room?"

"They've made portable models the last few years, Bishop. What I wouldn't give to get my hands on one. Someone donated a small generator for us to use here at the clinic, but I haven't even turned it on yet because we don't have any equipment that requires it."

The two men walked into the hotel lobby and found a half pot of coffee that was still warm. Bishop wanted to get back to the market and check on how Terri and the kids were getting along. He thanked the doctor again for his efforts and walked out onto Main Street.

As Bishop headed toward Pete's, he could feel the desperation building inside. Seeing David with his two young admirers earlier had only fueled the fire in Bishop's mind. Meraton, its market, and the community as a whole had to survive. It was more than just a symbol of hope for Terri and him. It was important for the future of his child, or children. Bishop often wondered how his son or daughter would find friends and perhaps a love of their life. He had thought about what his child's life would be like so many times. Who would teach them to read and write? The answer was always Meraton. He had even considered moving here at some point in the future.

Now that he knew more about the current state of the outside world, Meraton became even more important. Its isolation and general population were probably a rare combination. While he had no way of knowing if there were hundreds, or even thousands of such communities scattered around the country, his heart told him this town was probably one of but a handful of places that was actually moving forward, not falling deeper into the abyss.

Even if there were hundreds of places like Meraton, what would help the town survive – no, even thrive? What had made the difference for the towns of the old west? How come some of the early settlements thrived while others became ghost towns? What allowed some communities to withstand the test of time? The country as a whole could easily end up in a civil war in the next few weeks. Bishop believed that scenario was more likely to be the outcome than any sort of reconciliation or compromise between the two sides. If war broke out in the metropolitan areas, the survival of smaller villages like Meraton would become critical for normalcy to be restored.

As he walked down Main Street's sidewalk lost in thought, Bishop didn't notice that the market was winding down for the day. People had to travel back to their homes and ranches, some several hours horseback ride away. He saw Terri closing up shop, and her body language and expression indicated she was a happy girl. He had to smile as he watched his wife go about packing everything up. She was not only a beautiful woman, she moved with a sense of grace and confidence that made him proud. He had fallen in love with her the first time they had met and never looked back.

While she was about four months pregnant, their diet and workload had caused them both to lose weight. Terri was wearing a pair of blue jeans that had fit her before their bug-out from Houston and she seemed to be comfortable in them. Her normally flat abdomen was just beginning to show a bulge, and it would require a careful observer to realize she was with child.

126

Bishop knew all of that would change soon. While he hadn't said anything, he had been eating a little less than normal in order to let her get all she wanted. She was eating for two after all, and he was always worried about their food supply. His face was a little thinner, and he had had to adjust his load vest and other equipment. While they were nowhere near suffering from malnutrition, they didn't exactly have pepperoni pizza or rocky road ice cream in the kitchen freezer anymore either. Bishop had been hunting more often and trying to store more food for his growing family.

West Texas jackrabbits were their primary meat. The plentiful critters were easy to snare, and Bishop was still paranoid about shooting any game because the sound carried for miles. Rabbit meat was fat free. When Bishop had discovered a full-grown longhorn heifer wandering through a nearby valley, they enjoyed a tasty feast. The animal was exhausted and carried no brand. They had eaten beef for almost two weeks.

Thinking about food brought his mind back to that word "finite." It was basic items that worried Bishop the most. Salt, for example had been a big concern. While the couple left Houston with enough to spice meals, they were completely unprepared for the amount of salt that was required for homesteading. Drying meat, baking and many other household activities required salt. They had a single one-pound container at the camper, purchased long ago to refill the table shakers. Bishop happened to come across a five-pound salt block while hunting one day. It had been set out for cattle to meet their daily needs. It was pure luck he had wandered across the badly needed mineral; and in just a few short weeks, they had used almost half of it.

"Finite." He was beginning to hate that word. It seemed like every day some routine activity would drive that word back into his thoughts. Anything touched, used, worn, or eaten seemed to be finite. While the first deer he brought down was buried with so many of its body parts that it fertilized the ground, burying the last carcass barely required a trowel to dig the hole. At first, the fledgling homesteaders had taken the prime cuts of meat and buried the rest of the animal, including the hide. It was a few days later that Bishop caught the side of his boot on a sharp outcropping and tore the leather. The incident reminded him that he would no longer be able to run to the store and buy a new pair of boots. The ones he had were going to have to last a lifetime, or he would have to make his own moccasins. Every single animal harvested for food since had resulted in a hide being dried and cured in the sun. Even that process had been frustrating. There were so many basic things Bishop wished he had paid attention to before the collapse. He had not scraped the first hide well enough, and it had wrinkled and smelled to high heaven as it cured. The resulting hide was worthless and buried in the garden plot. He had gotten better at the process by trial and error. He knew there were a *finite* number of errors they could make.

Terri looked up and smiled as Bishop approached. They hugged each other and enjoyed the moment. She couldn't wait to show Bishop all of the items she had bartered for. Her most prized possession was three sets of children's shoes, mostly in good condition. At first, Bishop was a little taken aback, but as he thought about it, he realized their child was going to need shoes just like they did. There were certain times of the year where even the most calloused soles couldn't walk on the desert floor. Her second most prized possession was a stack of old dish towels. Some were heavily embellished with Christmas décor while others were clearly intended as a housewarming gift. When Bishop gave Terri a questioning look about the stack of towels, she said one word – "Diapers." Bishop was somewhat embarrassed that he hadn't thought about that aspect of having a baby around and realized Terri's motherly instincts were way ahead of his.

Terri started to show him the rest of her prizes when Pete joined them. "Hey, Bishop, there you are. We're having a town meeting inside the bar. I sure would appreciate it if you'd join us. We would like to have input from Terri and you."

Terri immediately answered for him. "We'd love to join in Pete, thanks for inviting us." Terri closed up her bags of goodies and looked at Bishop. "I'll show you the rest later. I got several things we needed."

As Bishop and Terri entered the bar, several of the townsfolk had already gathered. Many were sitting around the bar, while others scattered among the available tables, drinking water or whatever else they had. Bishop found a table toward the back and the two sat while more people continued to wander in.

After about five minutes, Pete looked around and then asked for everyone's attention. He had a small stack of papers in his hand. "Okay everyone, thanks for joining us today. I have several notes here from all of you, and we'll go through each and every one of them today. First up, is a note from George and Cindy Beltron. They want to discuss the topic of school and educating the children."

Bishop sat fascinated as the day wore on. The town meeting covered everything from schooling the young ones to maintaining the cemetery. The town had a small elementary school before the collapse, with the middle and primary school located an hour and a half away in Alpha. A couple of the school's teachers were still in town, and the local people who had smaller children wanted to see what would be involved reopening the school. The discussion was eventually tabled because the teachers were struggling to put food on the table and keep their households going. Without pay, there was no way the town could reopen the school. Three people volunteered to deliver ideas on compensating the teachers at the next meeting.

Security was another hot topic. There had been a handful of incidents since Bishop and Terri had left town. While the community had formed a loosely organized group of men as a posse, volunteering time was difficult because folks were struggling with day-to-day demands of this primitive lifestyle. The men who manned the roadblocks at each end of town all reported that the time required was becoming a burden to their families.

And so it went the rest of the afternoon. Some issues were resolved quickly, while others required more thought and analysis. Bishop would have normally been bored to death with the entire affair, but it was interesting to watch the process. More than anything, it gave him optimism for the future, something he badly needed.

Were it not for the final speaker, Bishop would have left the meeting believing things were positive and upbeat. When Doc Hopkins was given the floor, everything seemed to grow darker inside the room. The man reported in a monotone voice, and everyone in the room felt his pain. He wasn't saving many patients, and it was clearly pulling him down.

After the physician's report concluded, several hands shot up, and one man spoke out, "Doc, what do you need? We're so lucky to have you here, is there anything we can do?"
"Please excuse my attitude today. I'm especially tired, and the last few weeks have been somewhat demoralizing. Short of our having equipment and supplies, I can't think of anything that will improve our success rate for treating people. It's not going to get any better as time goes by, and I can see the day coming soon when we'll be even more restricted in what we can do."

Another man asked, "What do you need, Doc? Maybe someone around has some of what you need?"

"I sincerely thank you for the thought, but what we need is the equipment that would only be found in a hospital or well-funded clinic. Everyone has been so kind and brought me whatever medicines and supplies they have had lying around. But I need x-ray capabilities, blood transfusion, pumps, monitors, and other machines. I don't think anyone has that sort of thing in their garage."

"There's a hospital in Alpha...," someone volunteered.

129

Bishop looked around the room and noticed everyone looked down at the floor. The reaction struck him as odd, and he couldn't help but speak up. "What's wrong with Alpha? I mean, I know there was an explosion at the chemical plant, but the air should have cleared by now. What's going on there?

No one seemed to want to answer Bishop's question. It was finally Pete that looked up and volunteered information. "Bishop, no one really knows what is going on there. A lot of the people here have family and friends in that town, and a few of us have tried to see how things are there."

Another man interrupted Pete. "Tim Rollins and his brother left to explore Alpha a month ago; no one has heard from either man since. They were both pretty good hands and capable men."

A lady in the corner spoke up. "Riccardo Mendez rode his horse to Alpha, but he didn't even get close before someone started shooting at him. He left and came back."

Pete looked at Bishop and added, "Two houses on the outskirts of town were raided three weeks ago. Everyone inside was killed, and the places were cleaned out. The tracks led back toward Alpha. That's when we set up the roadblocks and had everyone move into town that could. The Benton ranch has been hit twice. They believe both times it was people from Alpha."

Bishop noticed everyone was looking at him, waiting on some sort of reaction. The only thing he could think to say was, "I see."

The town meeting broke up, and everyone started wandering home. Bishop and Terri walked back toward The Manor, each lost in their thoughts. It was Bishop who broke the silence, "Terri, I have so much I need to talk to you about. Let's get some chow and relax in the gardens. I want to see what you got at the market, and I'm sure you'll want to hear about my day."

Terri nodded and looked at Bishop. *He has that look again…that look like the entire world is resting on his shoulders.*

Both analytical thinkers, Samantha was in hot pursuit of David's queen in the most rousing game of chess The Manor's lobby had seen in years. Betty had some beef tips and peppers cooked on the hotel's open fire pit. As Bishop and Terri entered the lobby, the aroma hit them and both realized how hungry they were. Terri presented Betty with six eggs she had bartered for, and the hotel manager seemed thrilled. She made a plate for each, and they retired to a garden table with beef, peppers, corn bread and roasted pine nuts. It was a feast like they hadn't enjoyed in months.

After they finished eating, Terri offered to help Betty clean up before she talked to Bishop. As they were carrying the dishes into the kitchen area, Betty announced she had one more surprise for Bishop. She opened a drawer and pulled out a metal tube containing a cigar. Bishop responded with a look of "*for me?*" and Betty pushed the rare item into Bishop's hand.

As Terri helped with the kitchen duties, Bishop returned to their table and carefully snipped the end of the cigar with his fighting knife. In no time, he had the cigar puffing nicely and sat back to relax and enjoy the luxury.

Terri appeared a bit later and teased Bishop, "Would you care for some Port with your smoke, sir? Is there anything else I could do to make your experience here at The Manor more enjoyable?" Bishop choked when her eyebrows went up and down. Terri sat next to her husband and watched him take a puff from the cigar. When he exhaled, a bit of the smoke drifted her way, prompting her to scoot her face away from the odor. "For all the glamor those things have, they sure do stink. You're not kissing me with that mouth until you gargle with some kerosene, mister."

Bishop started to put out the stogie, but Terri waved him off. "Enjoy it babe – just keep downwind of me. My nose seems to be working overtime since I've been pregnant, but really, I don't mind."

Bishop handed her the Colonel's briefcase, unlocked. He showed her the folders, and then focused on his smoke. It took Terri about an hour to read through all of the material. When she had finished, she looked at Bishop with a blank look on her face.

Her voice was ice cold. "So my love, what does this have to do with the price of cheese in China?"

Bishop responded without emotion. "Not a damn thing, I guess."

Terri wasn't going to let it go that easily. She tapped her fingers on the tabletop, waiting on Bishop to expand on his last comment. When it was clear he wasn't going to do so voluntarily, she pushed for more details. "Bishop, he wants you to deliver his report, doesn't he?"

"Yes."

Terri stood up and walked around the table with her fists balled on her hips. Three times she stopped and pointed her finger at Bishop, but no words came out. Twice, she stopped, pointed her finger at the Colonel's room, but no words came out. Bishop just sat with a neutral look on his face, not daring to say a word. She continued working up a good head of steam.

Finally, she stopped her pacing and looked at the sky, spreading her arms wide, "This is bullshit...pure, U.S.D.A Government inspected table grade bullshit. How could he do that to you? How, in heaven's name, can he lay this on *you*?"

Bishop shrugged his shoulders. "It's important, Terri...I guess that's why."

Terri spun and leaned into Bishop's face, "No, it's not important!" She moved an outstretched arm in a wide arch, pointing at Meraton, "*This* is important. *This* is what matters. These people are what counts, not some bullshit power game being played by a bunch of government fucks who aren't risking anything but their egos. The guys who carry the guns and die are what matters, not those elected pukes and all of their cronies – they don't mean shit anymore. They had their chance and fucked it up."

Bishop simply nodded and pretended the rocks at his feet needed to be arranged.

"Come on, Bishop. Remember how we saw people eating dogs on the way out here? If the fucking President of the United States will sit at that table and eat a dog in front of me, then I will reconsider my point of view. Until then, he is nothing, means nothing, and will never be anything again."

Bishop had expected a major reaction from Terri, but not this strong. She was as mad as he had ever seen her, and the anger seemed to be growing. He was in new territory here and was trying to think through how to handle it, when her mood suddenly changed and her voice went monotone cold.

"So, you are supposed to find the president, deliver this report, salute, and head back home?"

Bishop looked her in the eye, "Not exactly. The president is coming to Fort Bliss, a few hundred miles from here. The Colonel wants *me* to convince the Commander in Chief to compromise and work with the Independents. Why he is convinced I can do this, I don't know."

Terri sat down at the table and crossed her arms over her breasts. "Bishop, I have agreed...no, *supported* your doing some pretty crazy stuff since we left Houston. I've watched you put on that rifle and walk off I don't know how many times. You don't know what it's like to sit and wait for you to come back. It's worse than your being in the Army or going off to war. At least some chaplain would knock on my door and let me know you were dead or wounded or missing or whatever. At least if you came home from the Army missing a leg, they would help me take care of you. Not out here, Bishop. Not now. We are on our own out here. If you had gotten yourself killed at Big Bend, I would've never known. I would still be sitting at that camper night after night, waiting for a blessed rock to hit the roof. I would always wonder what happened to you. There would be no closure Bishop, no flag-draped coffin, no honor guard, no wives coming over and letting me cry on their shoulders. That's the worst of it – not knowing."

Bishop just looked down at his feet again. He wanted to remind Terri that the same thoughts raced through his mind just two days ago when he considered whether or not to check on the plane, but thought better of it. This all needed to be out in the open.

Terri wearily sat on Bishop's lap. She sniffed a few times and sighed deeply. She looked up at the stars and wiped the tears from her cheeks. She looked at Bishop and then pointed skyward. "There, by the way, is Orion's Belt. I promised you the other day we would find it. I didn't have anything to do after you left to get Samantha, so I got out the book and found it."

It took Bishop a while to finally see what Terri was pointing at. She was always so much better than he at abstract things, like connecting the dots of stars.

Bishop reflected, "The ancient people must have been very bored most of the time, Terri. To sit at night and look up at the sky and find those combinations, make up those shapes and create legends out of just a few pinpoints of light. I wouldn't have been much help to them. I just don't have the imagination, I guess."

The couple sat and looked up at the stars, pointing and enjoying the view of the ultra-clear Texas night. The change helped calm Terri's mind.

"Okay, Bishop, we need to finish this conversation. What do you want to do?"

"I want to go back to the ranch as soon as possible. I want everything to be like it was two days ago before we heard that airplane. Unfortunately, that's impossible. We have David and Samantha to think about, as well as the Colonel."

"What about his files here? What about the president and civil war and all that?"

"I thought we were in agreement that was bullshit?"

Terri jumped off his lap and pointed her finger at him again. "Ohhhh no, you don't, Bishop. Nope, no way," Terri replied, shaking her head. "You are not going to put that on me, mister. I never said you couldn't go. I'm just mad this fell on your head like this."

Bishop chose his next words carefully. "Terri, I don't know how I would get to Bliss. The route goes right through El Paso, and everything we have heard indicates that's not the place to be these days. Even if I went around El Paso, I would imagine Fort Bliss is locked down tighter than a fly's ear."

Terri started to speak when a distant popping noise interrupted her. Before she could even ask what the noise was, Bishop was moving, "Fuck! Those are shots! Get the kids, get your rifle, and get everyone into our room. I am going to see what is going on."

Terri started to say, "Be careful," but Bishop was already gone.

Chapter 13

Bishop rushed to his room and grabbed his equipment. It took him a few moments to switch to a full fighting load. He attached his night vision onto his rifle, verified everything was secured, and jogged out into the night air. He could see Terri, Betty and the kids heading to the room as he left.

Others had heard the shots, and a group of men was gathering on Main Street. Bishop ran up and found Pete pointing west toward the roadblock. More individual shots sounded, followed closely by a long rattle of automatic weapons fire.

Bishop asked, "Do the guys manning the roadblock have auto weapons?"

One of the men answered nervously, "No – someone from the outside is shooting."

A pickup truck started its engine nearby and quickly pulled up to the group of men. Bishop recognized the driver from the town meeting earlier in the day. All of the men started climbing into the bed, handing up their weapons as they pulled themselves into the back of the truck.

Another single shot, followed by a rattle of automatic fire sounded in the distance.

Bishop shook his head, "I don't think this is a good idea."

One of the men looked up and protested, "We have to help 'em...everyone swore they'd come and help if there was trouble."

Bishop thought for a moment, "You men stay here and spread out. Don't let them into town. I'll ride out and help our men. I have an orange glow stick. If you see an orange light, don't shoot us coming back."

The intensity of the shooting down the road was increasing as Bishop climbed into the passenger side of the cab. He told the driver to turn off his headlights, and grabbed the wheel using the night vision to steer. The men of Meraton started spreading out as the truck sped off.

Bishop had the driver stop about a quarter of a mile from where the roadblock had been put in place. The shooting was louder now, and he could see the twinkle of muzzle flashes in the distance.

He told the driver to turn around and go back halfway to town, shut off the truck and keep a sharp eye out for anyone not wearing an orange glow stick. The driver nodded and quickly did as Bishop asked.

Bishop moved off of the road about 100 meters and then turned toward the roadblock. He found a slight rise in the terrain and took cover behind what was a small knoll rising from the desert floor. He was scanning with his night vision, trying to grasp the tactical situation in front of him, when a noise very close-by made him freeze.

He moved only his eyes slightly to the side and made out three men moving toward the road not more than ten feet away. They were going to step on his rifle if they kept going. Bishop thought there were only two Meraton men guarding the road. He didn't think anyone else from the town would be out here, but he didn't want to get into a fight with allies. When the men were less than five feet away, they stopped and crouched down. Bishop thought at first they had seen him, but they stayed put.

As slowly as his could, Bishop moved his arm and reached for his flashlight mounted on his vest. While the light was small in size, the LED bulbs were very bright and he hoped he could reach it without the men's eyes detecting the movement. After his hand closed around the handle of the light, he gradually shifted his weight to one side so as to unhook and remove the torch.

Again, moving only his eyes, he checked to see what the three men were doing and could make out their heads scanning from side to side. *They are either waiting on someone or something to happen.* Another exchange of shots occurred down on the road, and Bishop used the noise rolling across the desert floor to click off his rifle's safety.

The men were to his right and the M4 was in his right hand, flashlight in his left. In one motion, Bishop rolled onto his left side while swinging the rifle around one-handedly. His left hand hit the switch on the light, and he pointed it at the stunned men only a few feet away.

As the light swung an arch caused by Bishop's rolling motion, it crossed the faces of three men, all holding MP5 submachine guns. The light in their eyes caused them to raise their arms and turn their heads and that gave Bishop the time he needed. His rifle started barking at pointblank range, and hit its mark even though he could manage only one hand on his M4. He kept firing until all three men were down, turned off the light, and quickly moved away from the knoll. He hadn't traveled three strides away when the ground where he had been lying erupted in small geysers of sand caused by the impact of incoming rounds. *They had been waiting on someone. How many Columbians are here? What are they doing?*

Bishop had now lost the element of surprise. He was up against an unknown number of foes, and although he didn't believe they had night vision, he couldn't be sure. Zigzagging away from the knoll, he could hear voices behind him. He was trying to lure them away from the roadblock and gain a little breathing room. A small outcropping of scrub and cactus was the first cover he could see, and he dove behind it.

He used the night vision to scan behind him and could not see anyone following him. He breathed deeply and as quietly as possible. He used the moment to take a long pull from his water bladder. He hadn't drawn any of the attackers off and needed time to determine the next move.

Estebon was not happy. It had taken his men most of the next day to recover from the rescue of the girl and the ensuing firefight. They had to find new shelter for their families since the hotel could no longer be occupied. They initially searched the smoking ruins for car keys, but gave up and hotwired the remaining vehicles. There had also been the wounded to attend to. As soon as the first truck was running, he had sent two of his best to scout Meraton. They were not to make contact, nor allow themselves to be discovered, only to gather information.

He had calculated that Bishop would head directly to the safety of the town with the girl. No doubt, the injured man from the plane crash was there as well – if he still lived. Estebon's men had scouted the town and reported back that the Hummer was indeed parked at the hotel.

His plan tonight had been to draw some of the town's men out to the roadblock and then spring an ambush. His captain had carefully set up a fishhook shaped formation, and all of the men had been in place without the two sleepy fools on the road even knowing anyone was around. Once the signal had been given, a few random bursts of fire were sent toward the roadblock while most of his men waited for the rescuers from the town to fall into the trap.

Estebon could only guess who had blown their ambush. This gringo, Bishop was beginning to get under his skin, and every single man that had done that before had met tragic deaths. As Estebon and the captain sat on the roof of a park service truck with their binoculars, runners were sent to change everyone's position. Three more of his men were now dead, their bodies lying in the back of one of the trucks. The captain had sent instructions for half of their force to encircle the roadblock and kill the two guards. All of the remaining men were to hunt Bishop.

Bishop could tell something was going on, but couldn't get a clear picture in his mind. He could make out some movement through the night vision in the distance, but even with the light gathering device, it just wasn't clear what was happening. *No matter what it is, I need to move.*

His instincts told him to head back toward town, but he remembered the promise made to the two guards and couldn't leave them behind. When a sudden volley of fire appeared in the area of the roadblock, he knew they were still alive, but probably pinned down. From the volume of fire being leveled at the roadblock, Bishop guessed there were at least six or seven shooters. He had taken out three, so there had to be at least two cars or trucks parked around somewhere. He guessed that was where the head of this snake would be located. He moved to cut off that head.

He tried to remember as much about the surrounding countryside as he could, but really had not paid much attention. He decided to risk raising up to see if he could locate the position of the vehicles. He raised the rifle and looked through the starlight scope, immediately ducking back down. A line of men was approaching his position. There were at least five of them, probably more.

Bishop thought about Estebon and his Special Forces Captain. They had clearly brought most of their people to Meraton, and he imagined the reason had a lot to do with him. Even with the advanced warning, this number of skilled attackers could do a lot of damage to the town, perhaps even take it over. At minimum, several of the townspeople would die. The fact that Terri and the baby were there was the final straw – he had to break up this attack out here, regardless of the risk.

There was no way he could take on the number of men moving toward him in open terrain and with no cover. Bishop figured he could get two of three of them, but the rest would close and shoot him down. He was so badly outnumbered his only chance was to make them fight on his terms or get around them.

He took one last look at the hunters approaching his position. They were moving his general direction cautiously, with two or three covering while others edged forward a few steps. They kept repeating the process over and over again. Their caution reassured him a little. *I think they're a little worried about me.*

Bishop, bending to keep low, ran away as fast as he could. After he had gained a little distance, he slowed his pace and studied the landscape in front of him. This was the last place on earth to be outnumbered in a gunfight. He had been moving through an area of random patches of scrub and short cactus, but in front of him was nothing but flat hardpan sand. There wasn't a gully or significant alteration for hundreds of yards. He would be easy to spot crossing this open area even if his pursuers didn't have night vision. He might as well turn around and face the approaching killers like a gunfighter at high noon in the old west. The thought struck him as humorous because he knew gunfights in the old west were actually very, very rare. After pondering that action for a few moments and feeling the chill that went down his spine, he understood why. No matter, it wasn't time for drastic actions just yet.

Since there was no chance of winning a gunfight out here, the only other choice was to get behind the attackers. He needed to come up with something because they were pushing him further away from the roadblock. The problem with a flanking move was the open terrain and the fact that he wasn't sure how wide their line was. More gunfire coming from the roadblock reminded him of the urgency in helping the trapped men there.

Todd and Jake were very scared and almost out of ammo. Jake had been dozing in his truck while Todd was on guard when the first shots had been fired. Initially, both men believed it was either a random, wandering soul lost in the desert or perhaps another raiding party. They both had taken cover behind their trucks and returned fire.

Things had gotten a little more serious when automatic fire had started pinging off of the pavement around them. This wasn't some wanderer with a hunting rifle, this was serious. Todd had served in Iraq, but hadn't seen much combat. Jake had planned to go into the Army the very next year before the world had all fallen apart.

At first, they hadn't been overly concerned because they knew help would be coming from town. As soon as a bunch of men from Meraton showed up, the people shooting at them would probably fade away into the desert night. They'd be able to brag and tell stories at Pete's for months to come, maybe even impressing a couple of the local girls with exaggerated tales of bravery in the line of fire. When no help from the town had arrived, all thoughts of glory quickly vanished and both men began to get worried.

Still, the people shooting at them had seemed more intent on harassing, than actually killing them. Sporadic spits of bullets would zip through the air now and then, but nothing concentrated or sustained. The two would shoot back at the muzzles flashes and moving shadows, trying to hold the attackers at bay. This volleying back and forth had been going on for over ten minutes, when they had heard shooting north of their position.

Everything got quiet after that, but they could hear and sometimes see movement around them. Todd warned Jake, "Hey man, something ain't right here. Let's get under one truck together. You take the west and I'll take the east. I think they're going to try and rush us."

Todd's instinct had saved their lives. No sooner than the two men had crawled behind the rear wheels of Jake's old Ford, than several men popped up and began spraying heavy fire at the vehicles. The steel wheels provided them some protection, and after the initial shock of the assault, both men started sending rounds back at their assailants. The rushing attackers made it to within about twenty feet of the trucks when they finally broke off the attack. Todd's AR15 was cutting into them and three were lying on the ground moaning or already dead. While Jake's pump action shotgun was slower to shoot, its buckshot proved deadly as well.

Jake was wounded in that first wave, taking a bullet to his upper thigh and another to his foot. When Todd had a moment to check on his friend, Jake groaned that he was okay, and could still shoot.

Both men reloaded the few rounds they had left and waited for their attackers to hit them a second time. Both said a silent prayer that help from town would arrive soon.

Bishop cut to his right while there was still scattered cover around. He guessed that the Columbians had been concentrated close to the truck in some sort of ambush configuration, so heading right back toward the road was his best bet. With any luck, he could find somewhere to hide and the line of pursuers would pass right by him.

He could see the occasional head pop up through the night vision and knew his hunters were still a few hundred meters behind him. They were taking their time, checking each clump of vegetation that had taken hold on the arid desert floor, probably expecting him to be hiding in one of them.

As Bishop moved toward the road, he realized he wasn't going to make it. The line of hunters spread out behind him was too wide and as the scrub thinned out, their speed over ground was increasing. Bishop went prone to take cover behind a small mound of dirt less than one foot high. He banged his elbow hard on exposed rock, which surprised him, and he barely kept from letting out a yelp. As he looked at the source of his pain, he saw the top portion of a very large formation of sandstone barely peeking above the otherwise featureless desert floor. Right beside him was a burrow, probably the home of a jackrabbit that had been dug underneath the sandstone ledge. *If I almost missed that, there's a good chance they won't see it either.*

Bishop started frantically digging around the rabbit hole as fast as he could. His goal was to dig a ledge underneath the outcropping of rock - big enough to hide in. The soil was a mixture of crumbled stone and hard packed sand. Even though he was wearing gloves, the effort hurt his hands. He pulled his knife from his vest and used it to pry, dig, and scrape away the resisting earth. Every so often, he would raise his rifle to peer at his pursuers and see how close they were. It took a few minutes, but Bishop eventually dug out a small area underneath the big rock. He squeezed his body into the opening, using his feet to push out more earth and soil. In the dark, he couldn't tell how much of his body was exposed, or if any of the freshly dug soil was different enough in color to indicate that someone had been distributing the area. There just wasn't enough time to do everything right.

Bishop slowly moved his arm out and tried to pull back as much of the loose dirt as possible back onto his body. He had a fleeting thought, hoping there weren't any scorpions upset about his intrusion into their domain. When he heard the first footfall not far away, he became still and silent and held his breath hoping they wouldn't discover his position. If they did, he was a dead man as there was no way he could get his weapon into a firing position or even move. *If they find me, I've done them a favor – I'm already mostly buried.*

A boot landed a few inches in front of Bishop's face, quickly followed by its twin as a man stepped down from the small ridge of rock. The pair of boots stayed right there for what seemed like an eternity, the owner's weight shifting from one foot to the other.

In a few moments, Bishop could see a second set of boots a few feet away. He heard whispers in Spanish, but couldn't make out what they were saying to each other. The man standing right in front of Bishop's face turned slightly and Bishop could hear him fumbling with clothing. A stream of urine started

141

splattering on the desert floor right in front of Bishop, some of the offensive liquid splashing onto his face and hat.

After relieving himself, the hunter fumbled again with his clothing before trotting off into the desert night, trying to catch up with his friends.

Bishop waited for several minutes making sure there wasn't a follow on group of Colombians. Another round of gunfire from the now distant roadblock motivated him to move out of his hide and head toward the stranded Meraton men.

Estebon was pacing around the park service trucks about 300 yards away from the roadblock. The captain was getting a briefing from a runner who had just returned from the roadblock. After quietly whispering new instructions, the runner had disappeared to deliver the latest orders. Estebon looked at his watch and made a decision – they would remain engaged for another ten minutes, and then he would honk the horn of one of the trucks three times to sound recall. This plan wasn't working, and he was sure everyone in Meraton was now awake, armed, and waiting on them to come into town. *Sometimes you get the jaguar, and sometimes the jaguar gets you.*

Bishop was moving as rapidly as he dared, darting between lumps of cactus and small mounds of earth. He repeated the same actions - move, scan, listen, and move again, as he ate up the distance to the besieged men at the roadblock. There hadn't been any firing for a few minutes and that was normally a bad sign. Either the two guards were dead, or the attackers were regrouping for another attempt.

Estebon's captain had changed his tactics. He ordered the runner to gather everyone on the same side and rush the defenders, rather than continuing to come at them from different directions. Casualties had made the enveloping attack no longer a possibility.

As all of the Columbian's assembled on the south side of the road, Jake lost consciousness and Todd didn't realize it. Luck would have it that Jake was watching the south.

All of the attackers rose up at once, some 50 yards away from the two trucks. The remaining six men moved rapidly toward their objective and were surprised that no one had started shooting at them as they got closer. After watching four of their comrades fall, the lack of bullets whizzing past provided much needed motivation, and their pace quickened. It was the scratch of a noise less than twenty feet away that alerted Todd. He realized what was happening and spun his rifle around, firing blindly at the approaching men. The attackers, a little confused by where the defender was hiding, began firing around the two trucks.

Bishop was less than 25 meters away, looking at the roadblock through his night vision when he saw the Colombians rise up. He had started to move toward the trapped men but paused, realizing they might think he was one of the attackers. Bishop didn't have time to communicate with the defenders and shouldered his rifle.

Todd took a round in his shoulder and his arm would no longer respond. Bullets were tearing into the truck above him and sparks flew off of the wheel where he had taken cover. He was blinded by bits of blacktop flying into his eyes as a stream of rounds flew past his face. He was trying to move his rifle to the other hand, but the low clearance under the truck hindered the attempt. Movement from behind drew his attention, and he recognized a figure suddenly go prone on the roadway, looking like he was peering underneath the truck. He started to yell, "I give up, don't shoot," but the man, staring right at him, didn't move. Another man sat down next to the first and then toppled over. A third screamed close by before landing face first on the pavement.

It took Todd a moment to realize someone was killing these men. After a few more seconds, he could see the legs of the remaining attackers running off into the desert.

A soft crunching noise alerted Todd that someone was walking onto the roadway behind him. Confused, he didn't dare make a sound. He saw the outline of legs approach the dead men lying in the road, and then the newcomer leaned over, picked up their weapons, and threw them out into the desert. He watched as the legs moved around the trucks and then stopped again at the rear of the vehicle where he was hiding.

Suddenly a hand reached under the truck and pulled Jake out by his shirt. Todd could see the hand check Jake's pulse and then pull him further out into the roadway.

A whispered voice broke the silence. "Hey, you alive under there? Can you hear me?"

Todd responded, "Yes...thank god...I can move... I think."

"Well come on, they might not be finished. Get your ass out here."

Todd pushed out his rifle and someone grabbed it, pulling it the rest of the way. A second later, a hand was under the truck helping him out. He was pulled up rather roughly and handed his weapon. "Your buddy is in pretty bad shape. Watch my back, and let's get the fuck out of here."

Todd watched as his rescuer bent over and heaved Jake up and onto his shoulders. Without another sound, the man moved off the road and out into the desert. He had to hustle to keep up. Off in the distance, a horn honked three times.

Pete rushed to the street from behind the telephone pole he had been using as cover. The townspeople had been listening to the gunfire, waiting to defend their homes and businesses. A pair of headlights, flashing in the distance, indicated friendlies were on their way in. As the pickup truck skidded to a stop in front of The Manor, Pete was relieved to see Bishop hop out of the back and help Todd jump down. Bishop looked up at Pete and yelled, "Get the doc. I've brought him more business." The request was really unnecessary because the doctor was already on his way, rushing to the back of the truck to see the injured Jake lying in the bed.

Bishop turned to Pete, "I think they've left, but I can't be for sure. It was the Colombians from Big Bend I was telling you about. We took out a lot of them, but they may still be back. I'd keep everyone standing guard for a while."

Pete nodded and moved away quickly to spread the word around.

Bishop made sure the doctor was getting help moving his patients and then headed toward his room. He grabbed the latch and pushed open the door about three inches when bullets splinted the doorframe right in front of his face. "Fuck!"

It seemed like everyone started yelling at once. Bishop thought one of the Colombians was in his room holding Terri and the kids as hostages. The shouts and screams coming from inside only added to the confusion.

Bishop was squatting about three feet from the doorway when Terri's voice finally overrode the bedlam from inside, "Quiet! Quiet! Everyone just settle down!"

Bishop yelled, "Terri – it's Bishop. What the hell is going on?"

Terri was relieved, "Bishop, that was you?"

Bishop exhaled, "Yes that was me. Are you guys okay?"

Terri answered in an unusually loud voice. "Yes, we're fine. We didn't know it was you."

"I'm coming in – don't shoot, please."

"Okay."

"You're *not* going to shoot – right?"

Terri sounded annoyed, "It was an innocent misunderstanding, Bishop. We aren't going to shoot."

Bishop slowly rose up and moved to the doorframe. He could see light through two holes in the door.

He couldn't help himself and warned again, "Coming in now; don't shoot me, damn it."

He pushed the door open just a tad and popped his head around the corner. He saw a snapshot of Terri, Samantha, and Betty all hiding behind the bed, with Terri and Betty pointing their guns at the door. David was behind then, aiming the MP5 from the bathroom.

Deciding to milk it for all it was worth, "Okay, did you see it was really me?"

Terri had had enough, "Quit being such a drama queen, Bishop, and come in. We didn't know it was you before."

Bishop put his hands in the air and walked into the room. Terri put down her rifle and climbed over the bed, throwing her arms around him. She kissed his cheek and hugged him, then pulled away and hit him on the chest with both fists. "You scared the shit out of me. I love you. What the hell were you doing walking in on us without warning us first? We could've killed you. Oh my god, I'm glad you're back safe. Bishop that was stupid, what were you thinking? Are you okay? What happened? Baby, I love you. Is everything okay in the town; we heard lots of gunfire. I was worried about you. Are you okay? Let me look at you. I love you. If you ever scare me like that again…"

Bishop held his wife close and let her go on. While hugging Terri, he looked over her shoulder and noticed Betty just smiling at them. She winked at Bishop and then leaned the weapons against the wall. Bishop felt another set of arms wrap around him and looked down to see Sam had joined the embrace. He could also tell she had been crying.

"Mister Bishop, I'm glad you're back safe. I can't hear anything, but I'm glad you're okay."

Terri looked down at Sam and in a loud voice said, "What, baby? What did you say?"

Betty came over and yelled as well. "We can't hear anything. When David shot at the door, it was awful loud in here. I think we're all deaf."

Bishop winced at the thought of the gunfire in the small room, but then realized what Betty had just said. He looked at Terri and said, "That wasn't you shooting at me?"

Terri scowled at her husband, "You think I would've missed?"

Chapter 14

After everyone had settled down, Bishop managed to wash up and get a few hours' sleep. When he awoke, it was already daylight, and he busied himself getting ready for the day.

As he left the room, Terri was still deep in dreamland, and he quietly closed the door behind him. He checked around The Manor's grounds and noticed one of the town's men standing guard at the corner of the hotel. The two men nodded at each other and then Bishop headed to check on all of the patients. The doctor was nowhere to be found, and the Colonel was sleeping. Jake and Todd both were being watched closely by family members, and Bishop was informed both would survive. The news started off the day the right way.

Betty was evidently still asleep as the kitchen and office area of the hotel were still dark and quiet. Bishop decided to check on Pete and see if anything more had happened after he crashed for the night. He could smell the coffee at Pete's Place before he even knocked on the door, and a muffled voice answered him, "Come on in."

Pete was brewing coffee for the men helping guard the town. Bishop was impressed at the organization and communication the town's guardians displayed. Pete's Place, being in the center of Main Street was the logical headquarters, and while Bishop was downing his first cup of Joe for the day, two different runners had come and gone delivering status reports and coordinating shift changes.

Pete came around from behind the bar and motioned for Bishop to step outside. The two men meandered down the street to get out of earshot of the constant traffic in and out of the bar. Pete looked Bishop straight in the eye. "We've got a little problem brewing, and I want to let you in on it first thing. A lot of the men are worried about you and Terri being here. It seems you're a magnet for trouble, young man."

Bishop was hurt by what Pete said. It must have shown on his face because his friend continued in a gentle voice. "Now I tried to tell everyone it wasn't your fault. You did this town a great favor cleaning out those hoodlums, and I know you wouldn't bring trouble here on purpose. I'm just letting you know some of the men are concerned about this."

Bishop took a sip of coffee, "They're right, you know. I seem to have trouble chasing me around. I should've known those guys would come here looking for me. Maybe Sam and I should've hidden out at the ranch. Let things cool down."

Pete patted his friend on the back. "Hindsight is always twenty-twenty, my friend. Don't make more of this than what it is. I just wanted to let you in on what folks are thinking. Todd has a wife and two kids. His bride was in here already this morning worried about feeding them. Jake lives with his granny and takes care of her. We'll figure out a way to make sure everything works out, so don't let it trouble you."

Despite Pete's words, Bishop felt like shit. He remembered Billy, and how it had been his fault the old cowboy had been murdered the last time he was in town. He was tempted to go load up Terri and get out before someone else got hurt, but he couldn't do that just now. The Colonel, the country, and the kids all weighed on his mind.

Bishop knew the Colonel wasn't going to make it. It was a testimony to the man's willpower he had survived this long, but even that wasn't going to be enough. It also wasn't right to just up and leave the town with two teenage children. Food was hard enough to come by, let alone the responsibility of raising two kids.

Terri and he were barely surviving at the ranch, and he knew Terri's need for calories was going to do nothing but increase. He didn't know, but assumed she would continue to need extra food while breast-feeding the baby. While they had not gone hungry so far, they weren't gaining weight either.

As Bishop continued down Main Street, he was deep in thought about how to solve all of these problems.

When Terri and he had first arrived at the ranch, they had busied themselves setting up their new home and tending to the basic needs of life. While even the simplest of daily human needs could be challenging, they were essentially happy, and moreover – content. The routine of rebuilding their lives was therapeutic in a way. Establishing daily routines, constant hard work, and the challenges of living without modern conveniences, healed their minds and bodies after the ordeal of the trip west.

At first, Bishop had trouble settling down and focusing. He had constantly felt the need to patrol the area, set up tripwire alarms, and monitor the surrounding countryside. After a few weeks of never seeing another soul, he finally reached a point where he could relax a bit and go hunting. The first deer he encountered escaped to live another day. Its good fortune had nothing to do with Bishop's capability using a rifle. The shot would have been easy and his skill with a rifle had been proven time and again since the collapse. Bishop froze because he didn't want the noise of the shot to give away their location.

When he returned to the camper empty-handed, Terri had not questioned his decision. She had learned to trust his judgment on such things, despite their dwindling food supply. She was, however, beginning to worry that his paranoia was never going to fade. She supported his attempts to set snares and bring home some food silently, and never complained when the traps were always empty.

Eventually, he started bringing home meat from his hunts, but they couldn't survive on meat alone. The book they had found on useful desert plants had helped some, but they still weren't very good at harvesting from the land.

Bishop wished he had paid more attention in school. One of his classes covered local mineral deposits, but he had blown the topic off as boring and not useful. He would give anything to have that textbook now. Were there any salt deposits in the local mountains? What about sulfur for wounds? Coal for fuel? There were so many things he simply didn't know.

He had read in the book that pine needles were an excellent source of Vitamin C. Since they couldn't go to the market anymore and buy oranges, he had gathered up a bagful on one of his trips to the mountains. Terri and he had spent an entire day trying to figure out how to make the things edible. It finally dawned on them to boil the green needles in water and make a tea. It was so bad they could barely swallow it, but when they added some roots that tasted like lemons, it was palatable. Now they made pine tea once a week and forced it down.

There was simply no way the land around the ranch could feed two more mouths. He liked Sam and David just fine, but felt like their need for food, medical care and parenting was beyond his reach.

Bishop's thoughts were interrupted by the sound of a motor, and he looked up to see a truck towing in one of the shot up vehicles from the roadblock. He watched as the wrecker pulled into a gas station down the street.

Curious about the condition of the vehicles and what was going on down at the scene of last night's fight, Bishop turned toward the gas station. Besides, he needed a distraction and realized he hadn't been to this side of town lately. Along Main Street to the east, the storefronts and commercial buildings thinned out quickly. The gas station was the first business one would encounter if driving into town from that direction. Positioned in the midst of an open area, Bishop was surprised to see that the place now more closely resembled a medieval castle than a spot for a fill up or repair. The owner had built an impressive ring of fortifications around his business, and Bishop didn't blame him one bit. The below ground tanks held probably one of the most valuable, sought after resources in the entire world right now – fuel.

As he approached the station, Bishop realized just how much work had gone into fortifying the business. The entire perimeter surrounding the buildings was protected by a ring of junk cars. Carefully placed bumper to bumper in a complete circle, there wasn't even room to walk between them. Strung all around the cars was barbwire, probably acquired by bartering with a local rancher. The roof of the main building was a typical flat commercial roof with a raised edge all around. There were tents set up on the roof and Bishop wondered if the family of the owner lived up there. He could see the top of sandbags at each corner, indicating that at minimum they could defend their property from the elevated positions.

As Bishop approached, he noticed that the exit drive was blocked by an old delivery truck. As he got nearer, he heard another engine start. Then a younger boy ran to the delivery truck, and started it as well. The kid moved the blocking hulk out of the way, and the wrecker pulled out onto Main Street, obviously headed back to the roadblock to retrieve the other shot up pickup. As soon as the wrecker had pulled onto the street, the big delivery truck rolled back into its blocking position and was shut off.

Bishop recalled the owner of the station was of Mexican descent and had a large family. He couldn't remember the man's name, but knew he mostly kept to himself. Seeing Bishop outside his perimeter and no doubt noticing the rifle he wore, the wrecker driver stopped next to Bishop and looked him up and down. "Could I help you, Senor Bishop?"

Bishop smiled, trying to be friendly. "I was just curious what it looked like in the daylight at the roadblock. I thought I would stop by and ask you what was going on."

"I'm heading that way; ride with me if you like?"

Bishop unslung his rifle and climbed up into the cab. He extended his hand to the driver, "Bishop."

The driver shook his hand, "Roberto."

The two men rode to the roadblock in silence. As they approached, Bishop could see several of the town's men were already wandering around the site. The dead men he had left on the road were no longer there, the only remaining evidence being large dark pools of blood. As he walked around the area, he absent-mindedly bent over and picked up spent cartridges, placing them in his dump pouch. He had reloading equipment back at the ranch, but the *finite* supply of brass had been yet another item that concerned him.

A short distance from the road, Bishop observed three mounds of freshly turned dirt. The last resting place of the Colombian men he had killed the night before. As Bishop walked toward the graves, one of the men from Meraton joined him. "I didn't want to bury them. I wanted to hang their bodies from a sign post with a warning on it – 'This is what happens to looters,' but I got voted down."

Another man soon joined them and asked Bishop what had happened. As Bishop recounted his story of the night's events, he remembered throwing the dead men's' weapons out into the scrub. After finishing his story, Bishop toured the vicinity and retrieved the weapons. He was gathering quite a collection of submachine guns.

Roberto had the remaining pickup in tow and was getting ready to head back into town. One of the men whistled, and everyone started climbing into the bed of the wounded truck. Bishop took his scavenged weapons and started to climb in when Roberto approached him. "Senor, I am interested in those weapons if you do not plan to keep them. I can trade many things."

"Roberto, I will visit you soon and see what we can do."

The wrecker stopped in front of The Manor on the way through town, and all of the men hopped out of the back. Roberto casually waved and proceeded to tow the shot-up pickup to his station. As Bishop headed toward the hotel, Terri ambled out of the gardens and smiled at him. He gave her a peck on the cheek and went to their room to stash the extra weapons. As Terri joined him, she asked what he had been up too this morning, "Oh, I am thinking of opening a gun store somewhere nearby. I seem to keep finding these weapons lying around, and they're beginning to take up too much space."

Terri rubbed her chin and looked off into the distance. "Bishop's Gun Emporium, kind of has a ring to it."

"My problem is a good wholesale supplier. My current source is suspect because the previous owners are all dead."

"I guess that doesn't bode well for your products, does it? I mean, who wants to own a gun that lost the last fight?"

Without thinking, Bishop said, "I guess I could advertise that people were just *dying* for me to sell their guns." The remark earned him both an eye roll and a punch on the arm.

The couple rocked in the chairs in front of their room, and both seemed lost in thought for a while. Bishop then relayed what Pete had told him that morning about the townspeople beginning to wonder if Bishop's company were a healthy thing.

"Bishop, that's ridiculous! You saved how many of those people from being burned? How many of them would have died trying to root out those bank robbers from this very hotel?" Terri shook her head, "I can't believe anyone in their right mind would blame you for all this."

"You can't blame them. They are tired, worried, and frightened most of the time. This morning, when I went out to the roadblock, it seemed like the men all looked at me like I was the grim reaper or something."

Terri took her husband's hand and squeezed it. She conveyed him a look that meant, "*I'm so sorry.*"

Bishop decided to change the subject, "Terri, I've got another one of my crazy ideas. How about I go to Alpha and bring back some medical equipment? It might solve some of our problems and get me back in the good graces of the fine citizens of Meraton."

Terri started to blurt out "No!" She stopped herself when she saw the somber look on Bishop's face. "How would it solve some of our problems?"

"First of all, I would feel better about your having our child if the doc had better equipment," he said as he reached over and rubbed her tummy.

"Secondly, if the doc could save the Colonel, the kids would have their grandfather. It would also get me out of town in case the Colombians decide they want another go at me."

Terri's gaze was focused on two hummingbirds enjoying The Manor's gardens this morning. She watched the graceful creatures move from blossom to blossom and seemed to be ignoring the subject at hand. Bishop knew she was deep in thought and rolling the whole idea around.

Finally, she looked over at him, "I understand your reasoning. I guess I would feel better if the doc were bettered equipped. Not only for birth, but kids do get sick sometimes. It would help the town, and maybe people would excuse some of your bad habits. I just don't like the idea of you running off on some dangerous adventure and leaving me alone again."

Bishop nodded, "I understand, but I don't think it's that dangerous. I went to high school and college in Alpha. I know the town well. When I was growing up on the ranch, we went to Alpha almost every month. When I was dating, it was those Alpha girls we thought were hot. There used to be a clinic at the college. It's on the outskirts of town. If I could sneak in there, grab a bunch of medical equipment, supplies or whatever else looks good, I could be back in one night."

Terri digested what Bishop had just said for a few moments and then replied. "Okay, let's think about this for a second. What makes you think the clinic at the college has the equipment the doctor needs?"

"I can't be sure about that. It might already have been looted, or the entire campus could be burned down for all I know. There has to be someone in this town who went to college there recently or went to the football games or something. I would have to ask around and gather some more facts."

Terri gave him a questioning look. "How would you get the equipment back here? Our truck?"

"I would use the Hummer. The doc would have to draw me pictures and make a list of the stuff he needed. I can't take him with me – that would be too dangerous and slow me down. The Hummer has a big storage area in the back if you fold down the seats. I have an idea about how to make it even bigger. If the Colombians don't see the Hummer here in town, they'll think I've left and might leave well enough alone."

Terri stuck out her bottom lip and pretended to be hurt. "Bishop, I thought you brought the Hummer home for me? I always wanted one, you know."

"We can't afford the insurance on it, babe."

The concept of paying auto insurance in these times made both of them laugh.

Terri got serious again. "Bishop, I don't want you going by yourself. I hate it when you run off and do these things all alone. I'm in, if you take someone with you."

Bishop hadn't thought about that. It was his turn to watch the two hummingbirds having breakfast. After a bit, he said, "Terri, I don't know about that. The town is already short two men from last night. Everyone is on edge about the Colombians…I don't know if it's a good idea to ask someone to go with me."

"I'll go," a voice said from behind them. Both of their heads turned around to see David standing in the doorway. "I can drive *and* fly a plane. I know how to shoot, and I want to help grandpa. I want to go. I feel useless around here, and Sam's driving me nuts anyway."

A pillow flew out of the room and hit him in the back of the head causing him to turn around and snap, "Sam, quit it! Go back to sleep."

Sam's face appeared beside David in the doorway, "I'll go too. I can help. You'll see I'm not just some sissy girl!"

Bishop immediately began to tell both of them there was absolutely no way they were going, but paused. The Colonel had warned him about underestimating people just the day before. After all, if a man as demanding as the Colonel placed his life in the young man's hands, who was he to dismiss the notion? Bishop also remembered being sixteen and what a difficult time that was. He decided there was no way David was going with him, but he would break it to the lad gently, logically. Besides, one day soon, he might need the experience of working with kids, given he had one on the way."

Terri surprised the hell out of him by saying, "I think it's a good idea for David to go with you. I need Sam to stay here and help me, but he would make a good partner for you, Bishop."

Bishop gave Terri a look of "*What the hell are you saying*," but she wasn't messing around. She knotted her brows and simply replied, "Think about it."

Bishop was puzzled by Terri's reaction, but decided to avoid the subject altogether. "Well, no one is going anywhere unless we can learn more about Alpha. I'm not driving all the way there until we can be reasonably sure it's worth the risk."

No one could argue with that logic, and Terri was hungry. Bishop said he was heading to Pete's to gather information while Terri and the kids went to the hotel office to see if Betty were cooking.

Chapter 15

Pete's Place, as usual, was bustling with activity. As Bishop entered, he couldn't help but notice people were looking at him differently. *Maybe I'm just being silly, and it's all in my mind.*

It took a while for him to explain to Pete what he was thinking about doing in Alpha. There was a constant flow of people interrupting the two men with questions and status reports, and a few even wanted a warm cup of ale. After Bishop finished, Pete lowered his gaze to the floor. "Bishop, no one knows what's happening in Alpha. We know there was an explosion at the chemical plant, and that a lot of people were killed by a poison gas cloud. Since then, other than a couple raiding parties we *think* came from Alpha, no one really has any facts."

"Pete, there could be medical equipment there that would save lives. It might be just sitting there, rusting away. If I can find someone here in Meraton who knows the lay of the land, it could be worth checking it out."

Pete thought about what Bishop said for a few minutes and refilled a customer's glass. "Old man Parker was a season ticket holder for the football team there. We all teased him about watching the cheerleaders and not the game. He's the only person I can think of that went to Alpha all the time."

"Where can I find Mr. Parker?"

Pete gave Bishop directions and warned him that old man Parker had been a little quick on the trigger lately. He also added that the old man's eyes were not so good, and he had failed to hit anyone so far.

The Parker residence was only seven blocks away, close to the city park. As Bishop walked through this part of Meraton, he saw people were mostly outside working. Freshly washed clothes were being draped on makeshift lines, a few scattered children were playing, and the smell of roasting meat filled the air. The aroma made his stomach growl.

Mr. Benedict Jefferson Parker's residence was a small one-story ranch style home, covered in vinyl siding and in need of a new roof. Bishop, weary of Pete's warning, stopped some distance away and studied the layout, trying to determine how to safely approach Mr. Parker.

The yard was surrounded by a common chain link fence with red reflectors on the corners, and a rusty old gate stood in front by the mailbox. Bishop wondered if the weeds growing along the fence line were a recent addition, or if the place looked the same as it always had.

The front yard, that was mostly sand and gravel, was adorned with two neglected flowerbeds. Small clumps of green dotted the area, probably due to the recent rain. The driveway was occupied by an ancient pickup truck and an even older lime green Ford Crown Victoria. The car didn't look like it had been driven in years, and wore a thick coating of dust, topped by a peeling, black, vinyl roof. One tire was completely flat. The only unusual feature of the estate was a larger than normal hardwood tree that provided shade for the front of the house. Bishop didn't think the tree was native to the area and wondered how it had survived all these years. *You're not here to provide a real estate appraisal for the house – go talk to the man and get this over with.*

Bishop moved his rifle around to his back and proceeded toward the residence, careful to stay in the middle of the street, and keeping his eye on the ditch just in case the old man came out shooting. When he was even with the mailbox, he faced the house, yelling, "Mr. Parker, are you home? Mr. Parker, Pete sent me. My name is Bishop. Anyone home?"

A voice answered from an open window. "Tell that Pete I'll pay my bill as soon as my social security check arrives. No need to send a bill collector down here."

Bishop thought, "*That's not good. He thinks he is going to get a social security check. Worse yet, he hasn't noticed there isn't any mail.*"

Bishop tried to keep his voice friendly. "Mr. Parker, I'm not here to collect any bill. I'd like to ask you a few questions and then be on my way. Could I talk to you for a moment, sir? It's important."

Bishop heard movement inside the house, and then the front door opened, revealing an older man carrying a shotgun. Mr. Parker didn't come out on the front porch but elected to stand in the threshold. "What do you want?"

"Sir, the doctor in town needs medical equipment. I'm thinking of going to Alpha and maybe bringing some back. Pete told me you went to Alpha often, and I was wondering if you could provide any information about the town. I've not been there for years."

"My grandson played for Alpha State's football team until he got hurt last year. I went to the games, but that was about it. I don't know how I'd be of help to you."

Bishop decided to engage the man. "What position did he play?"

"He was the starting tight end – at least he was until his leg got broken. God, that was a nasty looking leg. I saw the pictures of the bone in the locker room and knew he wasn't going to play anymore."

Bishop's head snapped up. "X-rays? They took X-rays in the locker room?"

"No, it didn't look like those TV shows where the doctor holds up film to the light and whistles or such. This was a contraption that had a fancy computer screen. They rubbed his leg with a piece of equipment, and you could see the broken bone on that computer. When they rubbed his leg with that doohickey, that big kid yelped like a kicked dog. That's why I remember it so well."

Bishop had no clue what he was talking about. He tried to ask Mr. Parker questions about the layout of the town, where new buildings had been constructed, and anything else that may have changed. Mr. Parker really wasn't any help. At one point, Bishop moved closer to the man so he could draw a map in the dirt. When he took a step forward, the old gent raised his shotgun menacingly and warned Bishop off.

Frustrated, Bishop thanked the man for his help and spun around, heading back to Pete's. *What a waste of time.*

As Bishop ambled back to Pete's Place, his attention was drawn to the activity around him. A group of children was gathered at one house, playing on an outdoor swing set. Neighbors were talking over a fence, apparently negotiating an exchange of laundry and what appeared to be butter. It all looked so normal until a bright flash caught Bishop's attention. He froze for a moment, thinking it might be the sun reflecting off of a riflescope or binoculars. As he scanned, there didn't appear to be anyone or anything that would have caused the effect. He studied the terrain one last time when an arm waved at him from what appeared to be a rooftop air conditioner. Bishop smiled at the ingenuity of the hide. Someone had painted a box to look like a common AC unit, but inside was really an over watch sentry, keeping an eye on the neighborhood. Bishop waved back.

Bishop headed straight for The Manor to find Doc Hopkins. As he navigated the garden's path, the healer exited the Colonel's room. The doctor saw Bishop approaching and greeted him, "Good day, Bishop. Your friend in there is not going to be with us much longer, I'm afraid. The other patients you brought me are doing well though. They both would like to talk to you whenever you get time."

Bishop nodded. "Doc, I'll stop in and see everyone later. Right now, I need to know if you could draw me pictures of the equipment you need. I might have an idea where to find some medical equipment. A list of the drugs you need might help too – at least anything that doesn't need to be refrigerated."

A serious look came across the doctor's face. "You're not going to bring me more patients, are you, Bishop?"

"I sure as shit hope not. If anyone needs you this time, it's going to be me."

"I can do one better than give you horrible artwork, Bishop. I can get you pictures from some of the medical journals I brought from Houston. I'll also make you a list of medications. When do you need all this?"

"Early in the morning would be best. I plan on leaving at dawn."

The doctor considered that for a minute before answering. "You got it. If I don't see you before then, I'll leave it outside your door."

Bishop thanked the man and then verified it was okay to visit the Colonel. After he was informed that the patient was sleeping, he left to find Terri.

Chapter 16

Wayne, as usual, had outdone himself with the evening meal. All around the large dinner table, napkins were placed on top of empty plates while last sips of water were taken. It was almost as if every man and woman seated at the table were afraid to waste a single morsel of food given the starvation being experienced by the rest of the nation. The sound of chairs being scooted back from the table could be heard throughout the estate as the well-fed attendees rose and prepared for the serious business yet to come.

The twenty people staying at the senator's home had begun arriving by helicopter, private car, and even military escort some hours ago. For the most part, their leader had remained secluded, giving his guests time to acclimate to their new surroundings. When dinner had been announced, the attendees had promptly arrived and been shown to their seats. The meal had been consumed with little conversation. These were serious people, with a serious mission, during serious times.

The dignitaries included United States Congressmen, career military officers, academics, and even a Supreme Court Judge. Senator Moreland hoped that one day this group of distinguished patriots would be considered the founding fathers of their time. While the Constitution was never questioned by anyone in the organization, the interpretation or meaning would have been heartily debated given the opportunity. This night however, there would be no chance of that happening. They all understood that if the actions they had initiated failed, there wouldn't be a need to even read the founding document, let alone discuss its intent. They had to establish order and leadership in a significant portion of the country before it was too late. The recent news that they were going to have competition from the President of the United States was a little disconcerting. Everyone knew the significance of that information. Everyone understood the potential for civil war.

No one had to call the meeting to order. As the participants took their seats, Wayne distributed a packet of papers to each of the attendees. Inside each neatly bound bundle were intelligence briefings, strategic milestones, and lists of deliverables for each and every person seated at the meeting. After Wayne finished his deliveries, Senator Moreland waited for them to browse the contents within.

The senator casually strolled to the front of the room and cleared his throat. The room fell quiet.

"Ladies and Gentlemen, thank you for attending our conference. I know the journey here was difficult for many of you, but I felt the situation warranted the effort. As you all know, we've been extremely successful these last few weeks in recruiting others to our cause. We now control over 30% of the active duty armed forces and over 40% of the Reserve and National Guard units. Our brothers in the military have decided our cause is just. As of yesterday, Dade county Florida joined our network, and martial law was lifted by the commanding general of greater Miami. We are busily trying to reestablish basic services and provide food for the general population there. Our first tanker of fuel refined at the facilities under our control in Texas will arrive at the port of Miami tomorrow. We intend to have electrical power restored in a few days, as well as a reconstitution of the Miami police and fire departments. Already, the military units that were controlling Miami are making arrangements to withdraw and can be deployed wherever we feel is necessary."

Moreland glanced around the room at the approving nods and gestures. He had started this meeting on a positive note, even though everyone knew the tone was destined to change.

"Until now, we have not directly confronted the forces loyal to the president and the executive branch. Always, we have either offered leadership to areas ignored by the pentagon or recruited those who were disenfranchised by the illegal martial law being forced on the people."

Again, many of the heads in the room nodded their understanding and agreement.

"As you all know, that situation is about to change. Six weeks ago, our experts agreed and recommended that we focus our efforts on the Mississippi River Delta. We designated the plan Delta1. Once rule of law is established in this region, it will house a centralized base of operations, spreading out both east and west. Our plan had always been to use our strength in the geographical center of America as a negotiation point with the resident should a confrontation ever become necessary. Recently, we learned that our idea had been validated by none other than the Pentagon and those loyal to the president. They have arrived at the same basic conclusion. Our sources inside of the president's staff inform me that they still have no idea of our existence, let alone our plan."

The senator glanced around the room, after noting a collective sigh of relief from his audience. For days, there had been the fear that *the Independents* also had a mole inside of their operation.

The senator's tone became very somber. "There is an excellent chance the president is about to be briefed on our existence. One of his emissaries, sent to scout Beaumont, Texas, rejected recruitment, and worse yet, escaped interception by our agents."

Both Wayne and Senator Moreland carefully watched the reaction in the room. After a short pause, he continued, "Neither I, nor anyone else in the room, authorized the actions that were taken in an attempt to recruit that particular emissary. It was poorly handled, and those responsible have been relieved of their positions. Regardless, there is now a man who knows far too much information about our group, its plans and sensitive operations on the loose. We believe this man is trying to report back to the president. As of this afternoon, he has not, but that could change at any moment."

The senator took a few sips from a glass of water beside his chair. He used the time to gauge his audience's reaction again before he continued. "So my esteemed colleagues, we have a decision to make. Do we back down from Delta1? Or should we continue, knowing full well that eventually we will have a confrontation with our fellow Americans? This confrontation, as we all know, would most likely lead to civil war."

One of the guests raised his hand to comment. "Senator, what is the status of the Navy and the Air Force?"

Moreland nodded to one of the generals who were in attendance. The military man faced the room to make his announcement. "The Navy's carrier battle groups are in port, scattered prominently at major bases along the US coast, such as San Diego and Pearl Harbor. Most of the sailors have been retasked to secure the bases. We know that San Diego and Norfolk are having trouble hanging on due to the level of social unrest. We have several smaller vessels under our control, but the big ships are not operational at this time. From what I am told, the Navy can barely feed its own, much less put to sea and project any power."

The general officer cleared his throat and continued. "The Air Force seems to be sitting this one out. We don't believe either side has much in the area of large-scale air assets. They seem to be in a similar situation as the Navy in that guarding their own bases is about all their personnel can handle. We have a few Air National Guard units at our disposal, but nothing of consequence. If this turns into a fight, it is primarily going to be a land-based conflict."

Several heads nodded their understanding, and the general sat down. Senator Moreland returned to the front of the room and scanned the faces of the attendees as if to ask if there were any further questions. When no additional inquiries were made, a break was called to give the participants a chance to discuss what had been presented.

The senator had wanted everyone together due to the sheer gravity of the decision. He had expected hours, perhaps even days of serious debate. It came as a complete shock to both Wayne and him when, after only twenty minutes, a vote was taken and a path chartered. Operation Delta1 would continue, despite the potential threat represented by the military forces loyal to the president.

After the meeting had adjourned and the guests had all left, Senator Moreland relaxed in the great room while he surveyed the valley below. He replayed the day's events in his mind before deciding to retire.

The valley that sprawled below the mountain estate was blessed with wisdom more ancient than that of man. Often it had sustained life, when the mountains around it became barren. The decisions made during the gathering meant no more to the valley than the first Continental Congress had meant to the bedrock under Carpenter's Hall in Philadelphia. It wouldn't have mattered if the valley had shared its sage advice. Men had long ago forgotten its language.

Chapter 17

Bishop drove the Hummer to the Meraton gas station. After the blocking van rolled aside, he pulled into the compound, and the entrance immediately closed upon his passing. Roberto observed the deep stress lines in Bishop's expression and attempted humor to raise his spirits. The mechanic carefully examined the once beautiful car, kicking a tire for good measure, before he said a word. "Let me guess, your state safety inspection is expired, and you want an oil change?"

Bishop just looked at the man and blinked. Roberto decided to keep going, "I sure am seeing a lot of bullet damage these days. What do you have in mind?"

Bishop finally smiled and responded. "I will trade you two MP5's and six full magazines, if you will make some modifications for me. I need this done by tomorrow morning. Did you ever see an old western movie called "'The War Wagon?'"

Roberto smiled and tried to be funny again. "What a classic! I used to have the Spanish version on Betamax years ago."

"Well, sir, I want to create a slightly modernized version of the war wagon, minus the horses. I need to 'up armor' this vehicle."

Roberto's eyebrows arched, "Are you planning to haul gold like they did in the movie?"

Bishop shook his head, "Nope. I plan on hauling something more valuable, but not as heavy. I need the car to be bullet resistant, and I've got a few ideas about how to do that."

Roberto thought for a few moments about Bishop's request. "I don't have much steel plate around here, if that's what you're thinking."

Bishop shook his head, "No, that would probably take too long anyway. I'm thinking more about surrounding the passenger compartment with sand. I also need the top cut off and the back seats taken out. Remove all the glass; make as much space inside as you can. I'm visualizing something like a Baja dune buggy, only Hummer-sized. I want you to check all of the vital mechanics as well – this baby took some heavy fire, and who knows what got hurt in the process."

Roberto circled the Hummer again, scratching his chin, and then examined underneath the vehicle for several minutes. Bishop explained his ideas about filling the door panels with sand and creating another barrier behind the front seats that would protect them from anyone shooting from the rear.

After inspecting the engine compartment, he looked at Bishop and extended his hand, "Deal."

Bishop shook the man's hand and asked, "Can you have it by in the morning?"

"Yes, it will be ready. It's not like I have a long waiting list of customers these days." Bishop finally laughed.

After Bishop left the garage, he looked for Terri. The two had quite a few decisions to make and kept being interrupted. Bishop found his wife in the hotel pool swimming in a pair of his old gym shorts and a t-shirt. Bishop waited until she came up for air and then gave a long wolf whistle. Her head snapped around, surprised to see her husband sitting in one of the lounge chairs.

Terri rubbed the water out of her eyes and smiled. "Hey, babe. You okay?"

Bishop leaned forward. "I'm better now, sexy girl. There's nothing like seeing a pretty lady in a bikini at the pool."

Terri stood, pretending to model her swimsuit, "Do you like it? It's the latest Paris fashion."

"I think it looks great on you. I think it would look even better in a pile next to the pool."

Terri splashed water at him, "Pervert."

They both laughed, and then Terri's voice betrayed her melancholy. "Bishop, there for a few minutes, it was like being back when life was normal. While I was swimming, everything seemed to melt away, and I could even imagine our just vacationing at a normal hotel and taking laps in a normal swimming pool. If a waiter had approached me to see if I wanted something from the bar, I wouldn't have been surprised. You don't think I'm going crazy, do you?"

Bishop thought for a moment, "Terri, I think the occasional daydream is healthy. If we had been here back when the world was sane, and you had been daydreaming about being in Las Vegas, would you have been worried?"

Terri had to think about that. "I guess you're right. None of this seems real sometimes, Bishop. I can't wrap my head around everything that's happening. It seems like we were just getting settled down and mellowing out from that trip out here, and now it all starts again. Is there any way we can get back to a boring, old life again?"

Bishop laughed.

Terri gave him a quizzical look meant to inquire, "*What's so funny?*"

"Babe, I know you didn't realize it, but actually this existence isn't so much different for me." Bishop looked down at his feet and then continued. "I guess it's amazing what you can get used to."

Terri tilted her head in thought, "Bishop, look at us. You're sitting in what has to be one of the most beautiful places within 300 miles, yet you have all that gear on. I can't remember the last time I saw you without that armor, vest, rifle, and all those pouches hanging off of you. Don't you want to get back to a time when you watch a basketball game on a Saturday afternoon in a t-shirt and jeans? How long can people stay prepared for war every single minute?"

Bishop sighed. "Believe me darling, I think about it all the time. This crap is heavy."

Terri decided to swim some more while Bishop relaxed. She completed two more laps and then stopped in front of him, holding onto the edge of the pool and breathing hard. She pulled herself out of the water a bit more, rested on her elbows, and looked him straight in the eye. "You have to go to Alpha, don't you? You have to go do that thing for the Colonel, too."

"Terri, I won't do squat if you aren't one hundred percent cool with it. I'll stay right here with you and the baby, and it will never be mentioned again. Zero regrets."

She shook her head, "No, Bishop. I know I flew off the handle when you first told me, but I get it. I understand what it could mean. If there's any chance of life returning to something even close to what we all had, we need to take the gamble."

All of sudden, Bishop found his feet interesting again.

"Bishop, look at me please."

He looked up and ducked quickly as Terri's wet shirt flew through the air at him. He smiled and jumped up to hang the "Pool Closed" sign on the gate. As he strutted back, he had to duck again when his soaked gym shorts flew past his head.

Bishop woke up before the sun rose the following morning. After they had finished their "swim," Terri and he enjoyed another wonderful meal prepared by Betty. They had sat for hours studying Bishop's plan, and as usual, Terri had provided some excellent suggestions. They retired early because they both knew the next few days would allow for little sleep. Bishop was going on a trip, and Terri wouldn't rest well while he was gone.

Doc Hopkins was visiting his patients early, and Bishop wanted to review the information about the equipment he desired. The two found a candle and sat at one of the garden tables discussing all of the pictures and lists. As Bishop took a crash course in medical gear, one of the pictures caught his attention. It was a computer screen mounted on a small cart with some other boxy equipment and was labeled as an ultrasound machine. Bishop had heard the term before and something about the computer screen jarred his memory. "Doc," he said, pointing at the picture, "Would you be able to use this machine to look at a broken bone?"

"Oh yes, it's better than an x-ray machine in several aspects. Why do you ask?"

"I spent a little time with Mr. Parker yesterday. Turns out his grandson played football at the college in Alpha. He mentioned that he once went into the locker room when his grandson was injured. According to him, while he was back there, he could see the broken bone on a computer screen. He told me when the team doctor rubbed the kid's leg with 'some gizmo,' they got the picture right then and there."

The doctor's eyes brightened, "That's an ultrasound! That would make sense because that machine is very portable. It would be a good addition for a sports program because they are easy to use and can see ligament or tendon damage as well."

"So one of these would help you with the Colonel?"

"One of those would help me with the Colonel and just about everything else around here. They were developed to use on pregnant women because you can't use x-rays due to the radiation."

Bishop's head snapped up and he made eye contact with the doctor. "This would help you if Terri had a problem?"

The doctor was slightly taken aback by the intensity of Bishop's expression. "Most likely it would, but nothing is one hundred percent."

"Thanks Doc, that's all I needed to hear." Bishop stood to leave when the physician stopped him. "Bishop, wait. The Colonel gave me this for you. I almost forgot," and handed Bishop an envelope.

Bishop found two handwritten letters inside. One was addressed to the President of the United States and the other to the commander of Fort Bliss.

Bishop looked up from the papers, "Thanks, Doc. I hope to see you soon."

"Good luck."

Bishop knocked on David and Samantha's door. In order to avoid another friendly fire incident, they had agreed on a code, which Bishop thought was funny since he had removed the clip from David's MP5. A sleepy-looking young man opened the door.

"It's time to kick the tires and light the fires, young man. We're going on a trip. I need you to be ready in one hour. Make sure you get something to eat before we go."

David yawned. "That movie was lame, but okay. I'll be ready."

Clearly, the kid had no appreciation for the classics. Bishop rolled his eyes and headed for the gas station.

As he approached, he could hear hammering and observed a young boy on the roof with a big bolt-action rifle, complete with scope. The young man looked to be no older than twelve or thirteen. *This world sucks for the young and the old alike. That kid should be watching cartoons or playing video games, not pulling sentry duty.*

Bishop yelled a greeting at the building and was invited in. He maneuvered between two of the barrier junkers and was shocked by the vehicle before him. Parked in front of the bay doors was what used to be a Hummer and now more closely resembled a dune buggy.

The top had been completely cut off, leaving the seats exposed. The windshield, frame, side glass and even the back gate had all been removed. Bishop inspected the inside and smiled. The door panels were gone, and the space was now filled with several bags of sand. A plywood wall had been built behind the front seats, and the compartment behind had been packed with sand and dirt. The hood was open, and Roberto was welding two steel plates along the firewall of the engine compartment.

As Bishop admired the newly renovated SUV, he couldn't help but be impressed with Roberto's work. Bishop pulled on the handle, but the door wouldn't budge. Roberto joined his customer, wiping his hands on a rag. "I had to weld the doors shut. If you open them, the sand bags will fall out. You have to climb in using the running boards."

After Roberto slammed the hood shut, Bishop noticed another upgrade. A beautifully painted skull and crossbones graphic had been painted on the hood. Underneath was the word "Bones." Bishop gave Roberto a questioning look.

"My son is an artist and hasn't had any cars to paint for a while. I hope you don't mind. It cheered him up."

Bishop rubbed his hand over the lettering, "I love it, Roberto. It's perfect. Your son has talent."

"Thank you senor, I hope he has the chance to use it again someday. We'll have it ready for you in about 20 minutes. One problem though – this is a diesel, and I only had a few gallons of diesel fuel that we drained from an old tractor. You have only a half tank of fuel."

Bishop thought for a moment and decided that should be enough.

"See you in 20 minutes."

Bishop hurried back to the hotel to find Terri was already awake and going through her morning routine. She gave him a sleepy kiss, and he showed her the letters the doctor had given him. As she read them, her eyebrows arched more than once. Without comment, she folded the papers and handed them back.

Bishop asked if she would make sure David was ready and explained about the Hummer. "You've messed up my Hummer, eh? Don't worry about your truck while you're gone," and tried to produce an evil laugh.

He picked up the two MP5s and headed out the door wondering how serious she was about his truck. In a few minutes, he pulled up in front of the hotel with Bones. David and Bishop started loading a few random items in the back just as the sun was rising in the east. By the time they had finished loading, said their goodbyes and double-checked they weren't leaving anything behind, it was broad daylight. Terri, Betty, Pete, and Doc all watched as Bones headed west out of town.

Chapter 18

Colonel Owen Marcus stood on the front bumper of his command Humvee, watching the long convoy of equipment leaving the front gates of Fort Polk, Louisiana. His 4th Brigade Combat Team of the 10th Mountain division was deploying once again. More so than at any other time, Colonel Marcus was questioning his orders and himself.

The 4/10 was normally a "light" unit, meaning their order of battle didn't include heavy armor. For this mission, they had been supplemented by two platoons who had been at Polk for a training exercise. Those two units included eight M1A1 Abrams tanks, and the colonel was glad they were coming along.

Some years ago, the Army had begun reorganizing practically every single unit under its command. Before this program was initiated, a division was the smallest self-sufficient unit that could be deployed to any theatre. The war on terror, combined with the fall of the old Soviet Union had changed how the Pentagon planned for war. The first Gulf War had been the real catalyst; however, as it was the first major deployment of U.S. forces since WWII. The entire military was frustrated at the time needed to assemble, transport, and reassemble divisional-sized units. Even though Americans heard news reports that stated, "Elements of the 1st Infantry Division arrived in Saudi Arabia this morning," on television, in reality, it took weeks before all of the pieces of any division were in place. After the war, it became apparent that something had to change. Post-victory analysis documented what everyone already knew. Even several weeks after U.S. forces began arriving in the region, they would have been unable to stop Iraq's Army had it decided to invade Saudi Arabia. Some American units arrived piecemeal, a little more each day, while others would have all of their people, but none of their equipment for weeks on end. Had the Iraqis decided to invade Saudi, it could have been a bloodbath and might have resulted in total defeat for the coalition.

Afterwards, the Pentagon determined that regional conflicts and police actions were the future of the U.S. Army. Moving a division of 36,000 men and all of their equipment was difficult, expensive, and slow. The concept of the "modular combat team" had been devised as the solution. The resulting changes in how U.S. forces were structured had been tested, proven effective, and implemented across the entire branch.

These combat teams were really just small divisions. Usually numbering between 3,600 and 5,000 personnel, these self-contained units could be quickly deployed and possessed similar weapon platforms and capabilities as their divisional-sized predecessors – just wrapped in a smaller package.

With advances in firepower, air support, and combined arms command and control, the Army's new combat teams possessed almost equal capability to that of a full division just a few decades prior.

Colonel Marcus watched with pride as his troopers poured out of the gate. His men had been one of the last units withdrawn from Afghanistan just a few short months ago. They had been scheduled to stand down for a much-needed rest and refit when everything had fallen apart. After society failed, they initially deployed to Baton Rouge under orders to control the state capital. Fate would have it that the Louisiana State Police had been hosting a statewide law enforcement convention in town at the same time. The thousands of deputies, city police officers, and state troopers had been well led and spread out immediately in an effort to keep the peace. The efforts of the visiting officers had been enough to allow the regular city police, combined with some local National Guard units, to establish control, although barely.

When Colonel Marcus had reported to his superiors that neither martial law, nor the presence of the 4/10 was required in Baton Rouge, he was reprimanded and told to execute his orders to the letter. While still in shock at the response from higher up, he had been approached by the Independents. His old commanding general had suddenly shown up at the makeshift headquarters his unit had established in the city. They had talked through the night about the movement and what it represented. He had watched several video tapes and read through a stack of papers delivered by the three star officer.

The following day, Colonel Marcus had called in his senior officers. His men sat in silence as he delivered a briefing almost identical to the one he had just received the night before. It was his closing remarks that seemed to inspire most:

"Gentlemen, I am joining the Independents. I cannot sanction the actions we have been ordered to execute in this city. I feel it is an unlawful order and furthermore believe our Commander in Chief has left the reservation. Each of you has twelve hours to brief your units on what has transpired both here, and across the country. Each individual solider is to be allowed his own decision. Those who wish to stay with this command are welcome to do so with the full understanding that I am pledging the 4/10 to the Independents. Those who do not wish to stay with the unit will be allowed to leave. Dismissed."

Not a single solider had elected to leave the unit. When this news arrived, Colonel Marcus was honored that his men placed so much faith in his leadership and judgment. Everyone who has ever commanded men dreams of this type of reaction.

Without question, doubt had raised its ugly, divisive head numerous times since. When the orders were issued to assemble and head back to Fort Polk, many of the officers and NCOs had quietly discussed their decision among themselves. While Baton Rouge remained orderly, hunger and disease were a growing factor. Colonel Marcus attributed the lack of civil unrest in the city to the fact that many of the residents were transplants from New Orleans after hurricane Katrina, and somewhat immune to disaster. When the mayor and city council pledged their allegiance to the Independents, things settled down. The entire population seemed relieved when the 4/10 started pulling out of town.

Since Baton Rouge was firmly in control of the Independents, it was decided that the 4/10 would deploy to the Shreveport area and be in a position to control that general region. The agricultural and nuclear power facilities close by were of critical importance to Operation Delta1.

What was causing Colonel Marcus to second-guess his decision was a last minute briefing he had received just a few hours ago. Elements of the 1st Calvary Division from Fort Hood were known to be in control of the Dallas area. He was instructed to deploy in such a manner as to enable the 4/10 to be a blocking force should the 1st move east. While the Colonel had known there was the potential of engagement with forces loyal to the president, the order to be ready to fight his fellow U.S. Army soldiers brought an entirely new reality to his decisions. He had many friends in the 1st. Some of its commanders had been in his class at West Point.

Regardless, he had made a commitment and believed in the cause. No doubt, Grant, Lee and other officers involved in the War Between the States had experienced similar internal strife. He could only prepare for the worst and hope it didn't come to another civil war.

As they headed west out of Meraton, Bishop let David drive Bones so he could get used to the feel of the stripped down SUV. Bishop noticed the young man could carry on a conversation without looking at him and actually drove pretty well. Not that the deserted highway provided many challenges.

"David, we are going to the ranch first. I have some equipment we have to retrieve there, and I want to make sure you have everything you need as well. You said you were comfortable with distance shooting?"

The young man nodded. "I shot class F in the NRA juniors for the last two years."

Bishop whistled. "Class F is 1,000 meters, isn't it?"

"Yes, sir. Dad always said that if I developed the discipline to shoot longer ranges early, the other skills would come naturally."

Bishop had to agree. "I think I'd like your father, David. He sounds like my kind of guy."

David smiled. "He's a lot like you. He never thinks I can do anything good enough, but I know he loves me. He went up flying with me once and didn't let loose of the door handle for twenty minutes. Now, it's the first thing he wants to do when I see him."

Bishop smiled at the thought, "Well young man, I'm going to place my life into your hands, so don't think I underestimate your capabilities. I am, however, going to spend some time today showing you a few little tricks of the trade. Have you ever shot an AR10 piston .308?"

David moved his head indicating he hadn't, and then said, "I saw that rifle in your rack back at the cave. Is it accurate?"

Bishop grinned, "Oh, yes. It's what I call a factory freak. We received ten of them at work to evaluate. I took them all out to the range to zero and break them in. That one was a tack driver, and I assigned it to myself."

David's voice was all business now. "I noticed it only has a 16-inch barrel; that's pretty short compared to what I'm used to. Won't that take some velocity off the round?"

"Yes, it is about 50 feet per second slower out the pipe than a military issue sniper rifle. At 900, that means you have to add a little holdover. No big deal."

David thought about that a little bit and shrugged his shoulders, "It's just math."

That statement made Bishop smile again.

As they drove, Bishop started outlining to David how they would work together. Every now and then, David would interrupt and ask for a term to be clarified. By the time they were approaching the vicinity of the ranch, the two were communicating well.

Bishop pointed for David to pull off of the highway. The young man was a little confused. "I thought we were going to the ranch?"

Bishop nodded, "We are, but I don't want to go in the normal way. I don't trust those Colombians one bit. They may have someone up in the mountains watching the road, hoping to see where the ranch is located."

David thought that was a good idea.

Bishop guided David to park Bones under an overhang of rock where it would be difficult to spot. The two dismounted and began a long hike through the low-lying desert hills. On the way, Bishop took the opportunity to begin David's training.

"David, when you are moving through hostile territory, you always decide where your next cover is before you move. If you can, look for an alternative spot as well. Never leave good cover unless you know where you're going."

Along the way, Bishop explained a few more basic movement techniques to the novice and was pleased to see the lad learned quickly.

When they got close to the camper, Bishop had David take a high perch on top of a rock formation. "Go up there and stay low. Don't silhouette yourself. I'm going to move forward and disarm the tripwires. Your job is to make sure no one tries to follow me and to keep scanning around, seeing if you can spot any observers.

David nodded and began climbing up the rock.

It was almost noon when they finally walked into the Bat Cave. They fixed a quick, simple meal and then Bishop started laying out equipment for David. The boy's thin frame required adjustments to Bishop's spare gear. He used Terri's body armor and a spare load vest to get David ready for a little time in the field.

Before long, they were headed toward Bones, and Bishop couldn't help but notice the transformation in David. The boy seemed to be taking all of this seriously and paid close attention to Bishop's every word. *He understands what's on the line.*

When they had arrived at the Humvee, Bishop stopped David and handed him two balloons. "Here, blow these up." Bishop took a deep breath and began blowing up one himself. When they had six of the balloons inflated, they jumped into Bones and drove into the flat, open desert. Bishop kept looking over his shoulder and finally stopped David near a small patch of scrub oak. They carefully tied the balloons onto the branches, and David commented that it looked like a birthday party for the rabbits. Once all of the decorations were in place, they returned to the overhang. Bishop looked at David and instructed, "Pop 'em."

David extended the bi-pod on the big rifle and braced it on Bone's hood. He looked through the scope and adjusted the rangefinder. He flicked open the small notebook Bishop had given him and looked at the DOPE that was recorded in the pages.

The young man took a deep breath, flicked off the safety, and welded his cheek to the stock. The big rifle bucked against his shoulder, its discharge sending echoes rolling across the desert floor. One of the balloons vanished a full second and a half later. Bishop was pleased that the kid didn't even take his eye from the scope, and in a few moments, a second shot was on its way. After seven shots, all six balloons were gone.

David flicked on the safety and ejected the magazine from the rifle. He had a pure look of disgust on his face, "I missed. I knew I'd pulled it before I saw the miss."

Bishop reached up and grabbed his shoulder. "Son, that was some damned fine shooting. Don't worry about it. You're using a new rifle in a new environment. We'll be just fine if you keep that up."

"I wish we had some more time. I think another twenty rounds or so and I could hit six out of six from here."

"You're fine, bud. I don't think I could hit six out of six if we stood here until next Sunday. Now, here's the important question – do you think you can shoot a man if you have to?"

David thought about that for longer than Bishop was comfortable. He finally looked the older man in the eye and answered, "I don't know. I really don't know."

Bishop understood the hesitation. "Son, your grandpa, Terri, and I all need for you to take a shot if necessary. I'll try not to put you in that situation, but I need to know you will pull that trigger. We can talk about it some more on the way to Alpha. Let's get going."

Chapter 19

Alpha, Texas was an oddity. There was no logical reason for the town to have grown and survived when most others in the area had barely managed to exist. With a population just shy of 6,000 people, the town existed on the southernmost slope of the Davis Mountain range. At an elevation of 4,500 feet, Alpha occasionally received snowfall. Before the collapse, a ski resort had been built only 15 miles outside of town in the Alpine valley. While not considered a world-class ski resort by any means, the facility attracted visitors from the surrounding countryside and was a viable operation. It was not unheard of to see beginners heading down the slopes in cowboy hats.

Alpha State University added another 2,000 residents to the town. While the college had been absorbed into one of the larger state university systems some years ago, it still maintained its rural campus charm. Alpha had witnessed a decline in population during the 1980s. The city fathers decided that non-ranching jobs were a critical element to reversing the trend and established an industrial park just north of town. While the original expectations had never been met, the town did attract a small chemical plant, which added some well-paying jobs to the local economy. A large distribution center was also built in the community due to its centralized location. While the decline had stopped, it was still a stretch for any city manager to claim the town was booming.

Bishop and David were approaching from the south, traveling the sixty or so miles to the outskirts of town cautiously. Bishop attended both high school and college in Alpha. While he had known the lay of the land well at one time, he had only occasionally returned since. Bishop knew of a spot used by high school kids back in the day to park and make out. He hoped he could still find it.

David guided Bones over a roadway that was ever increasing in elevation. Their climb brought them to an elevated area where the lights in the evening were as close to a romantic vista as could be found in the Chihuahua desert. Careful to drive slowly and not kick up any dust, they finally found the site about a mile outside of the city.

Bishop took the big rifle from David, and they found a location to go prone and observe the town. It was the first time Bishop had been to Alpha in over five years, and from this distance, everything looked very much like Bishop remembered. The big rifle had a mounted scope that provided twenty-four

175

levels of magnification, and as Bishop focused the optic, he quickly realized the sleepy, little college town had indeed changed since his last visit.

The first thing he noticed was a gas station that had burned to the ground. Only the rusted skeletons of the pumps and the seemingly untouched sign identified the heap of scorched lumber and brick. The surrounding structures had apparently sustained quite a bit of damage in the fire as well. On the same highway that Bishop and David had just been traveling, there appeared to have been a roadblock at one point in time. Two smashed vehicles of some sort, accompanied by piles of old tires and a rusted piece of farm equipment had been all stacked to make a low wall across the highway.

Bishop wanted to enter Alpha at night, and they had arrived a few hours before sundown. They decided to stay put, have a meal, and then attempt passage to the north side of town where the university campus was located.

Bishop broke out a small German infantry camp stove that was about the size of a deck of cards. He unwrapped a couple of fuel pellets and began to prepare some food. David was assigned to keep an eye on the town and let Bishop know if he saw any movement. Bishop kept an eye on their immediate surroundings so no one could sneak up on them.

Bishop finished heating up water for soup and coffee and was about to invite David to join him when the two heard a distant popping noise coming from Alpha. Bishop immediately recognized the sound of gunfire. He moved quickly to David's side and watched as the young man desperately moved the scope from side to side trying to see where the racket was coming from. The source, he announced, must be hidden by all of the structures in the town.

The shooting continued for several minutes. Bishop thought he could identify several different weapons being discharged; although at this distance, it was impossible to be sure. As suddenly as it had started, the firing stopped, and then a revving engine noise could be heard in the distance. Everything was still after that.

The two ate in silence, each picking at his food. David was steady, but Bishop could tell he was nervous. Bishop didn't blame him one bit. After they had finished their meal, Bishop reviewed the plan again. The fuses had been removed from Bones so it wouldn't emit any light. They were going to maneuver like a caterpillar through the town, with Bishop scouting ahead on foot until a suitable hiding spot was found. He would then radio David to follow with Bones, and they would repeat the process until they were on the college campus. David, while parked, would watch Bishop with the night vision, and try to cover his back with the long-range rifle.

As the sun began to set, they packed up everything, rechecked their equipment, and proceeded toward the highway.

The President of the United States was furious. He stalked around the conference room, holding a thin stack of papers in his shaking hands. "This is treason!" he screamed. "Absolute treachery! Why would anyone do this? Why now?"

General Wilson replied. "Sir, we don't know who the man was feeding information to, or why. He killed himself as soon as he knew we were onto him. What we do know is that he transmitted all of the plans to Operation Heartland to an unknown location. There is evidence that he had been sharing critical information since we evacuated Washington."

"Why, General? What possible reason could someone have for wanting to know our plans?"

"Sir, there has been speculation of another group trying to organize various parts of the country. The data has been sketchy at best, and I had made the decision not to trouble you with rumor and innuendo. Perhaps that wasn't the appropriate course of action."

"Another group? What do you mean another 'group?'"

"Sir, some of the units that we no longer have contact with have been observed intact and conducting themselves as normal. It would seem as if the command structure were taking orders from someone other than my staff. The act of refusing communication while still able to do so is by itself a serious offense."

"General, are you saying a foreign power has taken over control of part of our military?"

"No, sir. I am not implying that whatsoever. I now believe the new group is domestic and most likely led by current or former political figures from Washington."

The POTUS had to digest that statement. "Any news of our emissary from Texas?"

"No, sir, no news. However, I did speak to the commander in charge of Houston. He is suspicious some of his officers are near rebellion. He also has been hearing rumors."

The president's temper boiled over, but one would have to know him well to tell. "General, we can't wait any longer. We are losing control of this situation. What is the first step of Operation Heartland?"

"The first step is to secure the nuclear reactors around Shreveport, sir. Elements of the 1st Calvary Division would vacate Dallas and proceed east to establish control of the area."

"Let's do it, General. I hate initiating this plan without having a complete picture, but we can't wait any longer. I'll sign the order."

"Yes, sir."

The Humvee bounced down the somewhat rocky incline to the highway where David turned left and proceeded toward Alpha. The sun was just slipping behind Twin Peaks Mountain off to the west, and some ambient pink light leaked around the 7,800-foot formations. When they were within sight of the abandoned roadblock, Bishop dismounted and proceeded on foot.

Bishop knew he was taking a risk by approaching the town while there was still visibility, but decided that it would be best to let David get accustomed to working their system. They hadn't seen any movement at all in this area of the city, and Bishop couldn't see any reason for anyone to even visit. They passed the charred debris that had once been a gas station without incident, and David did a good job of maneuvering Bones into a narrow alleyway behind the rubble of the building. They were entering a section that was partly residential with a few small businesses scattered among the homes. Bishop saw signs marking an insurance agency, a small clothing store, and a hair salon. He carefully moved from cover to cover, always looking for any sign of habitation or trouble. It was completely dark now, and after moving four blocks north, he spotted a car wash and radioed David to bring Bones and hide in one of the stalls. Bishop moved another three blocks away from the car wash when he saw movement ahead. Using his night vision, he spotted a group of people directly approaching his position. There were at least ten of them, and he could make out rifles. Bishop keyed his microphone and whispered, "David, we have a group of armed men heading directly at us. Get ready to get out of there."

Two clicks acknowledged David had received the message.

Bishop retreated toward David's stall at the carwash, taking cover in what had once been a dry cleaning storefront housed in a concrete block wall building. The front door was nowhere to be seen, and shards of window glass littered the ground. He entered through the doorway and ducked behind the front wall, looking out one of the window frames. He knew the concrete block would not stop bullets, but he was in a hurry and hoped the location would at least provide some cover. He watched as the gang of armed men continued to advance toward his position. A quick check revealed a back exit, which was

178

missing its door as well. An obstacle course consisting of trash, papers and steel racks turned on their sides lay between Bishop and the exit. An ornate, older cash register sat on the floor in front of the counter, its drawer extended and empty. He barely could pick up the enormously heavy machine and managed to place it next to the wall he was hiding behind.

The group of men continued down the street, and Bishop realized they would see David and Bones in the next few minutes. It was now too late for David to move without being seen. Bishop waited until the strangers were in front of the dry cleaners and fired two intentionally high shots at the men. He radioed David to get the hell out of there and meet him back by the burned out gas station.

He didn't hear the two clicks because he rose up and fired two more wild rounds in the general direction where the men had been. He was getting ready to run for the back door when the entire wall around him erupted inwards with dust, bits of concrete and lead flying through the room. Bishop dove for cover behind the cash register and could feel the rounds striking the heavy steel device. He was waiting for a lull in the fire when a large chuck of block was blown off the window frame and struck him in the shoulder. He looked up to see an entire section of the wall falling inward as its support had been eaten away by the volume of lead blasting through.

The last thing Bishop remembered was covering his head with his arms when the wall crashed on him. His vision went black with small white lines vibrating away into darkness.

Bishop's hands were on fire. His brain sent the signals to pull his arms back from the flame, but they wouldn't respond. He suddenly remembered the wall caving in and tried to jerk away, but couldn't move. He managed to open his eyes and saw a strange face a few feet away from his, staring at him.

"He's awake," a strange voice announced.

Another voice from behind him asked, "What's your name, hotshot?"

Bishop didn't see any reason not to answer, so he responded with the truth, "Bishop."

Bishop tried to move his hands out of the fire again, and then it dawned on him he couldn't move because his hands were bound. Whatever was being used to tie his hands was way too tight, and the burning sensation was due to loss of circulation.

"Well, Mr. Bishop, you look extremely well-fed to be one of the skinnies. How long have you been with them?"

"I don't know who the skinnies are. What are you talking about?"

A sharp blow almost knocked him out of the chair.

"Don't bullshit me. I'm going to kill you in a few minutes whether you tell me what I want to know or not. The difference will be a quick death or a slow one. Now, how long have you been with the skinnies?"

"I have no idea who the skinnies are, dude. I own a ranch south of town and am trying to just pass through."

"Bullshit!" Another blow soon followed, this time strong enough to knock over the chair Bishop was sitting on. Rough hands set him back up.

A third voice spoke from across the room. "Just go ahead and pop him in the head, and get it over with. Why do you give a rat's ass how long he's been with the skinnies?"

"I care because this dude had night vision, full clips, and extra food in his kit. If they've found a cache of supplies or weapons, I think we need to know. And if they are getting help from outside, I think we need to know."

Bishop tried again. "I'm telling you, I'm with nobody. I'm just trying to head north."

"Stop lying. You better talk to me, sweetheart. Deacon Brown will be here in a bit, and I'm warning you. I'm a pair of warm, fuzzy, bunny slippers compared to the Deacon. You won't enjoy that conversation near as much as mine."

"I'm not lying. I have no idea who the skinnies are. I'm just trying to get to Fort Bliss."

"Oh, yeah? Well tell me, Mr. Bishop, who was that with you? Why did they take off in that dune buggy? That sure looked like a skinny truck to me."

"That was my nephew. I radioed him to leave when I saw you guys." *Thank God, David got away.*

Again, that third voice spoke up. "He shot at us. If he was just passing through, he wouldn't have shot at us. Put him down, dude. I'm tired and want to go to bed. We can divide up his stuff in the morning."

Bishop heard a round be chambered into a pistol behind his head. *These guys are really going to shoot me.*

Bishop closed his eyes and thought of Terri. He felt the barrel of the weapon being placed on the back of his head.

A new, strong female voice filled the air. "Enough! Put that weapon away."

Bishop opened his eyes to see a woman placing a chair directly in front of his. She held a Bible in her hand. The woman placed the seat with its back facing Bishop, and then sat with her arms folded on the chair back, just looking at him. She rested her chin on the Bible.

With raven-colored hair and the blackest eyes Bishop had ever seen, she was stunningly beautiful. She appeared to be about forty years old with a clear complexion and thin frame. She just sat there, staring at Bishop, for what seemed like several minutes. Finally, she held out her hand and a giant man came into view and handed her some papers. Her piercing gaze continued to drill into Bishop, never wavering for even a second.

"I assume you are Bishop," she said, holding out the papers.

"Yes."

"My name is Diana Brown. Everyone around here calls me Deacon Brown. You are an interesting man, Bishop. I've read the papers we found in your pack, and if I understand them correctly, you desperately want to get to Fort Bliss."

Bishop had forgotten all about the Colonel's papers being in his pack. *So much for my security clearance.*

"I tried to tell these men I was just passing through."

"Why did you shoot at my people, Bishop?"

"I didn't shoot at them. I shot above their heads to pull them away from my nephew. If I had been aiming at them…"

Deacon Brown thought about Bishop's response for a little while. She eventually looked at someone standing behind Bishop's chair and instructed, "Untie him."

A few moments later, Bishop was rubbing his wrists and wincing from the pain of the blood rushing back into his hands. The large man moved closer to Deacon Brown, and Bishop looked the gentleman over while working on the circulation in his limbs.

He was at least six feet ten inches tall, and Bishop guessed he would top the scales close to four hundred pounds. He looked to be in his early 20s and clearly was a weightlifter. The tight t-shirt he wore indicated a lot of time dedicated to curls and bench pressing. Deacon Brown noticed Bishop checking out her companion and smiled. "Bishop, let me introduce you to my son, Atlas. He is of Russian decent. I adopted him through our church program several years ago when he was a toddler. I would advise you not to threaten me or move quickly in my direction, as he is naturally very protective of his mother. I wouldn't want an accident or misunderstanding to occur. He was raised in one of those Russian orphanages where the infants were never held or coddled. He isn't blessed with many social graces."

Bishop heard a few of the men standing behind him snicker at Deacon Brown's remark.

After a stern look from the woman, all of the men behind him became quiet. Atlas remained next to his mother, who eventually spoke again. "Can you stand?"

"Yes."

"Would you like a drink of water?"

"Oh yes, I would."

The Deacon didn't even have to ask, and in a few moments, a glass of water was held in front of Bishop's face. He started to take the liquid, but a sharp pain streaked through his head behind his eyes causing him to gasp and reach for his temples. When he touched his head, he felt dried, caked blood on one side and realized he had taken quite a blow.

Deacon Brown said, "A brick wall fell on you. You were out for almost an hour. I'm not a doctor, but I would bet you have a mild concussion."

Bishop looked at her and nodded, causing more pain. "Could I have my kit?"

This request required a look from the woman to the men standing behind Bishop. In a few moments, Bishop's load vest, minus knife and pistol, was placed in his lap. He could tell his blow out bag had been searched, but it appeared everything was still intact. He found a small packet of aspirin and fumbled with it trying to get his still numb fingers to work. One of the men behind him spoke up. "You're not going to let him waste those, are you? We've been out of aspirin for weeks. Why let him take those if we're going to kill him anyway?"

Deacon Brown looked at the speaker and frowned. "His fate has not yet been determined. I remind you we are still Christians here, even though the language I heard coming from this room earlier wouldn't prove it."

Bishop finally managed to open the stubborn wrapper, and then found the tube connected to his camelback water bladder. He took a quick pull of water and then swallowed the pain pills. Two more pulls of water helped his head start to clear.

Bishop's act of drinking from his kit drew a questioning look from the Deacon. He took another drink and explained, "I try to drink the water from home if I can. A stomach bug can ruin your vacation, and I was warned not to drink the water here."

Deacon Brown didn't even smile. "You don't have to worry about our water. We hold the springs. Water and our faith are about all we have plenty of. Still, the Lord provides what we need. Can you walk?"

"I think so." Bishop tried to stand, but his legs were a little wobbly. The third attempt succeeded and Deacon Brown motioned for him to walk toward the door. Bishop exited into a long hallway lit by a candle at each end. He turned, waiting on his host, and noticed a small sign on the room he had just left that said, "3rd Grade Sunday School."

Deacon Brown and Bishop walked down the hall, Atlas a few steps behind them. Bishop noticed the hallway walls were covered in children's artwork. They eventually came to stairs, and careful to use the rail, Bishop managed to climb without toppling over. Through another, wider doorway, and the small entourage entered the main assembly area of the church. There were two sections of pews facing a pulpit on a raised stage. A large statue of Jesus Christ extending a hand toward a child resided behind the choir box. Several candles illuminated the area, and it was ghostly quiet.

Bishop decided to break the silence and asked, "Who are the skinnies your men kept asking me about?"

Without breaking stride, Deacon Brown responded, "When the plant exploded, thousands died instantly. There were only about 500 people left as far as we could tell. Fortunately, by the grace of God, the gas cloud was released on Sunday morning, and our service here was especially full that day. I think the news reports and power outage caused a lot of the townspeople to try and get closer to their maker. That morning our sanctuary was overflowing with people. The good Lord and a light breeze kept the poison away from this building."

Deacon Brown turned and looked at the statue of Christ. "At first, we extended help to anyone who came to our doors. No one knew how far the cloud would spread or how long before it dissipated. It didn't kill everyone instantly. We had the entire annex building full of victims with damaged lungs who were barely breathing. Eventually, they all died, but for the first few hours, it was a horrible experience."

She turned to Bishop with an injured expression on her face, "Everyone was scared to return to their homes. Rumors started spreading that the poison could kill just from touching something exposed to it. The town had been without electricity for two days, but one member of the congregation was a HAM radio operator. He went to his house and sent out a call for help. We kept waiting on some type of emergency personnel to respond, but they never did. After a few days, some of the men decided to explore the town. They came back and reported having seen bodies everywhere. The chemical plant was still burning, as were several other buildings in the area. We all decided to stay here until help arrived. The church was always having a food drive for our missions. The basement was full of canned goods, and we managed to eat pretty well that first week."

Bishop could see the pain in the woman's eyes as she recounted the tale. Her voice remained strong and steady, as she continued. "I think it was about 10 days after the explosion when a group of men showed up at the front door. They claimed their families were starving and asked if we had any food. The pastor told them we could share a little and led them down to the basement where our storeroom was located. I wasn't there, but was told that a disagreement broke out about how much they could take with them. One of the men pulled a gun and shot our reverend. The men ran out with all the food they could carry."

Deacon Brown sighed and then continued walking. "That next day some of our men left our facility to return to their homes. People needed prescription medications, and we had two diabetics in our flock. It wasn't long before they came back here, panting and exhausted. It seems they found looters in their homes and had barely escaped with their lives. At that time, we were housing about 200 people in our congregation and another 50 or so of the townspeople who had come here to help. The next day, the looters showed up here again. There was a group of about twenty of them, and they didn't even ask. They just kicked in the door and headed directly to the basement storage area. A couple of our men tried to reason with them, and when that didn't work, a fight broke out. Two of our members were shot, and another was badly beaten. When word of that incident spread, several of the men banded together, to go back to their homes and bring back what they could. One of our members was the officer in charge of the Alpha National Guard unit, and no one had thought to raid the armory. He brought back the few weapons they had there and a small amount of ammunition. That ended up saving us."

Deacon Brown led Bishop to another set of stairs, this one rising upward. As they climbed the steps, the ever-vigilant Atlas switched on a flashlight. There were two flights that suddenly ended at an office door labeled "Reverend Brown." Bishop gave the Deacon a questioning look, and she said, "Reverend Brown was my father. I've taken over his office." *Now is probably not the time for any jokes about the preacher's daughter.*

The door opened into a spacious reception area that fronted a large, well-appointed office. The church had been constructed so that the windows of the pastor's office looked out over the main parking lot and off in the distance, the town of Alpha. Atlas turned off the flashlight, and Deacon Brown motioned for Bishop to take in the view.

The church grounds were extensive for such a small community. The main building where they were standing was surrounded by two other metal buildings of good size. A large blacktopped parking lot was in the center of the complex.

Bishop could see fires burning around the edge of the grounds. Someone had taken trash barrels and strategically placed them around the perimeter, each producing both heat and light. He could also see a wall had been constructed. Church busses, cars from the congregation, two large trees that had been cut down, and an assortment of other items had been placed to make a formidable barrier around the property. It reminded Bishop of the gas station in Meraton, but on a much larger scale. Deacon Brown motioned for Bishop to have a seat.

"Over the next few months, the town basically settled into two camps – our congregation and everyone else. Again, the Lord smiled on us, because the church's property bordered the city's water wells. We managed to extend our control over that area and eventually tapped into the supply after the power failed. For a while, a kind of barter system took place. If you wanted water, you could bring something you were willing to trade to our front gate, and we would provide water in exchange. That worked well until someone organized the people out in the town. Open hostility and pitched gunfights began to occur. That's when we built the wall around the church."

Clearly intrigued, Bishop asked, "Who organized the townspeople? Why don't you work together?"

"Oh, we tried. It was a group of prisoners who escaped from the county jail that took over. I tried to work with them – I tried several times, but they wanted to be in control. They wouldn't compromise."

The beautiful woman now sitting behind the desk seemed to drift off in thought. There was just enough light coming through the window that Bishop could make out her expression. He thought she was reliving some of the events that she had just shared, and he decided to remain quiet. Eventually, she looked up. "So Bishop, I've told you my story, how about you fill me in on those papers? I want to hear your story."

Bishop wasn't sure why, but he decided he could trust the woman. It took him twenty minutes to fill her in on the high points, including his quest to get medical equipment. After he finished, she asked a few questions and then drifted off again. When she had thought it all through, she said, "So, there is a 16-year-old boy out there in the desert somewhere alone right now? Aren't you a little worried about him?"

Bishop sat straight up, "David! Oh shit, I forgot all about David."

Bishop's language drew a dirty look from Deacon Brown, but she quickly got over it. "Do you know where he is?"

"I know where I told him to go."

Deacon Brown laughed at that remark. "Teenagers don't always follow instructions, I've found. Atlas, go get Bishop's equipment, would you?"

The huge man hesitated, clearly not wanting to leave his mother alone with this stranger. She sensed his apprehension and added, "It will be okay, son. He's not going to hurt me." Deacon Brown opened a desk drawer, pulled out a small automatic pistol, and sat it on the desk. "Go on, now. I'll be fine."

After he left, Deacon Brown seemed to make a decision. "You'll not be harmed here. If you wish, you can use that radio we found on you to call David. Tell him a group of my men will meet him and bring him into the compound. After you both have had a chance to rest, you are free to go on about your business. I must warn you though, the college campus is right in the middle of their territory, and I would advise against trying to go there. Chances are, the equipment and supplies you are after have already been discovered. Any sort of medicine is more valuable than gold these days, and I would imagine it's all been picked clean."

Bishop nodded and felt it was his turn to ask a question. "Why don't you expand your area? Are they that strong?"

She laughed at Bishop's remark. "We have lost over 70 men in the last few months trying to do just that. The patrol you ran into tonight was there to make sure they don't mass against us anymore. They have hit us very hard twice in the last week. They gather up dozens of men and try to overrun the wall. We patrol so we can have a little warning. I'll risk another one to get David inside the walls safely."

Atlas returned with Bishop's gear, including his weapons. As the big man handed Bishop his equipment, he hesitated before handing over Bishop's rifle, knife, and pistol. The deacon nodded to him, and the weapons were returned to the owner.

Bishop immediately picked up the radio and keyed the mic. "David, this is Bishop, can you read me?"

A few moments later, two clicks answered his call. "David, click twice if you can talk, once if you are in danger."

Click, click.

"Okay, son. How are you?"

"Bishop, are you okay? I did what you asked, but I saw all those men shooting at you. Are you all right?"

"I'm fine, David. Now listen to me carefully, I want you to meet me at the burned out gas station in…" he looked at the deacon, who mouthed the words one hour, "…In one hour. Do you understand?"

"Yes, Bishop, I understand. The burned out gas station in one hour."

"Okay, David. I'll meet you there, and I will have company. They are friendlies. Click twice if you understand."

Click, click.

Bishop took a few minutes to load up his gear. Deacon Brown had a washcloth and water brought to the office while she left to issues orders for another patrol. When Bishop had removed the blood from his scalp, he felt better. He gingerly applied a topical antibiotic crème to the cut and admired his rather large goose egg. *Terri always did think I was hardheaded. I guess she was right.*

Before long, Bishop was escorted down the steps and out the front door. Deacon Brown was standing with a group of eight men. As Bishop looked them over, he was struck by the mixture of weapons and equipment being carried. There were two M16 rifles, a couple of hunting shotguns, and several different calibers of deer rifles. One gent was carrying an M1 Garand. They all had makeshift slings, packs, and ammo pouches. A few camping canteens were hanging from belts, and two of them had matching bright blue hiking backpacks. The man who had hit Bishop during the initial interrogation was leading the group and clearly not happy about it. He gave Bishop a dirty look and said, "I hope you can shoot better than you did before."

Bishop stared the man down. "Let's hope I don't have too."

Bishop explained where they were going and told the patrol about Bones. Everyone nodded, and the group moved toward the perimeter wall where a car was pushed back just enough to provide an opening for the men to pass through single file.

Bishop took the lead because of his night vision. It took everyone a few minutes to adjust to his pace, but they managed to keep up. He noticed they tended to bunch up, as they got further away from the church. At one point, Bishop stopped at an intersection, taking cover behind a metal mailbox on the street corner. When he turned around, all eight men were right behind him, huddled up in a tight group. He shook his head and motioned them inside the empty building close by.

When everyone had settled down, he whispered, "Hey, look, don't bunch up like that. That is how I saw you guys coming before. We need to go down this street, so I want four of you on one side and four on the other. Stay about ten feet apart and leap frog each other. Scan right and left, don't just watch the guy in front of you. Keep some space between you. Got it?"

Bishop could see several heads nod up and down in the dim moonlight drifting into the building. After he checked it was still clear outside, they all moved toward the meeting with David.

They had moved a few blocks when Bishop heard the sound of an engine. He motioned everyone to take cover and watched as the patrol clumsily tried to hide behind cars, trees and even a picket fence that lined the street. *No wonder these guys are losing this fight, they have no idea what they're doing.*

They turned a corner and were almost to the car wash where Bishop had had David hide before. As they approached the building that had collapsed on Bishop's head, he noticed something was out of place. Ahead on them across from the car wash was a pickup truck parked along the street. He was almost positive it hadn't been there before. Bishop scanned the area on both sides of the street carefully with the night vision, but didn't see anything out of the ordinary. He moved quickly up to the new truck and took cover behind a wheel. He thought he saw movement out of the corner of his eye, but when he checked it out, nothing was there. *Something just isn't right here.* He motioned the patrol to continue moving up the street and was pleased to see that their spacing was improving somewhat. As the men were moving past him, his head itched from the cut, and he pulled off his glove to scratch. He absent-mindedly put his hand on the hood of the truck and felt warmth.

Several things happened all at once. When Bishop's head snapped up, he saw someone rise from the roof of the carwash. He raised his rifle and screamed "Ambush!" while trying to bring the target into view. Everything was moving in slow motion. It seemed like it was taking his arms forever to bring his rifle up to his cheek. He could see twinkling muzzle flashes from two other shooters out of the corner of his eye. Small holes appeared in the fender of the truck he was behind. Finally, after what seemed like minutes, the red dot of his riflescope was almost on the rooftop shooter and Bishop's brain sent the message to his finger to pull the trigger immediately followed by a warning to his arms that they had better center that dot quickly or he was going to miss. Just as the dot centered on the green outline of the target, the rifle pushed gently against his shoulder and he saw the man fall forward off of the roof. Quickly, Bishop centered again, where he had seen a muzzle flash and let go with three quick shots. He couldn't tell if he had hit anything. He swept the rifle left and fired where another shooter had been hiding and squeezed the trigger three more times. A spark flew off of the fender he was using for cover and he realized someone was behind him. He moved quickly across the road and scrambled for the raised concrete platform where the car wash vacuum cleaners had once been. As he slid behind the cover, bits of pavement and chips of rock flew into the air all around him.

Bishop was safe behind the low barrier for a moment and tried to collect his thoughts. The best way to get out of an ambush kill zone was to break through one end or the other. By pure luck, he had taken out one side of the attacker's setup and wondered where the other threats were hiding. Movement caught his eye and two of the men in his patrol scrambled around the corner of the building next to the carwash. They were dragging an injured member of the patrol. Bullets quickly followed them and Bishop saw muzzle flashes off in the distance. Whoever had planned this bushwhacking had known what they were doing. Bishop could tell their enemy had set up in a classic horseshoe formation. Bishop's patrol had walked right into the open end of the trap. Normally, he would have pulled back through that open end, but now some of his men were pinned down, perhaps even dead.

He spotted three more of his party to his right, hiding behind roadside cover. These guys had been at the rear of the patrol and hadn't made it into the kill zone. That left two more unaccounted for. Bishop broke cover and ran for the corner where the three men were hiding. As he got close, he yelled, "Make a hole!" and slammed his body against the wall of the structure. He did a quick snapshot around the corner and barely pulled his head back as the brick erupted from the rain of bullets. *This isn't good. They know exactly where we are, and if I had this advantage, I would rush this position.*

Bishop unsnapped his blowout bag from his vest and tossed it to the men trying to help their injured friend. They were trapped. If they tried to move away from the wall, they would expose themselves to withering fire from two sides. If they stayed where they were, eventually the attackers would catch on and flank their position. Bishop kept trying to figure a way out. Every time he poked his head around the corner, a volley of fire would spray brick and mortar fragments. Already a good six inches of the corner brick had been eaten away.

Bishop tried to alternate high and low when looking around the corner. Twice he stuck his rifle around and fired random shots just to keep the attackers off guard. When he poked around again, his blood froze with the image he saw. Five men were running down the middle of the street in a single file toward him. They were less than 50 feet away, and when they came around, it would be over quickly. He decided he would have to chance exposing himself again in an attempt to slow them down.

Despite the intense fire, Bishop went prone and popped his head and rifle around the corner. Clay shards stung his face and hands as he centered the red dot into the chest of the lead man, now less than 30 feet away and running hard. The shooters supporting the charging men leveled their rounds at Bishop, creating more dust and stinging missiles of brick chips. *I'm going to get off maybe one shot here.*

Bishop's finger started to squeeze the trigger, when a dark shadow appeared suddenly behind the charging men. In less than a second, the rear man's body was flying through the air, quickly joined by a second, then a third and finally all five. A flash went by Bishop's corner, and he recognized Bones as it careened past, going at least 60 mph. A sickening series of "thuds" and "crunches" sounded as the five already dead men landed on the roadway, some of them flying more than 100 feet in the air.

David slammed on Bone's brakes, and the big SUV skidded to a stop several blocks away. Suddenly, everything became quiet as the shocking results of David's move set in. A cheer rose from the surviving patrol members, and Bishop took the opportunity to gather the guys next to him and head out of the kill zone. Once reunited with the rest of the patrol, Bishop turned back to see their rescuer. Bones was sitting, immobile, sideways in the street. He couldn't see David behind the wheel. Bishop keyed his mic and said, "David, are you okay?"

No response. Bishop sprinted toward Bones as fast as he could, covering the four blocks quickly. As he approached the vehicle, he heard David before he saw him. The young man was lying across the front seats with his face buried in his hands, small convulsions raking his body. David was crying. Bishop wanted to console him, but there just wasn't time. In a strong, but friendly tone, he said, "David, no time for that right now. I'll help you handle the pain you're feeling after we're out of this. Move over, buddy. We still have work to do."

Bishop absent-mindedly tried to open the door, and then remembered he had to hop into the cabin. He climbed in and gently picked David up, moving him to the passenger seat. The boy was like a rag doll and unresponsive.

Bishop put Bones in gear and sped back to the remaining members of the patrol. It appeared as though David's action had broken the ambush, but the attackers could regroup and hit them again any second. The injured man was loaded into the back of Bones, and the other men all climbed aboard. Bishop was still worried about the missing men, but one of the survivors told him they were both with God now. The man was 100% sure.

Bishop turned Bones around in the carwash parking lot and sped back toward the church with all of the patrol barely managing to hang on.

As they approached the wall surrounding the church grounds, Bishop slowed down and looked at the men behind him. "Is there some sort of signal you use when coming back in? I don't want the guards on the walls opening up on us."

One of the men volunteered to get out and approach the guards with the signal. Bishop pulled over and remained parked until the man returned and waved them forward. In another five minutes, Bones was parked in front of the church steps, and people were rushing out to help the injured man. David hadn't moved. Bishop finally got David to snap out of it a little and helped the boy out of the Humvee. He put his arm around David and escorted him upstairs to the deacon's office where it was quiet.

Bishop spoke in a soft voice. "David, I know what you're feeling. I felt the same thing my first time. It's normal, and you should be feeling it. Sometime soon, you will want to talk about it. Find me. Until then, stay up here and lay down. If you have to puke, which is also normal, here is a wastebasket. Don't fight puking…it will help."

David nodded.

Bishop showed him to the couch in the reception area. After he was sure the kid was comfortable, Bishop left in search of water and to check on the injured man. He ran into Deacon Brown on the way down the stairs and told her where he had left David.

"He's in a bad way right now. It will take a few hours for the shock to wear off, and then it will all come spilling out."

Deacon Brown nodded her understanding and simply said, "I know. I'll say a prayer for him."

After Bishop made the rounds, he found a quiet corner in the basement and cleaned his rifle, repacked his gear and refilled his magazine. He washed off as best he could and set up his pack as a pillow and went to sleep.

Chapter 20

Major Owens was a happy man for the first time in two months. As he walked down the wide concrete steps of the Dallas City Hall building, he felt a new sense of purpose. His beloved Ironhorse Brigade was going into the field again, and it was way overdue. Halfway down, his senior NCO was waiting for him. "Well, sir, what's the skinny?"

"We're moving Frank. Finally, command has seen fit to get proactive on this mess, and we've got a mission - a real one."

"Outstanding, sir. Where are we going?"

"Do you like Cajun food?"

"These days, sir, I like *any* food."

As the two men continued down the board staircase, the major paused to take in the scene one last time. An M1 Abrams tank was parked at each intersection surrounding city hall. Between the tanks, precisely centered on the yellow traffic lines, were sandbagged machine gun emplacements. Between the tanks and the sandbags, razor sharp concertina wire was strung. Two outhouse sized guard shacks bordered a narrow gap in the wire, which was the only way to enter the once public building. A line of people waited patiently to be searched before being allowed passage. The major absent-mindedly spoke out loud. "My elementary school used to take field trips here to tour city hall. I got my marriage license here. I just can't get over how this has all turned out."

"None of us can, sir. Do you remember Baghdad in '05? We couldn't understand how people lived like that. At least *they* had food."

The Sergeant's comparison between the two cities was valid. In fact, the men had taken to calling city hall and its surrounding complex "the green zone," named after the fortified area in the Iraqi capital used during the reconstruction.

Major Owens wondered if the military would ever learn. He had been a young lieutenant when the unit deployed to Iraq. Their method of operation was to stay in a tightly guarded base during the night and conduct random patrols during the day. It didn't take long for the terrorists to figure that out. When the American patrols were not around, they squeezed the locals just like organized crime syndicates extorted entire streets. It was only after Washington finally realized they were losing control of the country did things change. The fact that American boys were dying by scores probably had some influence as well. Finally, when things looked very bleak, their mission changed. "Go out among the people," was the new method. "Live, eat, sleep and be a part of the community," was the theme of the new operational orders. It had worked, and the tide had been turned.

Just like Iraq, they were losing control of this city as well. Just like Iraq, they secured small sections of the city and conducted random patrols from their fortified bases. Just like before, it wasn't working. No one seemed to have learned any lessons, and the same mistakes kept being repeated. From what he heard, Dallas wasn't the only problem area. Why did the Pentagon think the Army could pull this off in the first place? Hadn't they learned anything from Iraq? It took thousands of troopers, private contractors and the kitchen sink to secure small sections of Baghdad, a single city. Why did command think they could handle forty such cities?

For the past several weeks, they had been in Dallas trying to keep the peace with a population that didn't want them there. It sickened him to see one of the most potent fighting forces on the planet reduced to the equivalent of mere grocery clerks. Day after demoralizing day, his troopers had been required to guard and distribute food. That in itself wouldn't have been so bad were it not for the fact that there never was enough food. Watching hungry mothers with small children beg for something to eat would break the spirit of any man. For all of their technology, firepower, and discipline, Major Owens knew his unit was quickly becoming a bitter, hollowed-out shell of disgusted men. For the first time in his military career, he was concerned he would lose control of his command if something didn't change.

He couldn't wait to get outside of the city limits and into the rolling countryside of northeast Texas. The air would be better, cleaner out here. The daily grind of watching thousands of his fellow Americans stand in line for half of the calories they really needed could get to any man. He wondered if he would ever shake the images of those pallid, dark-eyed souls staring at him, waiting to see if there would be food that day. To the once proud Texans who lived in Dallas, he and his men had evolved from being servants of the country to gods who controlled life and death.

The major had been with the brigade for three years and was less than eight months away from resigning his commission and entering an early retirement. He had planned to work at his brother-in-law's engineering firm to supplement his government pay. That new lifestyle would allow for as much fishing as he could stand. Well, that had been the plan anyway. Now, he wasn't sure if Kansas City even existed anymore. He hadn't heard from his sister since the grid went down.

194

Regardless, he was glad they were moving out. The Ironhorse was a combined arms brigade designated as "heavy," meaning they were armored. Equipped with the latest version of the M1A2 Abrams tank, the old Calvary unit was a mobile wall of steel that had proven itself in every major conflict since WWI. Soon enough he would be riding on top of his command tank with the wind in his face and a purpose in his heart. A mission he hoped would help him and his countrymen recover and start rebuilding once again.

Bishop awoke with a start. He slowly stretched the knots out of his muscles and rubbed his still sore head. It took him a bit more effort than usual to get up from the floor where he had been sleeping, and he had no idea how long he had been lying there. From the stiffness in his body, it had been a while. He pushed the button on his watch, and the illuminated dial indicated it was 6:00 A.M. *Holy shit, I slept all night.*

His mind was immediately flooded with several priorities, including finding a bathroom, checking on David, eating something, and figuring out how they were going to get to the campus and search for equipment. As he slowly worked his limbs, he decided on the coffee as the highest priority, right after the bathroom. *I'm getting too old to run around shooting and playing Army. I wonder if they'll ever re-establish Social Security.*

After stretching for several minutes, he finally felt human enough to put on his gear and ascend to the main floor of the church. There were several small groups of people clustered here and there in the pews. He asked one of the patrons where the head was located and was given directions.

After finishing his business, Bishop immediately sought coffee. Again, friendly brethren pointed him toward the kitchen, which was in a separate building. He walked into a large "cafeteria-esque" room and found a line of sleepy people waiting to be served what appeared to be oatmeal. When he inquired about coffee he was given a look of, "*You've got to be kidding,*" by the older woman manning the serving line. "We've got water, water, and more water, young man."

Bishop held out his plate and watched as the lumpy, semi-white blob of something was dumped on the plastic. He later overheard someone else comment, "Grits, again," but no one was seriously complaining. He took a seat at an open table and proceeded to enjoy his water and swallow the grits. He fought the temptation to pull out the small bag of ground coffee beans he had in his pack, worried it would cause a riot. A shadow fell over him, and he looked up to see Deacon Brown standing behind him. Atlas was behind her as usual.

195

"Good Morning, Bishop. Mind if I join you?"

"Not at all, ma'am. Please have a seat."

This was the first time he had seen the church elder in the daylight, and he had to admire her beauty. She seemed to notice Bishop staring at her and asked, "Do you have a wife, Bishop?"

"Yes, ma'am, I do. Her name is Terri, and she is with child right now. She is waiting for me to return to Meraton."

"I see. How long have you been married?"

And so the chitchat continued until both had finished eating breakfast. As they stood to take their plates to the kitchen, Bishop inquired, "Have you seen David this morning?"

Deacon Brown smiled. "Yes, he was still asleep on my couch when I went to the office a while ago. It's good he is getting some rest."

More and more people continued to enter the cafeteria as the hour got later. Bishop couldn't help but notice most of them looked drawn and tired. Eyes had dark circles, clothes hung loosely on shoulders, and strides were more like shuffles. Again, Deacon Brown's perception of Bishop's thoughts showed, "We are losing, Bishop. The other side, the skinnies some of the guys call them, have us pinned down here. We can't even send out men to hunt deer in the mountains. I'm not sure how long we can hold out."

Bishop looked around to make sure no one was within earshot. "You have an insider problem, Deacon. I was going to talk to you about it later in private, but since you brought it up – you have a spy among your people."

The woman across from him looked down at her lap. "I've been wondering about that for some time. But what makes you think so?"

Bishop kept his voice low. "Last night, they knew we were coming. It takes time to set up an ambush like that. Even if they had spotted us leaving the gate, which I'm sure they did, they still wouldn't have had enough time to set that up. Someone warned them we were coming and knew exactly where we were going."

Deacon Brown looked up, anger and fire in her eyes. "That's a pretty strong accusation for someone who just arrived here. We lost two men last night trying to help you and have a third injured." Atlas, sensing his mother's tension, moved a step closer.

Bishop was about to respond when a commotion at the door drew his attention. A sleepy-looking David was being led into the room by three men. Bishop noted that one of his escorts was the fine gentleman who had struck Bishop, twice, while he was tied to the chair last night. Bishop had learned later the fellow went by the name of Hawk.

Hawk had his arm around David's shoulder, and clearly, David wasn't happy about it. All smiles and happy, Hawk was showing off the hero of last night's rescue. "Here he is ladies and gentlemen, the creator of a new sport – BOWLING FOR SKINNY DOLLARS!" Hawk's comrades all laughed while David looked like he was going to throw up. Hawk went on. "You should have seen it, folks! This young man plowed into those charging skinnies like a bowling ball hitting pins. Those vicious killers flew through the air - it was a perfect strike!"

Bishop was moving. He could tell David was turning green, and clearly, the boy just wanted to get away from these creeps. Bishop approached them, taking David by the arm and gently trying to move him away. Bishop used an excuse. "Come on. David. I want to show you something." Hawk held onto the boy tightly. "What's the matter, Bishop? Can't you stand to see someone else get the credit for doing something right?"

Bishop looked at Hawk and said, "Some people don't like getting credit for taking human life, brother. It's not something the Christian soul relishes."

Bishop saw something odd flash behind Hawk's eyes as the man spouted, "Those animals aren't human. What the boy did was nothing more than put down some rabid dogs."

It all clicked in Bishop's mind. He had replayed the ambush in his head a dozen times and something just wasn't right. Hawk had been right behind him, as they had left the compound. He should have been in the kill zone with Bishop. Hawk dropped back for some reason and Bishop thought that was odd given the man's nature to want to be in charge. Hawk had been one of the main reasons Bishop had told everyone to watch their spacing and not bunch up. "Speaking of last night Hawk, where were you when we walked into the ambush?"

Again, an odd expression flashed momentarily over the man's face. "I was right there. You almost got all of us killed leading us into that trap. If it hadn't been for this boy, we would have all died last night."

Bishop looked at the two men with Hawk, and recognized one of them as having been in the rescue party. Bishop pointed to the man. "You were two men behind me, right?" The man nodded, wondering where this was going. Bishop continued, "Wasn't Hawk between us?"

Again, the man nodded and then gave Hawk a questioning look. "That's right, you were right in front of me. Where did you go?"

Hawk removed his arm from David's shoulder, but stood his ground. He protested in a shaky voice, "I had to tie my shoe. I was there; I just stopped for a moment to tie my shoe. No biggie."

Bishop looked down at the man's feet. He wore high-topped basketball shoes that had Velcro straps and no laces. There were several people standing around now, watching the exchange. Most of them looked down at Hawk's shoes and a murmur went through the crowd.

Bishop kept pressing. "Doesn't anyone else find it odd the skinnies knew where we were going? Doesn't it seem strange they had the time to set up an ambush? If I didn't know better, I would say someone warned them. From what I hear, they seem to know *every* move you folks make ahead of time."

Deacon Brown walked up. She had been listening to the discussion at the edge of the crowd and now decided to take charge. "Gentlemen, I think we should continue the conversation in my office. There's no need to disturb everyone's breakfast."

She started to press between Hawk and Bishop when Hawk suddenly produced a knife and grabbed Deacon Brown. Before anyone could move, he had the knife at her throat and was pulling her back toward the door. "Stand back! I'll kill her if you don't stand back!"

Atlas started to take a step forward, but Hawk yelled, "I'll kill her before you can move, big man. Stay back!" A small line of blood appeared on Deacon's Brown's throat as Hawk's pressure on the knife increased. Atlas froze.

Hawk was behind Deacon Brown, backing toward the door of the cafeteria. When he was in the threshold, he released the woman, pushing her toward Bishop before running. Atlas started to give chase, but Deacon Brown yelled, "Let him go!" The big man froze and then returned to his mother's side.

Bishop released the woman, "I think we found your spy, Deacon."

Deacon Brown looked at Bishop and then the crowd. "He'll make for the gate and go to the other side. No one is to try and stop him. We'll need to change our passwords and security."

Bishop put his hand on David's shoulder, "You okay?"

David gave Bishop a sheepish grin and nodded his head. "Is there anything to eat?"

Chapter 21

Estebon almost shuffled his way to the back of the last service truck where he looked at his men, or at least the few who remained. After the failed ambush, he had become withdrawn and seemed not to care about anything. The captain had taken charge and was now making all of the decisions for the group. He was shrewd enough to realize that Estebon was still respected by many of the remaining men, so he had let Estebon keep the façade of leadership, but the captain was really pulling the strings.

Since their return from the failed attempt at Meraton, the group had been busy burying their dead and consoling the widows of the fallen. Unknown to Estebon, the captain had sent two of his most trusted soldiers to a nearby town that advertised a mining museum. The idea had occurred to him while standing guard in the visitor's area of the main ranger station. The brochure for the museum pictured a display of gold bars on the cover. The photo looked real enough, and the idea had occurred to him that they might be mistaken for Bishop's gold long enough to free the hostages. Unlikely, but perhaps the diversion would distract the captors and allow a rescue attempt for his sister and niece.

He had convinced the now feeble Estebon easily enough. All of the remaining men would escort the "gold" out of the park and trade for the women. The captain had little confidence in the plan's ultimate success, but he had few other options. He felt compelled to try something to retrieve his family members, and this plan couldn't possibly be worse than Estebon's previous attempts.

Someone whistled, and he jumped into the back of the truck. The small three vehicle convoy embarked on its winding journey down the mountain toward the park exit and then on to Mexico.

Colonel Owen's 4/10 was deploying to its forward positions. He had received word that a large formation of the Ironhorse Brigade had left the Dallas area that morning, destination unknown. The Colonel knew where they were headed – right at him.

Even with the additional tanks assigned to his brigade, he was outgunned almost four to one with heavy armor. He knew the Ironhorse was a top-notch unit with a lot of combat experience in recent conflicts, and he dreaded the thought of any sort of confrontation with them.

His concern over fighting a superior force paled in comparison to the emotion he felt when he found out it might be his fellow Americans shooting at him. Battle against an enemy of the United States was one thing – fighting his fellow citizens was another.

Despite the internal turmoil, Colonel Owen had made a commitment, and the longer he was a part of the Independents, the better he felt about his decision. The people calling the shots had kept their word, as well as their vision, every single step of the way. He had even heard that a barge containing several tons of food had docked at Baton Rouge the previous day. "*I'm on the right side*;" he thought, "*let's hope it doesn't come to a fight.*"

The 4/10 did have two tactical advantages. The first was that having arrived first, they could deploy in defensive positions. The second was the speed of their Stryker fighting vehicles. These latest generation troop carriers were fast and carried significant firepower. While they were not armored like a tank, they had the advantage of maneuverability. The thought brought a slight grin to the colonel's face because he knew maneuver won more battles than actual combat.

Chapter 22

Bishop spent the rest of the day talking to some of the church's men about the skinnies. Several of them had been on scavenging patrols and tried to provide him information. A few even drew maps for him. Dusk was approaching when David and Bishop finished packing Bones and double-checking all of their equipment. Deacon Brown and Atlas watched. Bishop turned and pointed to the church's bell tower. "I have one more job to do before we leave. Is there any way to get up there?"

"There is a trapdoor in my office that leads to a ladder. There's not much room up there. We've tried to post a sentry up there, but it's so cramped, it was impractical to station someone there long."

Bishop peered at the tower again and asked, "Is there room to stand?"

"Barely, but yes, you could stand."

"Good enough," Bishop said, and reached into Bones, retrieving his big rifle.

When they arrived in the deacon's office, Atlas reached up to the ceiling and pulled on a small cord hanging in the reception area. An extendable ladder unfolded as the giant lowered the door. Bishop slung the rifle and proceeded to climb the narrow steps. Before his head disappeared into the opening, he paused and looked back at David. "I need for you to be ready to leave as soon as I come back down. I am going to find their lookouts and disable them. They will figure out what's going on pretty quickly, and we need to be out of that gate before they replace their sentries or send more people to see what's going on."

David nodded and headed back to the Humvee before things escalated.

Bishop climbed the steps leading to the bell tower. He estimated it was about four stories high, or roughly forty-eight feet. He reached the top, pushed open a second trapdoor, and stuck his head through the opening. Deacon Brown was right; the area around the bells was tiny. There was room for him to stand, but that was about it. Without touching the large bells hanging from a center pulley, Bishop braced the big rifle against a support and started scanning the area around the complex.

He found the first lookout easily enough. The man was lying prone on a rooftop a few blocks away. From ground level, he would have been almost impossible to spot, but from Bishop's height, he stuck out like a sore thumb. The second lookout was a little more difficult to find. It was an open window that gave him away. A small office building had four second-story windows, and Bishop noticed that only one was open. A rifle barrel resting on the window frame was the confirmation he had discovered another observer. The two lookouts were on opposite sides of the compound, and that was a problem. Bishop was sure that as soon as he shot the first, the other would catch on and try to escape. He scanned one last time, making sure there weren't three men watching the compound. In a space so small, he could quickly become a target himself, and there wasn't anywhere to hide.

Bishop decided on the man in the window first. The lookout on the rooftop didn't appear to have a weapon and was only watching the compound with binoculars. He wouldn't be able to shoot back and had further to move to find cover.

The man in the window was a concern. Bishop really couldn't see *him*, only the barrel of the rifle. He had to take a chance that the man was right-handed and had the rifle shouldered, watching the activity around Bones and the front of the church. He figured the angle and used the riflescope's built in rangefinder. The precision instrument indicated a distance of 650 meters to the window, and he had a downward angle of 25 degrees. A quick calculation told him he should aim five inches below the window glass. The second shot was simple. This man was only 200 yards away, and the downward angle had little impact on his aim at that distance. There was no bullet drop compensation either.

Bishop practiced moving his rifle from one shot to the other a few times, making sure he cleared the structure of the tower as he moved. It was now or never, and he steadied the big rifle against the support, flicked off the safety, and exhaled slowly. *Send it.* The rifle pushed against his shoulder, and he quickly placed a second and then a third round into the open window. Since he couldn't see the actual target, the extra rounds would increase his odds of disabling the man. Before the third spent brass even struck the floor, he spun the rifle around to the man lying on the roof. The sound of the shots had alerted him, and he was now searching the bell tower with his glass. As Bishop centered on the triangle composed of the man's shoulders and tailbone, the guy rolled away and scrambled toward a large air conditioner some ten feet away. *Send it.* The man flopped onto the roof and tried to stand. *Send it.* The man jerked, shuttered, and then lay still with his arms spread wide. Bishop swung the rifle back to the open window and was ready to fire again in case the first three shots had missed. The rifle barrel was now further extended out the window and at an odd angle. He could see the top of a man's head resting against the sill.

Bishop felt exposed in the tower and hurried to get down into the ladder well. After he had descended a few steps, he relaxed and made his way carefully to the bottom and into the deacon's reception area. He moved quickly out of the church to find David sitting in Bones, ready to go. He switched rifles and started to hop in when Deacon Brown appeared. She extended her hand and simply said, "Good luck."

"I'm sure our paths will cross again, ma'am. You guys have a fighting chance now. Reach out to the good people of Meraton if you can."

Bishop hopped into Bones and looked at David. "Ready?"

"Let's roll."

When they exited the compound, Bishop instructed David to head south.

"South? Isn't the campus north?"

"It is, but I want to wait until it's completely dark before we try and get up there. I just knocked out the skinnies' eyes and ears and if they have half a brain, they will send reinforcements thinking something is up. We will let them chill a little bit and believe we have left town. Then we can try to sneak in. Head back to where we stayed before."

David pulled Bones to the same location they had parked the previous evening. They took time to eat, clean weapons, and reload the five rounds Bishop used in the big rifle. Bishop told David he wanted to move through town the way they had before and both of them hoped for better results this time.

After it was completely dark, they moved out. Just as before, Bishop would scout ahead on foot and when he found a good hiding spot, radio David to follow. Whereas Bishop had tried to head directly north on the first attempt, he angled off to the east this time. The system worked well, and they made four moves without seeing anyone. Bishop could see the outline of the stadium on the horizon through the night vision, meaning the outskirts of campus were straight ahead. He radioed David to stay put, knowing Bones was practically invisible, hiding in an abandoned garage a few blocks away.

Bishop moved from shadow to cover into the campus. The street was littered with debris consisting of dead twigs and leaves, papers, shattered glass and the bones of a dog. The college bookstore was next to a strip mall, consisting of a pizza joint, a bar, and the student union. As Bishop passed in front of the bookstore, he scanned the utter destruction of the place through the broken window. Every shelf was overturned and hundreds of books were strewn all over the floor. The sales counter was smashed in several places. It looked like a tornado had hit the place. The Pizza Palace was in worse shape. Bishop could see a door from one of the walk-in freezers leaning against a table in the back. All of the chairs and tables had been randomly thrown around the dining area. Napkin holders, empty spice jars, and broken salt and peppershakers were everywhere. The cash register was in the street, evidently used as a projectile against the large front window. *Probably not a good time to call for delivery.*

Bishop found the first human remains as he turned the corner. A delivery truck with signage declaring it belonged to United Parcel Delivery was lying on its side. The driver had been pinned underneath, and his skeleton somehow managed to show the man's agony in death. The back doors were open, and the pavement was covered with dozens of opened boxes and shipping envelopes. Someone had cleaned out the van, opening every single package. *Probably looking for cookies that grandma promised she was sending.*

As he moved around the delivery van, he froze. At the end of the street ahead of him, movement caught his eye. He peered through the night vision and saw a fountain in the middle of the student union. While there was no water shooting through the statue in the middle, evidently the surrounding pool still held some liquid because there were three people dipping a bucket. They, evidently, were as concerned about being seen as he was because they kept looking around and were very quiet. After their bucket had been filled, the three silently slipped into the night.

Bishop backtracked, approaching the stadium from a different angle. The combination of the overturned delivery truck and the fountain made this route too dangerous for Bones and David. He moved back and down a few blocks in a zigzag fashion, entering an affluent residential area made up of ornate Victorian and plantation-worthy houses that was fraternity row. Across from the frat houses was a city park running parallel for several blocks. Bishop crossed the street and ventured into the overgrown park. He was amazed at how quickly nature had taken over what he remembered as being manicured, golf course-like grounds. There were patches of weeds almost waist-high, and the once well-trimmed shrubs rivaled Bishop's height. As he strolled the length of the park, he noted the overgrown landscaping would be perfect cover to bring up Bones. He kept moving in the general direction of the stadium, listening and watching for any sign of movement at all. He was so intent on the surrounding area that he stepped on the first body and almost fell.

When Bishop used the night vision to see what was beneath his boot, he physically jumped backwards. Lying before him was the grisly scene of a mass grave. There were hundreds of bodies in the park. Some were half-buried, while others appeared to have been simply dumped in the area. Animals had partially exhumed others. For almost a full city block, there were partial skeletons throughout the once picturesque gardens. As Bishop backed away, he had to admit it made sense. Most of the real estate around the campus was paved over. The park was the only grassy area available to accommodate such a large "cemetery," a pragmatic choice when there was still enough living to bury the dead.

He reached the edge of the park and took a knee in some thick grass before keying his microphone. "David, how ya doing back there, buddy?"

David responded with two clicks as usual.

Bishop stepped out onto the sidewalk of frat house row again and checked for any light coming from the houses. It was absolutely dead still and completely dark. *Should I risk driving Bones up this street?* Off in the distance, a motorcycle started, but the sound quickly faded away. The rattling motor caused several dogs to begin barking all over town. *I wouldn't bark too much, little doggies. You might end up someone's meal.*

Bishop decided to try one more route to the stadium, quickly moving past the frat houses and the bone yard. He crossed another intersection to a small side street that was actually more of a narrow lane than a roadway. He scanned the area carefully before spotting the large, green sign at the end of the alley, "Underground Stadium Parking." Bishop didn't like the route. There was no escape if he got pinned in there, yet he hadn't found a better path. In lieu of another option, he headed down the backstreet. About halfway through the alley, movement at the other end caused him to take cover in a doorway. He could see a shadow scurrying toward him. At first, he thought it was a large dog, and then it looked like a child. He couldn't use the night vision because raising the rifle would give away his position. The small creature scrambled from one side of the lane to the other, pausing to look back the way it had come. It, too, was about halfway through the narrow passage, when it froze again, a few feet from where Bishop stood.

Laughter, and then voices, coming from the end of the street had caused the scampering one to freeze. The small figure in front of him whimpered, and Bishop realized it was a girl. She started to run past him, but froze again when two torches came into view from the opposite direction. A distant voice jeered,

205

"Come out. Come out, wherever you are," followed by laughter. Two shadowy figures carrying torches rounded the corner.

Panting and struggling to catch her breath, the girl slid back the hood that covered her head, exposing an emaciated, young woman, perhaps eighteen years old. Her haggard look, complete with stringy hair and ripped clothing, looked more like a Halloween costume than casual dress for a campus co-ed. Her eyes darted nervously back and forth, trying to figure a way out, but it was no use. She was trapped, and so was Bishop. He could now see four shadowy figures advancing in the flickering light. The girl mumbled a frantic, "Noooooo," as the men approached. Their light finally illuminated her frail frame, as she backed against the alley wall, her head shaking. "Oh, please, no. Please don't."

The men now moved quickly to surround her. One of them stretched out his hand to graze her cheek. "I told you she was a pretty one. Looks healthy, too. The boss should give us a lot for her."

"Let's have our fun with her first, and then take her over to him," another man chimed in.

"We can't hurt her or nothing. Remember? The last one was all bruised up. We hardly got anything for those damaged goods at all."

A wicked grin spread across one of the men's faces as he handed his torch to his friend and started unzipping his pants. The girl's eyes darted from one of the men to another, and her breath was sporadic. When she saw the man's pants drop, she started to scream, but one of the guys covered her mouth and roughly pulled her down onto the ground.

Bishop didn't know what to do. *Just because I have a Bat Cave, doesn't mean I'm a superhero.* It was four to one, and the entire thing was none of his affair. He had David to worry about, and while a gang rape was something he didn't wish on anyone, he couldn't be the police all the time. On the other hand, wouldn't he hope for a Good Samaritan if the victim were Terri? He was barely concealed in a doorway less than 20 feet away. There was no chance of his backing out without being seen, and eventually one of these fine young gentlemen was going to turn around and spot him.

Deciding she wasn't going down without a fight, the girl kicked the "trouserless" attacker with all the strength she could muster. From her position on the ground, her foot landed squarely on his knee, and hit hard. The man let out a howl and fell, partially landing on the girl. This caused the others to guffaw at his lack of technique, and that really made him angry. Ignoring the warning of his friends, he rose and kicked the girl hard in the

206

ribs, causing her to utter a sound like a baby screaming. That piercing cry was the death warrant for the rape gang. *I might have a daughter like that one day. That could be my baby girl.* He disconnected the sling holding his rifle, unleashed the violence that flowed through his limbs and moved toward the men in a blur.

They were so focused on the girl they didn't see him coming until he was right in the middle of them. The first man was easy, a rifle butt to the back of his head. The second fell quickly as well, Bishop's rifle barrel caving in his left temple. A savage kick to the knee of the third while ducking a swinging torch temporarily disabled another. Bishop blocked a swinging torch with his rifle and then rammed the barrel into the man's solar plexus hard. He could feel the man's ribs give way. Someone tackled Bishop from the side, and the two men hit the ground. Bishop's head roared from the pain of the impact, and the rifle was knocked out of his hand. He managed to reach his fighting knife strapped across his chest and cleared the blade. The remaining foe lasted only a few seconds after that.

Bishop sat on the ground panting. His head and body ached, and he couldn't get enough air. His heart was pounding in his ears, and he thought he might black out. He wiped his knife on the body next to him and sheathed the blade. He crawled a few steps to his rifle and then sat back down trying to steady his breathing and gain some composure. Two of the men were still alive, moaning on the ground. The girl, recovering from the shock of Bishop's attack, stood up. She walked a few steps and picked up a brick recently dislodged from one of the buildings. Without even hesitating, Bishop watched her walk over to one of the injured men and smash the brick down into his head. She struck again and again and then moved onto the other man. Bishop started to protest, but decided to let her go. He just didn't have the strength, and quite frankly, didn't give a shit right at that moment.

He made it to one knee and was trying to stand, when she appeared in front of him. A whispered voice asked, "Are you okay?"

Bishop quietly replied back, "Yes, I just need to catch my breath."

The girl looked at both ends of the alley and said, "We can't stay here. I don't know where you're going, but these guys have lots of friends. We both need to get out of here."

Bishop nodded and stood weakly. He leaned back against the wall and steadied himself, trying to get his legs to move. The girl nervously reminded him again. "You don't want to be caught here with those bodies. Come on, let's go."

She helped Bishop get moving toward the end of the alley. The blow to his head was causing his vision to blur, and the petite woman had to brace him several times. She led Bishop around two corners and into the lobby of an office building. After checking that no one was around, she entered an ice cream parlor and motioned Bishop to join her in the back. She lit a small candle and then pulled a makeshift curtain across the narrow walkway to obscure the flame.

There was a giant walk-in freezer, complete with heavy metal door. The unit, once used to store the ice cream, was now the girl's home. Blankets lined one corner, and several burned down candles and spent matches littered the floor. There were protein bar wrappers, empty boxes of frozen food and other assorted trash along one wall. There were also small containers of water and an assortment of other scavenged items. The place didn't smell very good.

"I'm sorry it's such a pit, but I wasn't expecting company."

"You *live* in here?"

"I have since everything went to hell. My name is Sarah Beth."

Bishop held out his hand, introducing himself.

The girl ignored his hand and went about gathering up the trash. She pushed it outside the freezer door and into the walkway. Bishop was beginning to get his strength back and was curious about the girl.

"How did you come to live in an ice cream store?"

The girl shrugged her shoulders. "I worked here part time, you know, working my way through school. I'm a freshman at Alpha State. When the power went out the last time, everything in here started melting and I came in to help the owner clean it up. There was an explosion, and I saw everyone start clutching their throats and falling over on the street. I dove into the freezer and closed the door. It's airtight and that saved my ass."

Bishop scratched his head. "How did you get out?"

Sarah Beth laughed, "There's an emergency release on the inside. The door used to accidently close on us all the time."

Bishop smiled at the girl and looked at the freezer door latch. The girl stood with her hands on her hips and watched him move around. "You're not from around here, are ya? You have no idea what you did tonight, do you?"

Bishop shrugged his shoulders, and turned to face her. "No, what did I do tonight?"

She snorted and pointed her finger, "You killed four of the Ghoulish is what you did. That's what we call them anyway. Nobody messes with the Ghouls. When they find those bodies, there will be dozens of them looking for whoever hurt their buddies."

Bishop didn't react to the girl's comment as she expected. She put her hands back on her hips and observed, "I don't think you're scared of the Ghouls. You don't strike me as being afraid of much."

Bishop smiled at the girl, "You would be surprised at what frightens me, young lady. Now, I have a friend with a car not far away. He's hiding right now, but I need to get into the stadium."

Sarah Beth gave Bishop a questioning look, "Why the stadium? There's nothing in there – believe me. I've been all through it."

"I'm not looking for food. What were you doing out and about if the Ghoulish are so dangerous?"

The girl looked down at the floor and hesitated, finally deciding it didn't make any difference anymore, "I go to the park and climb the trees. I eat the bird eggs."

Bishop smiled at her embarrassment. "Young lady, you have nothing to be ashamed of. As a matter of fact, I'm impressed."

"There're not bad once you get used to them. Beats giving yourself up to the Ghoulish and being a sex slave to their masters. I'm not going to be able to go out for days now after you killed them."

Bishop reached in a pouch and pulled out a small bag of jerky. He pulled out two big pieces and gave them to the girl. She looked suspiciously at him. "What do you want for these?"

Bishop laughed. "You are a little young for me. Sarah. Besides, my wife is an excellent shot. Those are on the house. By the way, I think you killed as many of the Ghoulish as I did."

The girl eagerly started eating the jerky and rolled her eyes. "You have no idea how long it's been since I had any meat. Oh my god, this is good. I had to kill those guys, they saw my face."

Bishop walked out of the store and into the building lobby. He checked up and down both streets with the night vision but didn't see any movement. He keyed his mic and transmitted, "David, you still doing okay out there, bud?"

"Yeah, I'm bored though. It's been very quiet. How much longer?"

"I don't know, buddy. Hang in there. I should figure this out in a bit. Stay frosty."

"Stay what? I didn't understand that last?"

"Never mind that - Just stay alert is all I meant."

Click. Click.

Bishop went back to see Sarah Beth was finishing the last of the jerky. His tone got serious. "I need a route to bring up a car. My friend is out there and getting nervous. Come out here for a minute, please."

Bishop led her out into the lobby of the building where there was a map of Alpha in a glass case. Careful to turn on the red filter first, he then flipped on his flashlight. He shined the light on the map and pointed to where David was hiding with Bones. Sarah studied the map for a minute and then traced a route with her finger, "This would be the clearest way. There's not much out there but houses, and most of those people died in the poison cloud. The students looted that area early on, and I don't think anyone goes over there anymore."

Bishop studied the map carefully before arriving at a decision. "I'm going out to get him. You can stay here or go with me, it's up to you."

Sarah Beth thought about that for a minute and then proclaimed, "I'm with you."

Bishop keyed his microphone. "David, get ready. A new friend and I are on the way."

Click. Click.

They arrived at the garage where David was hiding after a 20-minute trek. Sarah Beth wore her hood and stayed back in the shadows, keeping a lookout. She had chosen the route well, and in a short time, they were pulling Bones up to a swing arm gate leading to the underground parking at the stadium. David stopped the Humvee and seemed to be waiting on the gate's arm to rise. Bishop grinned and walked over. "What are you doing?"

"Ummm, I don't know, I guess I thought you would raise the arm."

Bishop laughed, "Drive through. I don't think it's going to hurt the paint much."

David gave Bones some gas, and the heavy vehicle snapped the wooden arm right off. As David drove through the gate, Sarah Beth appeared at Bishop's side. "I found a good place to hide the car. Come 'on; I'll show you."

David followed along as Bishop and Sarah walked through the first level of the underground garage. She had picked an empty spot between two of the college's maintenance vans. Someone would have to walk right past the area to see Bones. Sarah Beth ran off to scout ahead while David got out of the car and stretched his legs. "Who's our new friend?"

Bishop said, "Oh, just some pesky girl I ran into. She was having boyfriend issues, and I helped her out. She's cool."

David tilted his head but didn't press. "Oh."

Before long, Sarah Beth was back and waved for them to follow. The threesome moved to a concrete staircase and climbed to the field level. When they emerged into the open air, Bishop stopped and looked at the football field. In perfectly straight lines, partially hidden by the now overgrown grass, were band instruments and bones. He gave Sarah a questioning look. "The band was practicing Sunday morning when the plant exploded. They all died right out there in perfect formation."

Bishop shook his head, and the group continued to another section of the facility. They descended another set of stairs and stopped. Bishop listened for several minutes before they entered the under section that had a sign on the door, "HOME Locker Room."

As they entered the locker room, Bishop's heart sank. The place had already been searched and looted. Locker doors were open, and their contents scattered all over the floor. Mostly clothing, uniforms, pads, ace wraps, and shoes. Very big shoes, Bishop noted. As they walked through the rather extensive facility, Bishop entered the empty shower room and looked around for some shampoo – there was none. David and Sarah Beth bent over now and then to pick up an item, but always seem to dismiss it and throw it back down.

Bishop picked up an overturned chair and took a seat. He was tired, hurting, and disappointed. They had come all this way for nothing. To make matters worse, they had to get out and back to Meraton. Bishop was shining the flashlight randomly on the debris that covered the floor, trying to find something of use to make him feel at least a little bit better. A small sign caught his eye, and he reached down to pick it up. It said "TRAINER." It was one of those small plackets normally found on a door. He moved a few steps, and there, behind an open locker and a pile of junk, was a door he had missed on the first pass. He quickly cleared the way and discovered the door was locked. There were pry marks where someone had attempted to bust the lock, but the door was steel and had two separate deadbolts. *That would make sense if they had any type of medications in there.*

Bishop looked around for something useful for breaking through the door; but couldn't find anything. He thought about it for a little bit and then turned to David. "Do you know where the tire jack is on Bones?"

David nodded, "Why?"

Bishop said, "You two go out to the Humvee. Bring the jack and the lug wrench…and hurry."

211

Sarah and David returned a few minutes later, carrying the tools and bringing bad news. Sarah, in a frightened voice, reported, "The Ghoulish must have found the bodies. There are motorcycles and people all over the place."

Bishop thought about that for a second and told David to go stand guard by the entrance. "Shoot anybody that comes down those stairs. Ask questions later." David nodded and headed off.

Bishop had Sarah hold his light and propped the tire jack against the door. He took the tire iron, and after instructing Sarah to hold her ears, swung and hit the door about thigh high as hard as he could. The impact dented the steel significantly. A second, and then a third blow soon followed. He took the jack and wedged it against the indentation. It took him a few attempts to get the angle right, but eventually he had the base of the jack against the concrete floor and the head wedged in the indentation. He started pumping.

At first, he didn't think he was going to do anything but bend the metal door. The jack was designed to lift 8,000 pounds of Hummer, so the tire could be changed. Bishop hoped that would be enough force to break down the door. As the jack extended, he heard a metallic groan and then the metal frame at the top of the doorway began to buckle. He adjusted the jack slightly and then pumped again, raising the head into the now quite large dent. A final grating of metal sounded, followed by a sudden pop, and the frame holding the steel deadbolt locks gave way. Bishop moved the jack aside and pulled the door outwards.

He shined the flashlight inside and immediately realized they had hit the jackpot. In the corner was a metal cart containing a fully intact ultrasound machine. The room was lined with small shelves stocked with everything from bandages to medications. Bishop quickly recognized two large duffle bags normally used to haul the bulky pads and helmets for the team. He told Sarah Beth to start filling one with any medical supplies she could find. He took the other and began gently packing the critical machine.

They filled three of the five-foot long bags. Sarah went to get David so he could help them carry the loot back to Bones.

When the teenagers returned, David admitted his concern. "I hear people moving around constantly out there. The place is buzzing like somebody kicked a hornet's nest."

Sarah gave Bishop a look clearly intended to say, "*I told you so.*"

The three carried the heavy bags back to Bones and deposited them in the back. Bishop said he would drive and told David to get in the front and be ready to shoot. He told Sarah to share the passenger seat with David. She defiantly put her hands on her hips and said, "I don't think so."

David seemed fine with the idea, and after Bishop explained to her that was the only area of the vehicle that was bullet proof Sarah Beth relented. Bishop pulled his pistol and an extra magazine and started Bones.

He exited the garage and turned toward the street that would eventually take them back to the ranch. He hadn't made it a full block when sparks flew off of the hood from someone shooting at them. As he sped around another corner, he saw their path was blocked by a semi-truck, abandoned in the intersection. There was no way around it. As Bishop put Bones in reverse, David's rifle started firing and Bishop looked up to see several men running down the sidewalk trying to keep up with them. Bishop spun Bones around and headed down a different street, navigating as best he could around the abandoned cars that seemed to be everywhere. More bullets thwacked into Bone's frame, and one hit the dash right in front of Bishop. A few blocks later, their path was again blocked by a three-car pileup probably caused when the drivers died after inhaling the poison gas. Bishop turned again, and this time noticed headlights behind him. Within a few blocks, two motorcycles had joined the chase. He yelled at David to shoot at the pursuers and tried to get some speed out of the heavy SUV. Bishop started to make another turn, but even more headlights were heading at them. His search for a path south to safety met with continued opposition, every route seemed to be blocked. He was being herded in. He narrowly avoided a collision when a pickup truck jumped into the intersection in front of him. Everyone inside Bones ducked as bullets tore into the engine compartment and cracked overhead. Bishop ventured down a wide four-lane street, and a sign caught his eye, "Highland Airport." It gave him an idea.

The trio turned toward the airport and found the roadway reasonably uncluttered. He drove as fast as dodging the legacy cars and trucks would allow and seemed to have lost the headlights chasing them. He knew it wouldn't last long. As they sped down the highway, Bishop noticed the city of Alpha was thinning out. Manmade structures were being replaced with open patches of high desert scrub and the occasional cluster of pines. A series of flashing lights on the dash indicated Bones had been badly injured and a minute or so later misty steam started pouring out of the hood. *Just hang in there a little bit longer, big guy – just a little further.*

They were about five miles outside town when another sign pointed toward the airport. Bishop didn't even slow down and busted through the chain link gate blocking the entrance. They hurried up the airport access road and pulled around a large tin-roofed building. An enormous door was partially open, revealing several private planes inside. Two more rows of aircraft lined the grassy area next to the building.

Bishop told David, "Go in there and find a plane you can fly. Make sure it has enough gas to get to Meraton. Hurry!"

Bishop grabbed David's big rifle and a spare magazine, hustling around the corner. He found a slight indentation where rainwater drained from the roof of the big structure. Bishop extended the bipod on the weapon and went prone.

A few minutes later, he could see headlights coming their way out of Alpha. From the looks of things, the Ghoulish had formed quite a convoy. He could hear David yelling instructions to Sarah from the hanger. They were looking for gasoline.

The convoy almost bypassed the airport. Bishop guessed the smashed gate gave them away when the line of six vehicles slowed down and then stopped on the road. Bishop watched several men hop down from the beds of pickup trucks and a discussion followed. He could make out some gestures in the headlights, and in a few minutes, a decision was made. One truck with two riflemen was appointed the lucky winner and turned into the airport lane. Bishop waited until the truck was even with the gate and began firing at the engine block. After the truck swerved and stopped, he then turned his attention to all of the men watching from the roadway. If the situation weren't so dire, it would have been comical. Through his riflescope, Bishop could see dozens of men scrambling for cover anywhere close by. Some of the men just laid flat in the road while others crawled to the ditch. One man ran around flapping his arms like a bird trying to take flight. He used up a full 20 round clip, slapped in the new one, and then stopped.

His radio sounded in his ear bud, "Everything okay out there?"

Bishop keyed his mic, "Yeah, I'm fine. We have company. I can hold them off for a little bit, but we don't have much time. How's it going with you?"

"We have a plane, but its tank is almost empty. We are draining the fuel out of other planes. It's taking forever."

Bishop thought for a minute, "Can you send Sarah out with your spare magazines?"

Click. Click.

Bishop heard someone coming up behind him and then Sarah dropped the three spare mags of .308 ammo beside him. She didn't say a word and ran back to help David.

Bishop watched as the men on the road began to regain their composure. He could hear voices shouting over the noise of the idling motors. He waited a bit more and decided it was time to add some stress to their lives. He centered the crosshairs on a visible headlight and fired again, watching the glass shatter and the light go dim. He spent the next few minutes randomly shooting at a tire or person or whatever caught his eye.

Someone down on the road finally got their act together, and Bishop saw two off-road motorcycles head up the access road. They swerved and jinked in an attempt to make a more difficult target, and Bishop ignored them. He laid the big rifle down and hustled back to the rear of the building, pulling the M4 around from his back. As the two riders slowed to make the turn toward Bones, Bishop shot them both. Their bikes made a shower of sparks as they slid across the pavement on their sides, the rider's bodies rolling across the ground from the momentum. Bishop waited a moment to see if they moved and then ran back to his hide. For the next few minutes, he randomly fired at the convoy in the road. He knew he wasn't hitting much, but was trying to buy time for the refueling he hoped was progressing well in the hangar. He noticed the sun was starting to rise behind him, and that wasn't good.

The men on the highway finally figured out Bishop's vantage point, and bullets started to pelt the area. It was only about 400 meters to the road, but they seemed to be having trouble finding the range. He tried to return fire when he saw a muzzle flash, but had no way of knowing if he were hitting anything. He was now down to a single magazine of ammunition for the big rifle.

His radio sounded again, "Bishop, we're ready. I need to preflight check this thing, but we finally have enough gas. I found some charts, too."

"What do you need me to do?"

"Sarah is loading the duffle bags right now. I just need about five more minutes. I have to let this engine warm up and check everything."

"Okay, I can buy you five, but that's going to be about it."

Click. Click.

Bishop heard David's voice shout "Clear!" from inside the hanger, and a motor sputtered, coughed, and then started running. The noise evidently could be heard on the road because Bishop started seeing frantic activity through his scope. Arms

215

were waving, and men were scrambling everywhere. Bishop did his best to keep their heads down, but they were determined not to let the prey escape.

Someone must have decided it was best for the convoy to rush into the airport, sniper fire be damned. As the assortment of vehicles began to line up for a charge, Bishop fired the last of ammunition for the big rifle. He decided he had worn out his welcome in his current position and began running back along the side of the hangar.

As he rounded the corner, he saw a small private plane rolling out onto the concrete. He caught up to the door and threw in the big rifle. David motioned him to get into the back, but Bishop knew there wasn't time. He looked David in the eye and shouted over the engine noise, "Get the fuck out of here. Tell Terri I'm going to Bliss, and that I love her. Now go!"

David nodded and revved the engine. The plane slowly started rolling toward the runway as Bishop sprinted to the corner of the hangar to buy them more time.

David guided the plane toward the runway and glanced behind him. Bishop was shooting at the approaching line of vehicles, and they were returning fire. He gave the aircraft more throttle and turned onto the long stretch of pavement he hoped would allow escape. He watched the speed indicator and as soon as the needle hit 80, he slowly pulled on the yoke, and then they were airborne. Sarah peeked out the window, then back at David, and smiled a little sheepishly. "I've never flown before. How old are you?"

David just shook his head, but didn't answer. He was concentrating on angles and pedals, and as soon as they were at 1,000 feet, he began a slow turn toward the sun. He glanced out his window and saw Bishop riding one of the downed motorcycles while being chased by two trucks. Bishop was heading north into the desert and waved as David zoomed overhead.

Terri had been tossing and turning all night. She opened her eyes and could tell it was daylight outside, but didn't feel like getting up. She hated sleeping in an empty bed and for the thousandth time, wondered if Bishop were all right. An odd noise made her rise up on her elbows and listen. It was a growling sound, and for a second she thought there was a dog outside her room. The noise continued to get louder, and then she realized it was an engine of some sort. Suddenly, an airplane zoomed overhead followed by several shouts from people outside. She scrambled out of bed and pulled on her pants, rushing for the door.

216

Samantha met her on the porch, and both of them hurried through the gardens and onto Main Street. Several of the townspeople had already poured out of their houses and were staring or pointing at the sky. Terri followed their gaze and spotted the airplane in a low, slow circle coming around for another pass. The plane lined up with Main Street and began to descend about a mile outside of town. The pilot touched down on the blacktop and bounded once before the aircraft was rolling on the ground, heading for downtown Meraton. Several people gathered on each side of the street as the small craft idled to a stop in front of The Manor hotel. Samantha yelled, "David!" and ran to the side of the plane as the propeller flopped its last few rotations. Terri walked around to the passenger side and her face showed disappointment when a young girl opened the door. Bishop wasn't with them. David hugged his sister and immediately updated Terri, "Bishop's okay. He said to tell you he was heading to Bliss and that he loved you very much." Terri perked up at the news and said, "He's okay though? Are you sure he's okay?"

David smiled. "The last I saw of him, he was riding a motorcycle off into the desert." Terri smiled at the thought of Bishop getting to ride a motorcycle; he was always telling her how badly he wanted one. David felt a small pang of guilt over leaving out the part about Bishop being chased. He'd have to tell Sarah not to mention it.

Everyone was sitting around the pool when the doctor arrived. He was smiling for the first time in several days. After the equipment had been unloaded from the plane, everyone had waited outside of the room while the operation on the Colonel was in progress. Several hours later, an exhausted physician had opened the door and announced it would be several hours before he could make a prognosis. The patient was still alive, but barely. The periodic reports had been the same until now.

The doctor strode over to the kids and reported, "I think your grandpa is going to make it, guys. He's one tough man, and his vital signs are still strong after the surgery. David, you can tell him later you helped save his life."

David was obviously distracted by Sarah Beth's efforts to get a winter tan, without even taking his eyes off of her he replied, "So the machine helped?"

"Oh yes it did. You also managed to bring back some stronger antibiotics than anything we had here. I actually can practice medicine now." The doctor then turned to Terri, "I expect you to show up this afternoon for your first prenatal examine young lady."

Terri saluted and smiled.

Epilogue

(From the upcoming novel *Holding Their Own III: Pedestals of Ash*)

Bishop was tired of pushing the dirt bike. He had run out of gas two hours ago and debated whether to leave the machine in the middle of the desert or push it in hope of finding some fuel. He estimated he had traveled about fifty miles northwest out of Alpha when the sputtering engine had finally shut down. The Ghouls had given chase in their pickup trucks until one of the 4x4's had lost a wheel in a blind rut, and the other had been discouraged by Bishop's M4 carbine.

He wondered if David and Sarah had landed safely, but decided to clear the worry from his mind. There was nothing he could do about it, and quite frankly, he was in a bit of a pickle right now. He glanced around at the terrain and shook his head. *"How do I get myself into these situations?"* He could see the southern tip of the Davis Mountains to the west; and far off in the distance, the Glass Mountains to the east. The high desert valley surrounding him was practically devoid of vegetation, and the day was already showing signs of being dangerous.

Even though it was mid-winter, west Texas still experienced some very hot days. Bishop wasn't concerned so much about the heat, but the lack of humidity in the air. On dry days like today, it wasn't perspiration or heat that caused dehydration - it was breathing. The humidity had to be less than twenty percent right now, and that meant the mandatory act of exhaling air literally sucked the moisture out of his body, and he was out of water.